MURDER AMONG FRIENDS:

A Mystery

By Charles E. Fager

Kimo Press

This book is for MaryLou,

And in memory of Mike Aun.

With special thanks to Asa David
for technical field assistance.

First printing, Twelfth Month, 1993
Second Printing, Sixth Month, 1994

Cover Design by Sandy Overbey,
Qubic Communications

ISBN 0-945177-08-9

Kimo Press
P.O. Box 1361
Falls Church VA 22041

This book is for MaryLou,
And in memory of Mike Aun.

With special thanks to Asa David
For technical field assistance.

Major Hawks: *The Yankees don't seem willing*
                  to quit Winchester, General.

Stonewall Jackson: *Winchester is a very pleasant*
                        place to stay in, sir.

--March 23, 1862
First Battle of Kernstown

CHAPTER ONE

"Sic Juvat Transcendere Montes." (Thus it is enjoyable to cross over the mountains.)

--Motto of Governor Alexander Spotswood's 1716
expedition, claiming the Shenandoah Valley for George I

"On a clear day in 1864," I said, pointing to the northwest, "you could see all the way to Winchester from here, twenty-some miles."

My arm swept a few inches to the left. "And even farther from over there at Signal Knob. That air almost won the Civil War for the South."

"It wouldn't help them much today," Eddie Smith said, squinting into the haze. "I can barely see the other side of Front Royal."

We were standing at the Shendandoah Valley Overlook, the first one after the northern entrance to the Skyline Drive. To a reasonably tuned-in observer of Washington area biped fauna, we would have been as easily identifiable as a whitebreasted nuthatch to a practiced birder:

Eddie in shirtsleeves and Levi's, mid-thirties, a short beard,

1

close-cropped wavy black hair and glasses. Me, William Leddra, in a battered Baltimore Orioles cap, prescription shades and chinos, pushing the mid-forties and the 190s. My beard was a little thicker and a lot grayer.

Then there was my veteran Toyota: Decals for WETA Public TV and Amnesty International on the rear window, plus a Greenpeace "Love Your Mother" bumpersticker. Added up, these signs left no room for doubt what we were: A couple of liberal policy wonks on vacation.

Mark that one off in the back of your Peterson's, Ethel. What? You say it's already checked? Figures. Too many of that kind around here anyhow. Oughta have open season on 'em, if you ask me. Clear some out.

Front Royal, Virginia lay a mile or so below us, squashed up against the rim of the Blue Ridge. From here the city looked mostly like a collection of roofs, streets, motel logos, and billboards urging us to visit various sets of commercialized caverns.

We were just far enough away, fortunately, that I couldn't see the yellow ribbons that, at ground level, had sprouted there, as they had everywhere, like some new variety of unstoppable kudzu.

The last big parades for Operation Desert Storm were, thankfully, a few weeks behind us. Americans were just beginning to notice that, after the months-long diversionary orgy of war-fever and pumped up patriotism, their country was still sliding quietly yet steadily down the tubes. The ribbons remained; but the sheen was wearing off, fast.

Beyond the city, the two shimmering forks of the Shenandoah River, North and South, came together at the end of their more or less parallel, twisting sixty-mile passages down the Valley's green expanse. On the other side of the river, the countryside was marked by rippling cornfields and dark stands of trees, but soon faded into a vague, impenetrable pollution grey.

That grey was the color of progress. It was also the color of the future, because we were headed right into it.

"Which one was Signal Knob?" Eddie asked. "And who was

it that climbed it?"

"It's the hooked nose on the end of Massanutten," I said, pointing again at the mountain a few miles west of us. "The big one there." Behind it, over in West Virginia, a line of slate-colored thunderclouds was building and moving slowly, menacingly towards us.

"And General John B. Gordon of Georgia climbed up it, October 18, I believe it was, 1864. He was planning an attack for Jubal Early on the Union forces, under Phil Sheridan. They were camped several miles north, across Cedar Creek. Gordon said the view was so good he could even see the sores on the Yankees' horses, and the pips on their uniforms. Now *that* was clean air."

"So did he do it?"

"Do what?"

"Figure out how to attack Sheridan."

"Sure did. They snuck up through the fog before dawn on October 19, caught the Federals mostly still asleep. Ran them all the way to the other side of Middletown, some of them stumbling in their underwear. Gordon even had a troop of cavalry assigned to swoop down and kidnap Sheridan."

I gestured dramatically to the north. "Hell, couple more lucky breaks for him and Early, we'd need passports to get up here. And Martin Luther King would have grown up picking cotton. Jubal Early almost turned the whole civil war around that day."

"Almost."

"Yeh. Turns out Sheridan wasn't there. He'd spent the night in Winchester, after some big meeting in Washington. When he heard about the battle, he jumped on his horse, galloped ten miles down the Valley Pike, rallied his troops and counterattacked. Pushed the Confederates all the way back past where they'd started. It pretty much finished off the Confederate army in the Shenandoah."

"Hmmmmmmm," Eddie mused.

"That's not all," I said, warming to the subject. "Sheridan's victory at Cedar Creek also guaranteed Lincoln's re-election a few weeks later. And that--"

Eddie cut into my lecture. "Isn't it a bit unseemly," he said,

3

"for a card-carrying Quaker, a conscientious objector during Vietnam no less, to be obsessed with the Civil War, the bloodiest American war of them all?"

I shrugged. "We all have our perversions. And besides, this one will be useful at the conference. That's what got me invited. I'm supposed to organize local history tours for the Friends from afar. Anyway, there's plenty of Quaker history in the Civil War too, though most of it's untold. Especially in the Shenandoah Valley. And particularly around Winchester. In fact--"

"I can wait," he interrupted again. "We should go."

Back in my car, winding down the mountain to US Highways 340 and 522, Eddie studied the conference brochure. "'The 1991 All-Friends Conference,'" he read aloud, "'will attempt to bridge the gaps of history, doctrine and practice that have divided Friends for generations, in hopes of beginning a process of healing, forgiveness and reconciliation.'"

He looked up at me. "You think he can bring it off?"

"Old Lemuel Penn?" I laughed. "If anybody can, he's the one. Remember, he spent ten years as a Quaker representative in Tel Aviv, shuttling from there through Cairo into Syria and Lebanon and back. And what better preparation could you have than trying to make peace between Arabs and Israelis in the Middle East for an even tougher assignment--making peace among Quakers in the Middle West? Penn's the closest thing to a Quaker statesman we've got."

I paused. "But, to be perfectly honest, I don't know if he can pull it off. Last time they tried it was back in 1977, out in Wichita, and that one almost went up in smoke."

"What happened?" Eddie asked.

"You mean you don't know?" I chided. "Oh, these younger Quakers, nobody teaches them their heritage. No wonder the Society of Friends is in a mess. Well, here's a hint: What was there about the summer of 1977 that's important in gay liberation history?"

He thought a moment. I glanced sidelong at him as he pondered: slender, carefully-groomed, good-looking but not one of your pretty boys. His temples were receding, and, just now, his brows were furrowed. But it didn't take him long to come up with the answer:

"Sure. Anita Bryant. The Miami gay rights ordinance fight. The orange juice boycott."

"You got it. Now: What do you suppose would happen to a Quaker conference that summer where you had not only the hardest core of our evangelicals coming, but also a group from Philadelphia that arrived under the banner of the H-word?"

He nodded. "Trouble."

"Nope," I said. "BIG trouble. The evangelicals threatened to walk out and picket, and the gays threatened to counterpicket."

"In Wichita?" Eddie was mildly incredulous.

"Yep. Turns out they'd just had Gay Pride Week in Wichita, with parades and the whole nine yards." I chuckled at him. "But why are you so surprised? You're the one who keeps telling me, 'We are everywhere.'"

He grinned back. "Yeah, but lots of us were still in the closet then, especially in the middle of Kansas."

"It was news to me too," I said, "but that's the truth. Made for great cheap entertainment, but it totally disrupted my own agenda there."

"Which was?"

"What else: Shopping for eligible Quaker women," I said. "Hell, man, I've got a sexual preference too."

"So how did it turn out?"

"A lot of behind the scenes mediation went on, and they managed to patch things up enough to get through the conference. Lem was involved in it, though I don't know the details. But afterward, most of the evangelicals said 'Never Again.'"

"No," Eddie said. "I meant, how did your search for Friendly females turn out?"

"Oh, you know," I sighed. "The old story. All the good ones were either married--"

"--or *straight,*" Eddie broke in. "I know how that goes."

"But hope springs eternal."

"You're a romantic," he said.

We were silent a moment. Then Eddie said, "I need some

5

music," and hit the power button on the radio.

But Washington's Number One classic rock station was gone, faded into the hazy ozone somewhere behind the Blue Ridge. In its place came a man's voice, so smooth it must have been slicked down with about half a quart of mousse.

"This is WVCR, Valley Christian Radio. And we're listening to excerpts from last week's conversation with the Rev. Ben Goode, pastor of the Good Life Baptist Temple in Harrisonburg."

"Jesus," Eddie swore, and reached for the dial.

I headed him off. "Wait," I said, "I wanna listen for awhile. Some of this stuff is interesting. And after all, the first rule of war is Know Thy enemy."

Eddie snorted. "It's *thine* enemy. And there you go talking about war again." He leaned back and looking out the window, pretending not to listen.

"--the crusade," said the announcer, dripping maple syrup all over the speakers, "is your biggest campaign so far, isn't it, Dr. Goode?"

A deeper, more authoritative voice answered. "That's right, George. We're going to put everything we have into a nationwide Crusade for Family Values, to reclaim American culture from the gays, the pornographers, the radical feminists and abortionists, and stop the promoters of godless secular humanist and New Age lies in our schools."

"That's a mighty tall order," said the announcer.

"Yes," Goode agreed, "we know it will be an uphill battle, but God has brought us important allies for the fight. We're in tune with the White House, and some of the finest pro-family talent in Washington will be on our team. Of course we'll need the prayers and support of all the Good Life Family members, here in the Valley and around the country."

"I think you know you can count on us," the announcer fawned.

"I *am* counting on you," Goode said. "Together, with God's help, we can win this war, take back our culture and uphold biblical marriage and families against the attacks of the gays and the media sex peddlers."

"Thank you, Dr. Goode," the announcer said. "I'm sure--"

"Christ," Eddie shouted, "this is awful. Do we have to listen?"

"Look," I said, "I can't help it. I find Goode and Falwell and all that crowd fascinating, at least in moderate doses. I think of broadcast evangelism as a marvelous indigenous American folk art form; like Elvis sightings, except that these guys are real, more or less. I never miss a supermarket tabloid article about Bakker and Swaggart."

But Eddie's face was serious. "That's easy enough for you to say," he insisted angrily. "You're safe. You don't run an abortion clinic or a gay rights advocacy group. You'll have options when the Christian fascist death squads come around."

He pointed a thumb at his chest "But I'm gay, always was, always will be. And I'm out--way out, the goddam Co-Clerk of the Lavender Friends Fellowship, for God's sake. You might as well paint a target on my ass. Where am I gonna hide when his Crusade crap hits the fan?"

I glanced down, and saw that his hands had balled into fists.

"I mean it," he went on. "Goode and his hate campaigns may be entertainment for you, but they're a matter of life and death for us. Have you ever watched him on TV? Just looking at his sanctimonious face makes me ill."

I felt a little shamed by his vehemence. "Well, all right," I said, "we can find something else."

Now a woman was talking. "--The plant closing will mean pink slips for 350 more Valley workers," she said. "It's the third major shutdown in the Shenandoah region this year." She paused and shuffled a paper. "Weather for the weekend coming up, right after--"

I hit the SEEK button, and kept punching it until it turned up a guitar riff that sounded familiar, dark and pulsing. It was the Rolling stones, doing "Gimme Shelter."

We listened to Jagger in silence, driving on into the grey afternoon.

7

CHAPTER TWO

Dear brother,
    I hope before long to see dear old Winchester safe and sound. I believe if our immortal Jackson were here, it would have been delivered from these vile invaders long before this....The town is just full of Yankee women, who act as if they owned everything in it.

--Letter from "Kate," June 12, 1863

Valley State College is just north of Winchester, about half a mile west of Interstate 81. The campus is compact and cozy, with nondescript red brick buildings ranged around a lush green oval lined with tall old oaks and maples.

"Welcome All-Friends Conference," read the hand-painted sign at the north entrance, with a black arrow pointing toward Mott Hall for Registration.

"It was started by Quakers from Opequon Creek Meeting, in 1867," I was telling Eddie as we turned in. "To train young women who were going South to teach former slaves. Lots of them went. After Reconstruction the meeting turned it into a normal school, for schoolteachers. It closed in the Depression, then the state picked it up."

I pointed across the oval, toward a tree-covered rise. "The Meetinghouse is over there, behind the trees. It goes back to before the American Revolution. Here's Mott Hall."

"That Lucretia Mott, I hope?" Eddie asked.

"Yep. This may be one of the few public buildings in the

8

valley not named after a treasonous defender of chattel slavery or a segregationist governor. Not that I'm prejudiced about the Old Dominion. I'll open the trunk."

With the obligatory nametags soon pinned on our shirts, we were quickly assigned to a room on the dormitory's third floor, and lugged our bags up the stairs.

From the doorway the room looked like an optical illusion, with two of everything: desks, beds, dressers and closets, arranged in sequence and exactly opposite each other.

I dropped my suitcase, flopped down on one of the beds and scanned the conference schedule, printed on a pink sheet in small type, while Eddie unpacked his bag. "There's a steering committee meeting going on now, in the auditorium," I noted. "I should get down to it, since I'm technically a member. You could come, too; it's an open session. Hey, what's that?"

I had glanced up and seen Eddie pulling out what looked like a sawed-off baseball bat from his bag. He grinned and tossed it at me.

"It's an authentic family heirloom and homophobia deflector," he said. "Got it at a yard sale outside Pittsburgh, cost me a buck. Look on the other side."

I caught it and turned it over, noting that the foot-long stump of a bat had been carefully sanded and varnished, except in one spot about halfway up, where there was a dark scribble. I peered at it. "Who--?"

"Roberto Clemente. And it's real, not stamped. One of the last ones he signed before he was killed."

I whistled. "A sacred relic, sure enough. But a homophobia deflector? Thee wouldn't be using this as a worldly weapon now, would thee, Friend? Thee knows what the Good Book says, 'Live by the bat, die by the bat.' Or words to that effect."

"What gives thee such an idea, Friend?" he bantered. "Though I admit I did show it to a couple of punks who tried to corner me in an alley over by Dupont Circle a couple years back. Worked like a charm, too, and I never touched them."

"Doubtless thee didn't have to," I said, lobbing it back at him. "But I hope it taught thee not to hang out in alleys."

He mugged. "What's life without a few adventures in alleys?"

He caught the bat and dropped it back into his bag. "Anyway, it's mainly for good luck." He stuck the bag into the closet by his bed. "Where did you say that meeting was?"

"In the auditorium."

"Is that where the exhibits are?" he asked. "I want to check my LFF display."

I looked at the pink sheet again. "Exhibits...Yep, 'Auditorium foyer.' Good location."

"Let's go," he urged.

"Right. I'll unpack later."

The auditorium was across the oval from Mott, in Woolman Hall. Like Mott, it was square and worn red brick, plain enough for its sainted namesake, a pre-revolutionary New Jersey Quaker tailor and mystic activist who refused to wear clothes colored with dyes prepared by slave labor.

The wide foyer was lined with long trestle tables, crowded with exhibits. But amid the clutter of unfolded displays for Quaker schools, colleges, retirement homes, conference centers and service groups, there was no sign of one for the Lavender Friends Fellowship.

"Where is it?" Eddie asked anxiously when we had walked past all of them. "We worked so hard on it, shipped it out here in plenty of time, and paid our fee months in advance. What could have happened?"

"Did they send you a receipt?"

He pulled out his wallet. "Got it right here." He unfolded the paper. "Says we're exhibit Number Three. Check the numbers."

I walked down the row of tables, looking for numbers marked on strips of masking tape.

The strip marked Number Three turned up on a table right near the main entrance; a great spot. But on the table was a display for the *American Friend* magazine and publishing house, a very orthodox outfit from Indiana. Its big feature was a blowup of the jacket for their latest book, provocatively titled *Quakerism and Biblical Truth: What Price Unity?*

I turned to call to Eddie, who had moved down to the far

end of the foyer, but then heard him muffling a curse.

"Here it is!" he declared. "What the *hell?*"

I walked over. He was tugging at the tape on a tall, thin shipping carton. "It's been put back in the box," he said angrily.

"Somebody took it down."

"Yeah," I said. "Number Three's over there. The *American Friend.*"

"What?" he shouted. "That's my table. I'm not gonna put up with this kind of crap."

Before I could say anything, he had rushed over and grabbed the corners of the hinged frame holding up the enlarged cover of *Quakerism and Biblical Truth*, and clumped them together. Pushing the stacks of brochures aside, he quickly lifted the shipping box up on the table, tore off the tape and pulled the cover flap open. "Look," I interjected, "maybe it's just some kind of a mixup."

He snorted, and unhooked the display board. The exhibit was considerably larger than that of the *American Friend;* the backdrop had four hinged sections, and as he unfolded it they took up the entire table, crowding the school and conference center displays on either side.

"GAY AND LESBIAN FAMILIES--LOVING AND FRIENDLY FAMILIES" the heading boldly proclaimed.

Below it, on each segment of board, was a large photo of a same-sex couple, two of them men, and two women. Everyone was smiling blissfully, I noted; ah, the innocence of young love. And each of female couples had a grinning child beside them as well.

"My, how things have changed," I teased, gazing at the photos. "Were the '70s really that long ago? Then the gays and lesbians were the insurgents, the radicals at Quaker gatherings. More and better sex, more often, with more people--wasn't that the message, or at least the subtext?

I pointed at one of the grinning male couples. "Now look at them," I recalled. "I was at their wedding, up in Pennsylvania. Hell, it was more traditional than any straight Quaker wedding at my own Meeting in fifteen years, except for that one minor point of both spouses being male."

I stepped back and surveyed the whole display. "The truth is, Eddie, your Lavender Friends Fellowship is rapidly becoming a conservative force among Friends. Marriage, families, kids--that's all you talk about anymore."

"That and AIDS," Eddie muttered, adjusting one corner of the display. "Plus the right-wing homophobes. Except not so much about them, not lately. Life is too short to spend all our time together fanning our paranoia. We even--"

A rumble of voices came from within the auditorium. "They must be taking a break," I said.

The doors burst open and out streamed a gaggle of men and women, most talking to each other, unaware of us at first.

Some of the faces were familiar to me; the rest fell immediately into two types: There were the pastors in their suits, which ranged from wool blend to polyester, roughly gauging their proximity to the evangelical end of the theological spectrum, and, of course, all men.

The liberals were just as distinctive; they looked like me: short sleeves or environmental tee shirts, numerous beards, and including several women, most likely librarians. Typical specimens of the two main species of *Quakerianus Americanae.*

For the most part, a group of Friends is a welcome sight to me. I felt myself starting to smile, and glanced reflexively at Eddie, expecting a similar reaction.

But his expression stopped me. It was frozen and hard and he was staring past me.

Looking back at the group, now dispersing toward the restrooms and the water fountains, right away I saw what he saw. Or rather, who.

Walking next to Lemuel Penn, chatting amiably and inaudibly, a yellow ribbon bright against the navy blue of his lapel, was a much taller, commanding figure: The Reverend Ben Goode.

CHAPTER THREE

Up from the South at break of day,
Bringing to Winchester fresh dismay.
The affrighted air with a shudder bore,
Like a herald in haste, to the chieftain's door,
The terrible grumble and rumble and roar,
Telling the battle was on once more....

--Thomas Buchanan Read, *Sheridan's Ride*

I knew Goode from his pictures, as, obviously, did Eddie.
"Christ," he muttered under his breath, "what's *he* doing here?"

"Beats me," I whispered back. "But I'll bet he hasn't come for training in silent worship."

"Wouldn't do him any harm," Eddie said.

"Hey, Bill," a woman's voice cried, "you made it! Gimme a hug."

I turned toward the door, just in time to be gathered into a bear hug by a large, smiling brunette.

"Rita," I said, reddening a bit. "You're here, too?"

Grabbing Eddie by one arm, I introduced them. "This is Rita Gillespie, Presiding Clerk of Metropolitan Half-Yearly Meeting in New York City. My old radical comrade."

"Don't say old," she objected with a laugh, stepping back and putting her arms akimbo. She wore a long, shapeless shift of brown and purple, and her dark hair made a convex frame for

13

her face. Then it twisted into a long, thick braid that bounced halfway down her back, held in place by a carved clip made from something like mahogany. I noticed, though, that now the braid was flecked with grey.

Rita wasn't even remotely fashionable in her look. Her figure, once trim and full, was rounder, its curves now more in line with gravity. She was, there was no denying it, older and heavier than I remembered.

But then, so was I. And with her grey eyes, full lips and good teeth, I found her very striking. Rita waved a long, strong-looking finger at me. "The Columbia student strike wasn't all that long ago. Barely twenty years." There was just a hint of wistfulness under her jocular tone, an inflection I was becoming increasingly familiar with.

"Right on," I said. "I think I can still make a fist, but I forget which one we were supposed to raise when we shout 'Power to the people!' I'm afraid they'll laugh at me at the next Sixties reunion."

"I have the same problem," she said, "so I just fake it and raise both fists. My ex-husband says it makes me look like a Trotskyite, but what does he know?" She leaned toward me and adopted a stage whisper. "Some committee meeting we're having," she said. "Lots of surprises."

"It certainly looks that way," Eddie put in. He gestured with his head toward Goode and Penn, now the nucleus of a cluster of suits across the foyer from us. "Where did *he* come from?"

"Curiouser and curiouser," Rita began, then the cluster of suits started moving in our direction. "Just a stretch break," she said, "and I gotta pee. Tell you all about it later." She hurried off toward the women's room.

Ex-husband, I thought. That was news. I remembered them from Wichita in '77; she had been one of the married ones. He was getting a doctorate somewhere and they were still almost newlyweds. Rita had been slimmer, and radiant in the way of recent, well-bedded brides. It had made me feel lonely just to look at her.

She was still attractive, I realized, and now, perhaps, eligible. This would bear further exploration.

14

Murder Among Friends

The pastors filed back into the auditorium. But they were silent as they passed us, and two or three gave us significant, distant stares as they passed. Lem Penn nodded, but there was an anxious furrow bisecting his wrinkled forehead.

The librarians came along behind them, smiling weakly; then Rita, who winked, squeezed my arm, and hissed, "Don't trust anyone over 30!"

"Well, that's a kick in the head," Eddie murmured when the doors had closed. "Let's go find out what they're up to."

"Wait a minute," I urged. "Why don't we center down a minute first. I think we may need it."

"All right," he agreed, and we stood there quietly for a moment, two Quaker initiates performing their secret cult ritual. He closed his eyes briefly. Then he opened them and nodded.

"Come on."

Pushing through the doors, we saw the committee, beyond the rows of old wooden seats, around a big rectangle of trestle tables set up on the stage. There were steps at the center and on both sides, the backdrop was white acoustical tile, and a podium with a microphone had been shoved to one side of the stage, next to a piano.

Notebooks were open, ballpoint pens were poised, and all eyes were on Lem Penn, who was just getting up, and saying, "Rita, will thee take over for a few minutes?" Then he turned and headed briskly down the steps in our direction.

"Could I see you outside," he asked quietly as he passed.

We followed in his wake out the doors and back to Table Number three. "William," he said when we got there, "good to see thee," and stuck out his hand.

I shook it, reflecting again on the fact that Lemuel Penn, the Quaker patriarch of the Alleghenies, was one of the few Friends I knew who could say thee and thou to me without it sounding affected. Like the handful of others I had heard using this old-fashioned Quaker plain speech, he was old, early seventies at least, and the practice would probably be gone forever with the passing of this quiet remnant, which surely could not be many years off.

Lem was not tall to start with, and his years had given him

a definite stoop. About half bald, his hair-streaked pate had a weatherbeaten look that reminded me of a rocky outcropping on one of the hillsides he owned a few hours drive from Winchester, where he grew some of the finest apples and cherries in southwestern Virginia.

In fact, it was apples that had introduced me to him, at a weekend Quaker conference in Boston. It was autumn 1969; he was the main speaker, but everybody shared the chores, and he and I were assigned to buy the food for the first night's dinner. We took the MTA downtown to the open air market in Haymarket Square to get it.

There we had cruised past the pungent sausages swimming in their own fat and stepped over the rotten cantaloupes and tomatoes in the gutter, dodged the flies and yellow jackets, ignored the stench of decaying vegetables, and picked up some eggs and several pounds of potatoes from one of the wheeled stands.

The harvest display was rich and colorful, but the glory of that season at Haymarket were the apples, red, yellow and greenish pyramids of them all around the crowded, smelly block. Northern Spy, Rome, the regional favorite McIntosh, others whose names I didn't know--and of course, mounds of the sleek, Establishment varieties, red and yellow Delicious.

While otherwise firmly anti-Establishment, this embarrassment of riches left me opting for the safe course, fruitwise. Opening a paper bag, I was about to start filling it with some shiny Red Delicious, when I felt a gentle hand on my arm.

"Not those," Lem said quietly. He was not bald then, only barely stooped, and wore a venerable fedora over a shabby brown suit. There was a retired, second string insurance salesman look about him, yet his hands, stubby, strong and callused, undercut any sense of softness. From more than a few feet away you wouldn't notice him; but close up, there was to his carriage a certain indefinable but solemn dignity that I could recognize as both uniquely personal and, at the same time, distinctively Quaker.

Murder Among Friends

He turned away from the pile of Delicious apples, and gestured for me to follow. I did, recalling that he had been explaining about his apple orchard on the subway downtown. The orchard did not produce much profit; but he did not need much. His wife was dead, his two children grown.

More than money, the orchard yielded time: most winters, with the branches bare and the hillsides chilly he was free to travel, while a neighbor kept an eye on the place. And travel he did, pursuing his many Quaker concerns, about four months of the year.

John Woolman had done that two centuries ago, using much of the time to visit Quaker slaveholders and plead with them to free their chattels, with some success. Woolman was something of a saint for American Quakers, and clearly a role model for Penn. Like Woolman, Penn lived simply and traveled lightly, unhampered by anxiety about Dressing for Success.

But Penn's interests ranged more widely than Woolman's. He was particularly interested in Arab-Israeli peacemaking, in what he persisted in calling the Holy Land. He was well read in the history and issues of that tangled and dangerous region, had travelled there several times, and was planning a trip back the following spring, adding the Quaker qualifier, "if way opens," the way a Muslim might say "Inshallah."

But Penn was also, by occupation, an expert in apples. And now I followed him in the bright autumn sunlight among and between wooden carts and rusty pickup trucks loaded with different varieties, pausing here and there to point out a batch that looked particularly glossy or ripe. Each time he shook me off and kept walking.

Finally he pulled up and said, simply, "There. These," and spoke to the vendor, who snapped open a paper bag.

"These?" I questioned, unbelieving. The fruit he proposed to foist on our unsuspecting Friends at the conference were small, colored an indeterminate brown and yellow, with only tinges of maroon, and pocked by what looked unscrubbed pores. And they weren't any cheaper than the Delicious or the McIntosh, either one of which would have been a safe bet.

He only nodded and plucked one from the pile to toss to me.

Murder Among Friends

I rubbed it on my pants and, still skeptical, took a bite.

It was terrific. Firm, sweet, with a unique tang, it was to the Red Delicious what technicolor was to black and white.

Penn saw my eyes widening as my mouth worked, and he grinned modestly. "It pays to know what's good," he said, selecting an apple for himself, and extracting a few dollars from an ancient wallet to pay for our produce.

On the way back to the conference, while I ate another of the succulent apples, he talked about one of his other main concerns: promoting greater understanding among the fragmented branches of American Quakerism. "It's not right for us to claim to be peacemakers in the world, if we can't maintain some kind of peace among ourselves," he insisted, his voice rising, the soft southern accent noticeable amid the hubbub of more nasal New England conversations around us. "It makes us hypocrites, scribes and pharisees."

In pursuit of this mission, he had recently gotten himself appointed as a representative from Tarheel Yearly Meeting to the North American Friends Association. NAFA, as it was commonly called, theoretically brought several of these branches together; but the union was an unstable one; ever since I joined Friends a year before meeting Penn, it seems that NAFA was always on the verge of flying apart, as one faction or another threatened to walk out over some theological or political outrage, real or imagined. In those days, with the Vietnam War in full bloody flower, such intramural Quaker quarrels seemed impossibly arcane and irrelevant. Later, I saw it differently: This peculiar Quaker community had helped me survive the war years. And as I settled into it, I could see how these schisms threatened that fragile community. So if they were still arcane, they were no longer unimportant.

Even so, to be honest, I must admit that understanding the course of the American Civil War was much more intriguing to me than tracing the various separations among Quakers. Federals versus Confederates, the Blue and the Gray, seemed like a much grander and more compelling saga than the squabbles between the Orthodox and Hicksite Quakers in Philadelphia 1827, or the Wilburite and Gurneyite Quakers in Ohio a generation later.

Murder Among Friends

So while Lem Penn, between trips to the Holy Land, stayed with NAFA and within a few years was its Presiding Clerk, I settled in Washington, worked as a reporter for obscure legislative newsletters, and spent my free time becoming conversant with such matters as the location of the little Dunker church in the Antietam Battlefield, identifying just where The Angle was at Gettysburg, walking the entire circumference of The Petersburg Crater, and puzzling about why McLellan was so reluctant to attack Lee during the Peninsular campaign.

Being a liberal, I also took pains to learn about the struggle of blacks to join the Union army; and being a Quaker, I had haunted the section of the National Portrait Gallery which had been used as a hospital, listening for the shade of the Quake-ish Walt Whitman moving silently and lovingly among the huddled ghosts of his many dying patients.

With such preoccupations, I hadn't thought about NAFA in years. Thus I was a little surprised when Lem Penn had called me last winter, just as the Gulf War was about to break out, wanting me to join the planning committee for the All-Friends Conference. "But Lem," I protested, "what do you want me for? This is a summit conference, a gathering of weighty Friends. Assistant Recording Clerk of Washington Monthly Meeting is as weighty as I get, and that doesn't remotely qualify."

This was not false modesty. Quakerism was my faith, true. I even managed to get to meeting on Sundays--or, in proper Quaker-speak, First Days--about three weeks out of five when in town; and I did send a check to the treasurer every month. When called on to fill in for the Recording Clerk, I took careful minutes of our business meetings.

But I was hardly a pillar of the Meeting. I was not, for instance, one of the dedicated cadre who always volunteered to teach First Day School(my one effort at it, substituting for a sick friend amid a roomful of definitely nonpacifist eight year-olds, had been a disaster). Nor was I among the sanctified elite who regularly arrived at our monthly potlucks with large serving dishes full of some steaming, aromatic and savory concoction whose main ingredient was something other than elbow macaroni.

Murder Among Friends

To be sure, I seldom missed the potlucks; they were one of the few places a single guy could get decent home cooking without unwanted romantic entanglements. But my typical contribution to them, if I remembered at all, was likely to be a supermarket pie from the day-old rack, or--if I had just read another article about carcinogens in processed foods--a bag of oranges, hastily sliced onto a plate at the last minute.

Only when Penn told me the conference location, and his idea for my role, did it begin to sound like fun. "I need thee to organize local history field trips," he said, "for the Friends from afar. Winchester is full of such history, as thee well knows."

So I did: The city that now styled itself the apple capital also had been the site of three major battles; several more had taken place nearby. The city itself had changed hands between Union and Confederate forces something like seventy times. "Now *that* sounds interesting," I admitted.

He waited patiently on the other end of the phone, until I let out a resigned sigh.

"Okay," I said, "as long as I don't have to come to meetings."

"No problem," he said. "I'll list thee as an alternate member from Potomac Yearly Meeting, and thee can start thinking about some easy daytrips to take."

Thus relieved of the need to take up the Quaker form of the cross--going to committee meetings--I had happily done as he had asked, and begun reading up on the Civil War in the Shenandoah Valley.

It was a rich field, I discovered, as well as a relatively underdeveloped one, at least historiographically. I didn't understand why it was so neglected, what with Stonewall Jackson, Jubal Early, Phil Sheridan, the cadets from Virginia Military Institute, raids by Mosby's Rangers, and lots more, with Winchester right in the middle of it all. But for my purposes, that only made it more interesting; it wasn't as well-worn as Gettysburg, or as exhaustively chronicled as Appomattox.

Of course, skipping the committee meetings also meant I had arrived in Winchester with no idea of what was actually going on with the conference. This, I realized as Lem Penn led Eddie

Smith and me out of the auditorium, meant I probably had a lot more to learn about what I had gotten myself into.

And when Penn turned and stopped at Table Number Three, pointed to Eddie's big display, with all its happily-married couples beaming out at us, and said quietly but firmly, "Friends, I'm afraid this can't stay here," I *knew* I had a whole lot yet to learn.

"What the hell do you mean?" Eddie demanded.

CHAPTER FOUR

The war began in 1861, and from that time until its suppression in 1865 we were, with brief intervals, not clear of one or the other of the armies in our midst.

--From a *Report* of Hopewell Friends Meeting, near Winchester, Virginia

"What I mean," Penn said calmly, "is that thy display is seen as inflammatory by several of the other participants, and in the interests of all I agreed to have it moved."

"Moved where?" Eddie demanded.

"We hadn't decided yet, but I think over there would be a possibility." He nodded toward the far corner where we found the display box.

"But the receipt says Number Three," Eddie insisted, brandishing the paper again. "We paid for it. We have a right to that space."

"Technically, thee may be right," Penn said. "But try to see it from my standpoint. What good does it do if thy display there means half the Conference delegates walk out? Thee knows how sensitive some of them are about this. Besides, they said they wanted it out of the foyer entirely, and I stood firm against that. So everybody will see it sooner or later anyway. Does a table really make that much difference?"

Eddie didn't answer. "Just who," he spat, "are 'they?' The Reverend Doctor Ben Goode? What is he doing here, anyway? He's not a Quaker. Thank God," he added.

"That's another part of it," Penn replied. "A lot of the

evangelicals were wary of coming here at all. This is outside their base, and they felt exposed. Look, I've been working on some of them for several years. When they said they'd come if they could invite Goode, I went along. I didn't think he'd accept. When he did, I was committed. Now he says he won't preach with thy display right by the main entrance, and the evangelicals are backing him up."

As he spoke, I was remembering a rueful comment Penn himself had made, in the closing session of the Boston Conference almost a generation ago. He had listened to us wrangle for several hours over whether to endorse the destruction of draft files as a form of antiwar protest: "Quakers don't believe in fighting," he had mused wryly, "except in committee."

I'd sat through my share of tough sessions since then, and while the current machinations all sounded pretty outrageous to me, they were not inconceivable.

But Eddie was having none of it. The more he heard of Penn's story, the more furious his face became.

"Preach?" he said, not quite believing what he had heard. "When is he going to preach?"

Penn shifted his feet and lowered his gaze momentarily. This surprised me. Was this pillar of Friendly firmness, who by his own account had pleaded for nonviolence and reconciliation face-to-face with both Yasser Arafat and Yitzhak Shamir, actually temporizing? How far had he caved in to these folks?

"Actually," he said, "Goode will be giving the keynote address tomorrow night."

"What?" Eddie's eyebrows jumped, and his face was livid. He pointed at the auditorium. "So now you're going to let that major league homophobe set the tone for the whole conference? This is too much."

He turned and took a few steps away, then whirled around and jabbed a finger in Penn's chest. "Do you realize what this means?" he shouted. "It makes a lie out of this whole goddam event."

"Now, I don't think there is any need for profanity," Penn murmured primly.

But this only make Eddie madder. He ripped the nametag from his shirt and waved it in Penn's face. "You want profanity? Look at this! You're gonna have to throw these away and make new ones that say, '*Some* Friends Conference.' Because you're giving a platform to a man who wants to make criminals out of me and all other lesbian and gay Quakers."

He gestured at the doors again. "Hell, everything that comes out of his mouth is a curse as far as I'm concerned."

"I realize this is hard," Penn tried again, "but the committee has agreed--"

"The committee?" Eddie said, and his expression changed, as if he'd remembered something. "Oh yes, the committee. You're right, they're all in on this, too. Very well then, they all need to know just what kind of genocide they're promoting."

Before Penn or I could protest, he had brushed past us and through the doors back into the auditorium.

Penn gave me a mournful look. "Perhaps it would have been better after all, William, if thee had attended some planning meetings. Thee might have helped prepare him for this."

But I just shook my head and shrugged helplessly as he moved toward the doors. I didn't have the same emotional charge about it, but Penn's disclosure was pretty shocking to me too. If I'd wanted to sit in on a Moral Majority meeting, I would have gone to Lynchburg. And I could stay home and watch Pat Robertson's rantings on TV. What did any of this have to do with a Quaker gathering?

Eddie's voice suddenly boomed loudly from inside, and I hurried after Penn back into the auditorium.

Eddie was on the stage, standing at the podium, where he had flicked on the microphone, giving him command of the scene.

"Doctor Goode," he was saying in a harsh tone, "it seems you may not have been fully informed about the Society of Friends in the United States when you accepted the invitation to speak here. This is supposed to be an 'All-Friends' Conference. But not all Friends have signed up with your anti-gay campaigns."

He waved toward the foyer. "Did you see my pictures, Doctor? In fact, many of our meetings abhor your attitudes, and

they welcome homosexuals, as does mine. Some of our meetings
even *marry* lesbian and gay couples. Yes, they do. And we're
proud of it, Doctor Goode. Did you hear me? We're *proud* of
it!"

Goode was seated exactly opposite Eddie, between two other
men whose suits gave them away as part of his entourage. He
was the incarnation of imperturbability, his thick black hair
carefully arranged, his large, smooth face impassive except for a
faint, fixed smile. He had been heckled before, and had stood
his ground well. He glanced toward Penn, hurrying up the
center steps to the stage. I stopped at the front row of seats,
uncertain where I belonged in this tableau.

"Mr. Chairman," Goode said calmly but firmly, heedless of
the fine points of our Quaker jargon, "could I ask what this is all
about, and who this gentleman is?"

"My name is Eddie Smith, Doctor Goode," Eddie said before
Penn could answer, "and I'm the Co-Clerk of the Lavender Friends
Fellowship. It is a recognized association of lesbian and gay
Quakers--"

"It's not a recognized Quaker group as far as *we're*
concerned," one of the pastors interrupted, in a stentorian voice
well-trained on many a sermon.

He was greying, fat, with a long, mask-like face. Doubtless
he could put on the hale-fellow bonhomie for evangelistic
purposes, but he looked forbidding now. Squinting at his
nametag, I could just make out the block letters: **Horace Burks.**
Under it were the initials EFC-WR.

I knew my Quaker alphabet soup; this was the Evangelical
Friends Church--Western Region, with international headquarters
in Whittier, California. Burks was its Superintendent, though
bishop or petty pope was a more fitting title from what I'd heard.

"We-we don't recognize it in Indiana either," said another
pastor, glaring at Eddie from behind thick glasses. **Lyndon
Coffin,** I read, Richmond General Meeting in Richmond, Indiana,
home of Earlham College and the largest Quaker center outside
Philadelphia.

Coffin's voice was high and thin, without any of Burks's

25

resonance. A bulbous adam's apple worked up and down the front of his prominent neck. His plaid polyester jacket was garish under the auditorium lights, and hung loosely on his sunken chest. He looked more than a little ridiculous. But I had heard of him; he was another superintendent used to getting what he wanted. "I-I think you should sit down and let us get on with our meeting," he piped. "We have a lot to do yet."

"Oh, I'll just *bet* you *do,*" Eddie said sarcastically, adding a campy lilt to heighten the effect. "What's next on your agenda, Friends? Approving the death penalty for sodomy? You're really big on capital punishment, aren't you Doctor Goode? *Leviticus uber alles* and all that? You and your church helped bring it back in Virginia, I believe."

He scratched his chin, mimicking thoughtfulness. "What was it you called the electric chair in one of your sermons, Doctor--Old Sparky? Very clever. And the governor's kept it busy for you, too. So *very* cooperative of him, don't you think?"

Now he aped concern. "But Doctor, are you sure you won't wear it out when you start sending all the gays and lesbians in the state there? After all, like they say, we are everywhere! What'll it be to keep track of us, Doctor, pink triangles? They worked quite well before. Or do you remember?"

Goode was shaking his large head. "My friend," he replied in a tone passably imitating compassion, "I can see you're in a lot of pain, and I did not come here to add to it. As Christians we try to love the sinner, even as we must hate the sin."

Eddie's tone veered from camp to shrill. "Oh, right," he sneered, "you'll cry all the way to the ovens."

Goode winced in distaste at this, and I did too. Troubling as the situation already was, Eddie's harangue was making me even more uneasy.

I had known Eddie Smith for five years, ever since he joined our men's group at Washington Meeting shortly after he began attending worship. He'd been drummed out of the Navy, where he'd been a crack computer operator, after being caught in bed with an ensign, and this turned him against the whole military system. He had put his computer training to work on a

26

Naderish, gay-oriented Personal Privacy Project. There he tracked
the ever-increasing number of ways government and corporations
can spy on people through database technology. His reward was
low pay, long hours, and a justified paranoia.

I'd listened to lots of his fear and anger about what was done
to homosexuals in our society.   Sometimes it all seemed
repetitive, even self-indulgent, yet mostly I sympathized with
him. But this tirade was getting scary.

I caught a glimpse of Rita, at the far end of the table. She
sat with her face in her hands, her braid hanging over her left
shoulder, clearly wishing she was somewhere else. The other
liberals were sitting stony-faced, their ecology tee shirts looking
faintly absurd at the moment.   None of them was good at
dealing with conflict head-on; no liberal Quaker I knew was,
including me. Passive aggressives, that's us. Besides, Eddie was
displaying terrible manners.

But the superintendents were not so timid.   "Lemuel, this
really must stop," Horace Burks declared loudly, banging a fleshy
palm on the table for emphasis. "Doctor Goode is our guest.
This is no way for him to be treated."

"Oh my, aren't we butch," Eddie mocked. "Is this where
Arnold Schwarzenegger comes in, 'Hasta La vista, baby', etc?"

Then his finger was thrusting again and the effeminate tone
was gone. "Well, let me tell you something, Superintendent. The
days when we hid in the closet and quaked when homophobic
fascists like you and Goode growled are past."

Rita finally spoke up. "Couldn't we have a period of silence?"
she asked, turning toward Penn. "If we could center down,
perhaps we could begin a time of healing."

"I'm afraid not," Eddie persisted. "The time for silence is past.
In my Bible--"

"Friend, would thee please be quiet."   Penn was moving
toward him, and raising his voice.

Eddie ignored him. "--In my Bible, Doctor," he repeated, in
what was almost a shout, "it says you reap what you sow. And
you had better watch your back, buddy, because--"

"My Bible says that, too," Goode shot back, "and that verse
comes back to me every time I read about AIDS."

"You bastard!" Eddie's voice was almost a screech, and he started to come out from behind the podium. But Penn had reached him, and deftly flipped the mike button off. Burks and Coffin were on their feet now, red-faced, shouting for him to get off the stage.

Eddie yelled something back at them, but I couldn't make it out. Burks pushed his chair away; it fell over and clattered off the stage. Then he was beside Penn, and the two of them were prodding Eddie toward the side steps, blocking his view of the committee behind them.

"Get away from me!" he yelled, and I could see his hands clench into fists. My own palms suddenly went damp. Were we going to have a brawl, for God's sake? I felt a pull toward them, and a thought, *Do something*, echoed in my head.

Then I was up the side steps, putting my hands on Eddie's shoulders from behind, not roughly but with a kind of tenderness, as if protecting him from the two menacing figures blocking his view of the group.

"Come on, Eddie," I coaxed softly, "let's talk about this outside. Come on now." Then I was guiding him down the steps and up the aisle, and he was crying and muttering something over and over, which I couldn't make out, but to which I repeated, "Yes, yes, I know," several times.

Back in the foyer, I kept an arm around him, and said, "All right, it's okay now, Eddie. Let's just take a few deep breaths, and maybe center down a bit while we do it. Count with me, okay? Inhale: One; now let it out. Inhale: Two--"

But then he was pulling angrily away from me.

"What was it you called Goode up on Skyline Drive?" he said bitterly, wiping at his eyes. "'A marvelous indigenous American folk art form?' Yes, that was it. Jesus, Bill, you really don't get it. This is not just talk. It's a matter of life and death for me. For us."

He raised his arm toward the display board behind us. But he was too close. His hand struck one of the grinning pictures, and the whole hinged assembly tumbled over in a heap.

"Oh, christ!" he shouted, and ran through the doors into the hazy late afternoon.

CHAPTER FIVE

As a member of the Virginia Convention, I voted against the
ordinance of secession on its passage by that body, with the
hope that even then, the collision of arms might be avoided
and some satisfactory adjustment arrived at. The adoption
of that ordinance wrung from me bitter tears of grief; but I
at once recognized my duty to abide the decision of my
native State, and to defend her soil against invasion.

--Jubal Early, *Autobiographical Sketch*

"So, do you know--what's his name--Mr. Smith well?"
I was not interested in this question, nor in the questioner.
Rita had just given me her quick version of the political layout
of the Planning Committee, while I nodded frequently and
shoveled in forkfuls from the mound of pastel green and
allegedly red salad on my dinner plate.

It's hard to be nutritionally correct in a college cafeteria, but
I was putting on a good front, figuring I'd find some potato chips
or cupcakes in a vending machine later and make up the
difference.

The cafeteria was noisy with the buzz of Quakers getting
acquainted and reacquainted, as were we. And there was the
hint of a smile on Rita's face as she talked, signaling the
possibility of more pleasure in our conversation than her story
deserved, something I was anxious to encourage.

We had reminisced a bit about the late Sixties, then caught
up on work (she was now Associate Curator of Special
Collections at Barnard); and family (she left her husband three

years ago; their son, now 12, was living with him in Queens). She had also given me her quick and dirty take on the leading evangelicals: "Horace Burks's dream is to plant a thousand new churches through telemarketing," she said.

"Telemarketing?" I gaped at her. "For *churches?"*

"Oh, yes," she assured me. "He did a briefing on it last night. It's the latest thing in evangelism. And Lyndon Coffin wants him to run a pilot program for them in Indiana. They've been losing members fast out there, and he thinks it could save their bacon. That is, as soon as every Quaker body gets out of the National Council of Churches."

"The National Council of Churches?" I asked. "Are we in that?"

Rita laughed, and it was a hearty, vigorous laugh. "I don't know," she said. "I think so."

I can't say I cared much one way or another about the National Council of Churches. But I liked the way this conversation was going.

It was at this point that Augustus "Gus" Murray arrived with his buttinski question about Eddie. He was, I had also learned from Rita, President of the Center for Public Renewal in Washington. And he sat his tray of roast beef and glutinous gravy down right next to her without even a by-your-leave.

I scowled and speared some more salad. So much for our getting re-acquainted at this meal.

Murray was scholarly-looking, with thick glasses, nerdily slicked back hair and manners much too refined for the assembly line food we were eating. In fact, he was a misplaced mandarin in our whole *deshabille* Quaker ambiance: the suit was too well-tailored for a Friends pastor, but the liberals wouldn't be caught dead in such getup either, especially away from the office.

And even the pastors, some of them anyway, wouldn't have called Smith "Mister." Avoidance of titles was one of the few classic Quaker traditions they remembered, at least at conferences like this one.

For Murray, though, it was part of the civility necessary to productive dialogue on issues, and he was big on civility. It was a key part of his Center's image, at least as I had heard of it around town. They were continually putting on forums and conferences on topics like "Social Issues As The Key to Realignment," "Recovering Authentic Values From the Wreckage of the Sixties," or, "Golden Age or Dead End? A Balanced First Look at the Reagan Years," in which a few well-patronized liberals were surrounded and out-talked by a phalanx of rightists. Ah, the fun you could have with right-wing foundation money.

So when he asked about Eddie, I was inclined to be guarded in response. I wasn't ready to pick up on Eddie's harangue; I wasn't even sure I wanted to be associated with it. But doing intelligence work for Murray wasn't my cup of tea either.

I swallowed the mix of limp lettuce and sallow tomato slices, gagging slightly on an extra-crunchy white-toast crouton. "We attend the same meeting," I said noncommittally.

Murray sipped from his water glass. "Is he often that, uh, vehement?" he asked. One eyebrow was slightly raised, emphasizing the understatement.

That was easier. "No," I answered. "In fact I don't think I've ever seen him that upset."

This was a line of questioning I was anxious to deflect, with one of my own. "How did you come to be here with, uh, Dr. Goode?" Skipping the title here seemed like going along with a PR image of affability that I found distinctly distasteful.

"He's working with us on the Crusade," put in The Reverend Tommie Lee Brewer, who was settling at Murray's right. Wiping his broad, perspiring face with a paper napkin, he smiled broadly, too easily for me. "Yep, Gus and the Center are gonna be the real brains of the operation."

Brewer was round and much more roughly-hewn than his partner. The effect of his expensive suit was spoiled by a tie which had "Jesus Is Lord" machine-embroidered on it in an italic, repeating pattern of silver and maroon.

Brewer put a dish of dark brown pudding on his empty plate and eyed it carefully. I could almost hear the interior dialogue. *On the one hand, it is probably mostly cornstarch and caramel coloring, with only a rumor of real chocolate. On*

31

the other, it is probably sweet.

He took a bite, savored it a moment, then put his spoon down. *Get thee behind me, sucrose. At least until I can find out if there's ice cream somewhere.*

"Gus is gonna run the office and handle the communications end," Brewer continued. "He's getting some real pros in on it. It was his idea to kick it off here tomorrow."

"Kick it off?" I asked, my throat feeling suddenly dry. "Kick what off?" I shot a glance at Rita; she looked embarrassed and wouldn't meet my gaze.

"The Crusade for Family Values," put in Horace Burks, beaming across at Brewer from over a cup of coffee.

All at once I felt surrounded. "It's quite an honor for us, really," Burks bubbled. "A chance to rededicate the Friends movement to genuine old-fashioned family values again. It'll give us a real boost in our church-planting, I just know it."

He turned toward Murray. "Do you think it will make the evening news shows?"

"We're hoping," Murray said modestly. "We could use a little publicity. This is a little more activist than our usual program," he added, reaching into his jacket and handing me a brochure about the Center.

I glanced obliquely at it; the heading read, "To Shape America's Future." I set it delicately down by my fork, and was not sorry when a drop of salad oil made a small dark spot on the textured paper.

Murray was droning on. "I've thought for some time we were perhaps getting too exclusively academic at the Center," he said.

"Policy debates in Washington are necessary, of course, but the pressure for policy change ultimately comes from the grass roots. So this will add a somewhat different approach to our traditional agenda. I'm looking forward to it. A press conference would be fun."

A press conference for Ben Goode at a Quaker gathering? And where, I wondered, was Lemuel Penn in all these machinations?

To be sure, I knew that his social views, shaped by the stern round of the seasons in a Virginia apple orchard, and his own mainstream Christian theology, were firmly traditional.

But he had learned to get along with the mixed bag retinue among the liberal Meetings. We had, after all, been the mainstay of support for his Middle East peace labors. The pastors didn't really care for the work, because it wasn't evangelistic, didn't "plant" any churches. As if you could better convert people after they'd all blown themselves to kingdom come.

Penn's broad range of contacts had in fact been the strength of his tenure as Clerk of the North American Friends Association, which so shakily straddled the great divide in American Quakerdom, and constantly threatened to collapse into it. He had learned to live and let live--judging not, letting the wheat grow with the tares--all the while gently coaxing the quirky, mutually suspicious bands of Quakers within it toward some group semblance of the understanding and mutual regard he had personally achieved with most of them.

"'You are my Friends if you do what I command you,'" I had often heard him quote from John's Gospel, "'and by this shall all men *[nowadays he sensitively said 'all people']* know you are my disciples, if you have love one for another.'" Said at just the right moment, it could bring a lump to your throat, and a wave of humility to your attitude.

The All Friends Conference was to be his chance to give this process a major goosing. But bringing it off would require a balancing act that would wear out all the surviving Flying Wallendas.

Surely, I thought, he would know how unnerving this alliance with Goode would be to one whole side of the family, wouldn't he? Eddie's reaction had been extreme, sure, but this talk of crusades and AIDS as the harvest of sin--well, it made my stomach turn. How the hell would I explain Goode's appearance when I got back to Washington Monthly Meeting? How could Penn have screwed it up this badly? How, I found myself wondering, could Rita have gone along with it?

I wasn't hungry anymore. Hearing a chorus of laughter, I looked around, and saw Penn at another table, with Goode and Lyndon Coffin. The three of them were chortling loudly at some unheard joke, oblivious in their camaraderie.

"Um," I said to Murray, fumbling for harmless topics, "where are you staying?"

Murray glanced down at the small print on the corner of his nametag. "'Mott 317,'" he read. "Up the stairs. Doctor Goode is on the fourth floor."

Oh great, I thought. We're practically roommates. Eddie will love this. If he stays around at all.

"Um, excuse me," I said, pushing away from the table, "I think I need a walk. See you all later." Rita looked up questioningly, but I turned away. As I reached the doorway, laughter erupted again from the table where Penn, Goode and Coffin sat. I was glad to put it behind me.

Outside, the evening light was slanted and softening, the tall old trees were rustling gently, and the edge of heat was off the air. In the southern distance, a thunderhead was floating toward Front Royal, its grey silhouette sporadically lit up by lightning bolts within it, too far away to be heard.

This was my favorite time of day, and as I walked aimlessly across the grassy central oval, my mood began to soften. Maybe there was some logical explanation for all the day's confusions.

At the other side of the oval, I looked up and saw the library across the street in front of me. Lights were still on, and I was drawn toward it like a moth to a flame. The sign by the entrance said summer hours were til 8:30, and that made it irresistible.

I went inside, found the New Books shelf, and wouldn't you know it, came upon a new tome on the Civil War in the Valley, *Jackson, Early and Sheridan: Titans of the Shenandoah*, by a professor at VMI. Within five minutes I was lost in its pages, retracing yet again the course of the many rivers of destruction that had poured through and out of this cut of land between the Blue Ridge and the Alleghenies.

The chapter on Early's string of daring successes in the summer of 1864 was particularly compelling. Once Lee gave the word, his troops raced down the Valley, brushing aside every Union force they met, spilling out into western Maryland to threaten Washington itself in mid-July. Lincoln himself watched the fighting one night from a parapet at Fort Stevens on the city's perimeter, coming briefly under fire and almost giving his generals heart failure.

Then Early turned and made a daring raid into Pennsylvania, burning much of the town of Chambersburg in retaliation for the sacking of VMI and the burning of farms in the Valley. When he galloped safely back into his Shenandoah stronghold, Grant had enough, and ordered Phil Sheridan to go in and stop him, no matter what. It was a hell of a story.

"The library will be closing in five minutes," said the student librarian quietly. She was slim, bespectacled, pretty, but I didn't like her message. I could easily have spent several more hours reading and ruminating on such weight matters as whether Sheridan really had miscalculated so badly in sending his troops through the Opequon Canyon in September, 1864, and whether Early was even more at fault for failing to leap through that window of opportunity, which cost him the victory in what became known as Third Winchester.

Closing the book with a sigh, I put it back on the shelf and headed for the door.

But I was not in fact forced to let go of my militaristic musings, because coming down the steps I practically ran into Lem Penn, walking with a much taller man I had not seen before. The man was waving his arms and talking excitedly.

"Sometimes, Mr. Penn, I swear to God I can almost hear them," he said. He stabbed a finger into the thickened dusk across the oval. "Sheridan and Early fought each other right across this campus during Third Winchester," he announced, "and there were encampments of both sides all around here, first one side and then the other, all through the war."

Penn glanced up and saw me. "Bill," he called, "thee should hear this. I've found a man after thine own heart. Fred--"

But the other man was already around him, bounding up the bottom steps to seize my hand. "Fred Harrison," he boomed, a bit too enthusiastically for my taste. "I'm the president here, and Valley State's Civil War heritage is one of my favorite topics."

Once he mentioned his job, I recognized the over-hearty tone:

it was the call of the hungry academic fundraiser picking up the spoor of a prospect. Not that I could blame him; it's a jungle out there in academia. The wonder is that he had time or energy to be interested in anything else.

"Are you a scholar of the war?" I asked innocently.

Harrison laughed. He had the hearty middle-aged good looks a viable college prexy needed, with a craggy face and upswept gray hair that were vaguely reminiscent of the Old Dominion's senior senator, John Warner. It was a look which couldn't have hurt him with the local establishment.

"A scholar?" he replied. "Not really, Bill, though I will admit to committing a few research pieces to print. I'm more like a fanatic. And why not? That war, with all the awful bloodshed, made America. For better and for worse, no denying it. And so much of it happened right around here, it's unbelievable."

He raised an arm, as if unveiling some mighty diorama that only he could see in the darkness. "From up the hill you can practically see--" then, interrupting himself, he started walking again and beckoned to us. "Come on," he urged.

We followed, I happily and Penn evidently willingly, though I didn't think he was particularly a buff. That's the slot he had recruited me to fill.

Harrison led on around the oval, past the Bartram natural sciences Building, to where a sidewalk angled off past it up a grassy slope and into some trees. I knew that beyond the line of trees stood Opequon Creek Friends Meeting, where the College had started over a century before, as one small, but constructive outcome of the war. Was Harrison taking us there?

He was not. There was a wooden bench near the trees, and Harrison stopped there, turning back to gaze across and beyond the quiet campus. The buildings were indistinct in the darkness, but beyond them we could see the lights of cars and trucks moving north and south along Interstate 81.

"You can't see it from here," Harrison said, "but just beyond and parallel to the interstate is US11, the old Valley Pike. It's as close to being the Main Street of the War as any route ever was. Lee passed up it going to Antietam and Gettysburg. One Yankee general after another chased Stonewall Jackson down it, but he always came back, sucking lemons and spitting fury. Jubal Early came through here on his way to raid Washington and Chambersburg."

"Yes," I chimed in, caught up in his rhapsodizing, "and then old Jubal almost kept Lincoln from getting re-elected."

Harrison smiled at me beatifically, recognizing a kindred spirit. "Cedar Creek," he murmured. "Third Winchester. The Burning. That was an epic duel, Sheridan versus Early. Sadly neglected, too, overshadowed by Lee and Grant. But really, for months those two were bogged down around Petersburg, Grant's troops shivering and sick, Lee's shivering and sick and starving. There was no nobility to it, no drama.

"But here," again Harrison's arm rose toward the night, "in the Shenandoah you had continuous action against a magnificent natural backdrop. Just think of Mosby's men. How many nights like this did they swoop down out of the darkness on a supply wagon train over there on the Pike, or maybe right behind us camped around the meetinghouse?"

He slapped his side and turned abruptly, almost fiercely to Penn. "That's why," he hissed, "there *must* be a center, a Valley Center, and it should be *here.*"

Penn nodded slowly, a stubby finger stroking his chin, mulling it over, but clearly impressed. "Thee may be onto something," he admitted.

"A what?" I asked. "What sort of center?"

"The Shenandoah Valley Civil War Memorial Center," Harrison said, savoring the words.

"But aren't there centers in the Valley already?" I persisted. I've been to New Market, and there's a big museum there. And down at Staunton, VMI--"

Harrison would hear none of it. "Those are monuments to individual battles and leaders," he demurred. "Fine in themselves, don't get me wrong; but none of them pulls together the whole four-year saga of the war in the Valley."

He straightened up, almost striking a heroic pose. "No, the Valley Center will not be just another marker for a particular battle, but the energizing nucleus of a whole renaissance of history and remembrance in the entire Valley."

He paused, and grinned shrewdly.   "And that's not to
mention that it would be a focal point for the increased tourist
revenues   a project like this would be sure to generate."

"Sounds good to me," I said. "Where do I send my resume?"

The president's grin turned rueful. "At this point, I'm afraid,
it's not a question yet of when, but still a matter of if," he said.

Now Penn was looking a bit mischievous, I thought. "Which
is to say," he added, "the Center is still a dream.   Or more of a
sales pitch.   At least I think that's what we've just heard."

Harrison chuckled. "I suppose you're right," he acknowledged.

"But that's what they pay me for. And anyway, it will soon
be more than just an idea.   I've been talking to community
leaders all up and down the Valley, and there's a building sense
of support for it.   Even enthusiasm, I think it's fair to say."

"Yes," Penn added, "and when thee joined us, William, Fred
was just telling me that he's about to get Ben Goode on his team
as well."

That news put something of a damper on my nascent
excitement about the scheme. "Why him?" I inquired.

"Why not?" Harrison shrugged. "Goode is just about the
biggest name in the Valley these days. If he signs on, he'd bring
a lot of others with him.   Besides, he's a Valley native, and had
ancestors in the war. He can see the good it would do for the
area. We're going to talk about it tomorrow at lunch."

I can see it now, I thought, The Rev. Dr. Ben Goode Wing of
the Valley Center. Maybe it would specialize in Baptist bigotry.

"You don't suppose," I said, with a certain edge of malice,
"that maybe he'd support an exhibit on the southern clerics who
defended slavery so strenuously as a God-ordained, biblically
certified institution, something only infidels and incendiaries
could oppose?"

Harrison's smile seemed to grow a bit tight and thin as I
talked.   This was perhaps not quite what he had in mind.   It
could be somewhat more difficult to sell to the local gentry. But
his silence only egged me on.

"Now that would be interesting, Fred, if a bit chilling," I said.

"Or how about an examination of the way fear of slave
rebellions, and especially talk about black assaults on white

38

women, were used as the Willie Horton ads of secessionist politics. That would be a hell of a lot more interesting than another collection of faded uniforms, old swords in need of polishing, and powdery-looking minie bullets wired in rows behind plate glass. I'm as fascinated by the Civil War as you are, but I've seen enough of that stuff already."

Harrison was fast on his feet, I had to give him credit for that. "There would be a place for such studies at the Center," he said quickly. "I want to see all kinds of creative scholarship taking place there."

It was an astute response. Keep such unsettling stuff out of the exhibits, where the donors would see it, and in the obscure journals, which were read mainly by graduate students under doctoral duress.

Harrison looked at his watch. "Time for me to take my evening jog and then turn in," he said. "You know your way back?"

Penn nodded gravely. "I think so," he said, deadpan. "My mother graduated from here in 1917. And I was thinking about a constitutional myself, up to the meetinghouse. Where she's buried," he added dryly.

"Well, then," said Harrison, a bit nervously, "I'll see you all tomorrow. Great to meet you, Bill." He shook my hand and strode back down the walk, around the sciences building toward the oval.

"Care to walk with me?" Penn asked.

"Sure," I said. "Why not? Maybe there are some peaceful ghosts up there, after all this war talk."

"Not entirely, I'm afraid," Penn replied, moving again up the walk. "Opequon Friends were not always as good about the Quaker Peace Testimony as they might have been, especially with each other. Doesn't thee know about the great Quaker fight of 1828?"

"Never heard of it," I said. "You're kidding, right?"

"Nope," he said, "I'm afraid not," and he shook his head in a sad sort of way that made me think he was talking of something that had happened last month.

Or maybe right before dinner this evening.

CHAPTER SIX

"The humble, meek, merciful, just, pious and devout souls are everywhere of one religion; and when Death has taken off the mask, they will know one another, though the diverse liveries they wear here makes them strangers."

--William Penn, *Some Fruits of Solitude*

On a crisp and sunny autumn afternoon in 1828, wagons began rolling west off the Valley Pike. They were headed up the dusty Old Creek Road to where the driveway angled up the rise to the Opequon Creek Meetinghouse.

Many of the drivers laughed and snapped the horses' reins as they made the turn, and conversation with the wives and children at their sides was lively. It was if they were heading for a picnic. In fact, not a few were bearing baskets filled with provender.

But a quiet family outing under the turning leaves was not what the riders had in mind.

Instead, these Valley folk were coming to watch the Quakers fight.

In keeping with their anticipated entertainment, besides the food a few fugitive jugs of liquor also sloshed unnoticed under the bench seats, stuff that would never have been permitted on the property on any other day.

The meetinghouse they approached loomed like the architectural antithesis of everything vulgar or noisy. It had sat on this ridge for more than sixty years, since before the

Murder Among Friends

Revolution; George Washington, it was assumed, had probably slept there sometime during the war. Its mien was as solid, substantial and sober as the reputation of its weekly congregants.

The walls, of grey flagstones, were outlined raggedly with white mortar, matching the color combination of the typical Quakeress's dresses and collars. The slate roof sloped to a sensible, unadorned peak.

Below its northeast corner, stone walls spattered with lichens and moss of orange, yellow and dark green diverged and then joined to enclose the large rectangle of the hillside that was the Meeting's cemetery. Already the remains of three generations of Friends lay within its confines, though the burial ground looked more like an empty pasture. The scores of unmarked graves were yet another silent Quaker challenge to the prideful pomp of the vain, passing world outside.

Opequon Creek Meeting was a place of thunderous quiet and truculently conspicuous peace, gaudily austere, almost histrionically serene. It was home to a people wordlessly conscious of the fact that their house of worship was senior to the nation of which they were citizens. On any other day, those looking for an afternoon's vulgar carousing and brawling would have automatically given it a wide berth.

But not this day.

The wagons' passengers did not disembark as they topped the rise and approached the meetinghouse. Instead, they pulled up under the larger trees, seeking shady vantage points from which to have a good view of the building.

They could not have got inside anyway. The place was full, packed to the walls. Bonnets and broad-brimmed hats crowded against the windows from the inside, as men and women jostled about, abandoning their usual segregated seating. Similarly-clad people milled around the doors, trying to get in.

There was sound coming from inside, too; not calls to prayer, or the singing of hymns, but angry shouts and the muffled echo of loud harangues, punctuated alternately by cheers and catcalls. The arguments fascinated the watching rustics, even though only occasionally could they make out a word.

The excitement increased when three new wagons, loaded

with young Quaker men, trundled heavily up the drive. The youths began jumping off before the wagons stopped, then formed a phalanx around an older man who stepped down slowly from the seat of the leading carriage.

"Here they come!" shouted a watching farmer, already loosened up with several nips of the sauce. "They's the, whatchacall, Hicksites. Hoooeeee!"

The young men ignored him, striding into the circle of crude gawkers toward the west door, where a rank of dark-clad defenders blocked their path.

"The clerk is here!" boomed a voice from among them. "Let the clerk come in!"

"No!" came the reply from the door. "The true clerk is at the table. Keep your imposter outside where he belongs."

In a moment there was pushing and shoving at the doorway. Broad-brims were knocked off, and a couple of youths went sprawling. The farmers began whooping and cheering, not really for one side or the other, which they couldn't distinguish by appearance or opinion anyhow, just egging on the show.

The phalanx of Hicksites, after being momentarily stymied at the door, was forcing its way in. Their champion was moving inexorably towards their objective, the presiding clerk's table set up inside, in front of the bare wooden facing bench at the head of the meeting. Control of the table meant control of this grey stone redoubt.

As the Hicksite vanguard disappeared, the din within increased. A window above the west door flew open, revealing two men pummeling each other in its space. A fist connected, and one of the man suddenly tumbled out.

Glancing off the angled roof of the narrow porch above the door, his fall was broken by a large bush. More cheers went up from the assembled viewers as he shook his head, pushed out of the bush, staggered a few steps, and then headed defiantly back toward the door.

Now people were being shoved out the west door: bareheaded, swearing men and screaming women, the crimson in their cheeks accentuated by their white bonnets. As the hoots of the farmers reached a crescendo, more Quakers hurtled out of the entrance, gathering in angry circles in the grass to rub their bruises, dab at their eyes, and shake their fists at their assailants.

A loud rending sound of breaking wood increased the exodus. A woman screamed and fainted as she came through the crowded entrance, and for a moment it seemed she might be trampled in a general panic. But someone scooped her up, and behind her several hands began pulling the door closed. It clunked shut, then a moment later opened briefly to permit the ejection of a grey-haired, bespectacled Friend of singular, and singularly insulted dignity.

The howling yokels fell silent as this Friend came out at a half-trot, propelled by several young bucks behind him. He reeled forward a few steps, tripped over a tree root and fell on his face.

"I'll be damned," a farmer swore, greatly impressed. "If it ain't ol' Mahlon Evans. Now that really beats all."

And so it did. Evans, a prominent and prosperous miller, was the clerk of Opequon Creek Meeting, these past twenty years, as was his father before him.

Had been clerk, that is. He now sat before the world deposed, fumbling in the grass for his spectacles, his thinning hair askew and carefully-tailored plain black suit ripped at the shoulder and streaked with dust.

His hands found the spectacles and raised them toward his face. They were broken, one lens gone and the gold frame bent crazily.

Evans put them on anyway, then stood up unsteadily and began slapping at the dust on his clothes. A woman rushed up to him, weeping.

"Oh, Mahlon," she cried, "what have they done to thee? What have they done to us?"

Evans looked at his wife for a moment. But before he could answer a young buck stuck his head out the open window behind and above them.

"Hey, Friend Evans," the youth mocked, "is thee missing thy clerk's table? No need to--here it is!"

Laughing, he tossed out several pieces of wood: the dark polished legs, and a slat from the clerk's table, which had been completely dismembered in the struggle.

Evans moved to dodge the missiles, but one table leg struck him on the arm. His wife cried out again and stroked the spot. But he shook her off, bent over and picked up the wooden leg, and waved it at his tormenters in the window.

"Is this what you ruthless heathen call true religion?" he shouted, and let the leg drop and bounce in the dirt.

Then he turned, straightened his back, offered one arm to his wife and began walking with her past the now silent farmers toward his own wagon, tied up in the meeting stable beyond the brow of the ridge. Despite his torn clothes and skewed spectacles, with every step he seemed to regain some of the dignity of which the assaults of the hour had deprived him.

The farmers watched the couple go with a kind of awe. Only after the Evans and their wagon were gone did they start to talk again, and turn to open their picnic baskets.

The battle for Opequon Creek meeting was now over, they realized, but as they passed around the chicken, and the beans and cornbread, they were not disappointed.

They had seen something strange, strange to the point of being unimaginable. And they knew the time would come when they would tell their grandchildren of the day they had watched the Quakers fight. And as the young eyes grew wide with amazement and disbelief, they would nod their old heads and vow that it was true, yessir, every word.

CHAPTER SEVEN

11th month 2d [1863].   Engaged with father preparing memorial to present to the [Virginia] legislature, on exempting Friends from [Confederate] military duty.
11th month 14th.   Detained until late before the military committee of [Virginia's] House of Delegates, who treated me respectfully, but declined to do anything for Friends.
2d month 14th [1865]. Went to see about the cases of several Friends who were suffering for the non-performance of military duties.

--From the *Diary* of Friend John B. Crenshaw

It was dark and getting late, but I was as spellbound as any antebellum farmboy as Lemuel Penn told this story. The great Separation among Friends had first sundered the Philadelphia meetings in 1827, and finally arrived in the Shenandoah Valley after surging across the American Quaker landscape for a year, building up momentum like a tidal wave whipped by a seabed earthquake toward an unprotected shore.

"Jesus," I said when he had finished, "how come I didn't hear about this in my Quaker history class?"

"They usually leave it out," he said. "Our historians are still embarrassed by it, and a little afraid of the intensity of the whole thing. You can find it in small print in back numbers of the *Annals of Quaker History.*"

He rubbed his hands meditatively. "Both Mahlon Evans and his wife kept journals, and the Winchester paper ran a long article based on the farmers' accounts. But it happened just about that way. Evans held his head up afterward, but it broke his heart and he died a year later."

"And tell me again what it was about?"

Penn waved a hand dismissively. We were sitting on a bench on a long porch that ran half the length of the meetinghouse from the northeast corner. Around us the night was warm black velvet. In front was the cemetery, where the crescent tops of headstones--the testimony against them having faded--showing over the stone fence. Through the trees a scattering of lights showed in the dormitories, and behind them were the white headlights and glowing crimson taillights moving on the interstate. An early cricket chirped from somewhere nearby.

"Why, the heart and soul of the true Christian faith, what else?" His voice was sardonic. "What is any such fight about?" he asked rhetorically. "Money, sex and power, isn't that the usual list? Well, there wasn't any sex here that I know of, and while the property was worth something, land was cheap and there was rarely more than a few hundred dollars in the meeting treasury."

He sighed, as if it had all happened last week. Maybe for him it had. "So that leaves power," he said. "In this case, the power to answer two questions: Who's right, and who gets to be in charge."

He leaned forward on the bench, elbows on his knees, a posture which I knew was a sign of strong feelings. He cupped both hands in front of him, as if holding a bowl which contained the essence of history, the elixir of understanding.

"Thee must always be grateful for the Peace testimony, William," he said abruptly. I didn't quite follow the turn of his thought. Then he added, "Without it, Friends could easily have been shooting each other over this. Religious wars and civil wars, they're always the worst kind."

"Aren't they usually related?" I wondered.

"Yes!" he said fiercely, nodding approvingly in my direction. "As far as I can see, they always are. The Holy Land is nothing else, once thee digs under all the nonsense about the Cold War and oil and so-called vital national interests. And surely the Civil War that our Friend Harrison wants so much to lift up was just that."

Murder Among Friends

"Do you suppose he'll want to look at that in his Center?"

"A good question," Penn said more quietly. "It won't be worth much if he doesn't. There's plenty of Quaker stories yet to be told in any full history of the War in the Valley. Men who died in prison rather than be drafted into the army. Women and children nursing the wounded of both sides in the middle of battles. And many families that lost everything."

A realization came stealing over me as Penn talked. The vividness with which he had told the story of 1828, and the intensity of his reflections on it and the war, clicked with other, inarticulate impressions to form a question I hadn't thought about before. "Is that what's so important about this conference for you?"

He nodded slowly, and I could sense a slow rueful grin. "Thee begins to detect the method in my madness," he said.

But then he leaned forward again, shaping his palms around his invisible bowl.

"Can't thee see how strained the fabric of our whole culture is nowadays?" he asked. "Friends are only, so to speak, a tiny thread in the social fabric. But all around I see that fabric being stretched and frayed and beginning to tear...." His voice drifted off as he gazed into the bowl again.

"It certainly was this afternoon," I agreed.

He nodded. Then after a moment's silence another thought took shape in my mind.

"And you think that's what happened before the Civil War."

Another nod. "Essentially, yes. Look at the major denominations. One after another, they split apart, Methodists, Presbyterians, Baptists. American society slowly but surely polarized, opening up more and more space for madmen and manipulators to operate in. John Brown in the North; William Lowndes Yancey and the Fireaters in the South. Eventually peaceful solutions were discredited, then finally abandoned completely."

"But Quakers didn't split over slavery," I objected. "We were politically correct on that a century ahead of time. And so humble about it too."

"True," he said, "though there were plenty of arguments

about just how far a good Quaker ought to go in opposing slavery. The Underground Railroad, which we brag about so much today, caused endless arguments among Friends in its heyday.

"No, in 1828, I think Friends were again--what's the current phrase--ahead of the curve, even in their conflicts. Though given my biblical bias, I'd call the riot here a prophetic sign. Because the struggle that caused it was between two groups that were carrying the seeds of what we see today."

"You mean the liberals against the evangelicals?"

"Yep. The two factions here at Opequon Creek finally reconciled in the 1930s. The descendants of the old families forgot what all the shouting had been about, and newcomers like you never knew about it. Same for the Methodists and Presbyterians, after a fashion. For awhile, in the fifties and early sixties, it seemed like we might actually be making some progress. Protestants started talking to Catholics and Jews. Even liberal and evangelical Friends got together now and then.

He shook his head. "Not anymore. Not really. Now everywhere you look the polarization is increasing. Where and how things might break apart this time, I can't guess. But I'm afraid it's coming."

He looked out over the headstones. "Sometimes I think I'm in a time warp," he said. "All the big churches are coming apart again. Same fights--abortion, gay rights, the Bible, you know the list. Quakers used to be different, peculiar; but now we're just like the rest. And it's making plenty of room for today's madmen and manipulators. They're hard at work, too."

At this, though, another, jarring question occurred to me. "If you believe all this," I demanded, "why invite someone like Ben Goode to speak at the Conference? Of all people, he's fuel to the fire."

Penn sighed. "Like I said to thy friend this afternoon, I was sure he'd never accept. Friends were much too small a group for him to waste time on. I was certain of it. But if I agreed to invite him, I knew Burks and Coffin would commit to come; their quid pro quo, thee might say."

"You mean their price," I retorted, thinking *thirty pieces of silver.*

He grunted, then added, "Their names on the program gave the conference credibility with the evangelicals."

"But what about the liberals?"

"Most of them weren't going to know, because Goode was going to turn us down, and that would have been that." He sighed again. "Besides, you liberals normally don't like to quarrel. Thy friend Smith is the exception that proves the rule."

He chuckled quietly at himself. "So much for trying to play Henry Kissinger in a broad-brimmed hat."

"Why *did* Goode accept?"

He turned his palms upward, admitting ignorance. "I'm not entirely sure, but it seems he has a soft spot for Valley State. I think he also had a favorite aunt who went here. And it turns out, I just learned today, that Horace Burks went to seminary with him. He must have loaned Goode money or something back then, so Goode owed him a favor, and Burks lobbied him to come across."

He paused again. "I also suspect," he said, "that a better offer for this week somewhere else probably fell through, and we happened to be in exactly the wrong place at just the wrong time. We're close to home for him, thee knows; the Good Life Baptist Temple is just down in Harrisonburg. It's no big deal for him."

He shrugged. "Who can say, in the end. Maybe it was just a whim."

"Do you mean," I said, "that maybe he wanted to see if Quakers were still dressed in grey and ate oatmeal all the time?" I hate that.

Penn grimaced. "There is that. The peculiarity factor. But I doubt it." He leaned back on the bench, dropping the imaginary bowl. "Actually, I think thee and thy Friend Smith misjudge brother Goode," he said more cheerfully. "He's probably not nearly as much of a monster as you think."

"Don't bet on it," I said grimly. "Smith may have lost his temper and exaggerated, but if you ask me--"

I stopped at the wail of a siren, in the distance but getting louder. Peering toward the highway, I saw the flashing blue and red lights come into view on I-81 from the south. Reflections off a square cab identified it as an ambulance, but a police car was close behind it. Penn was staring at it too.

Such caravans and their shrill noise were common enough back home that I barely noticed them. But here in the Valley nighttime, on the veranda of a building well into its third century, the sight and sound seemed utterly discordant.

"I wonder if a truck turned over," I mused, "the way they roar down the highway."

"I don't think so," Penn replied. He was leaning forward. "They're slowing down."

The lights swerved to the east and briefly disappeared from view.

"That's our exit," Penn said quietly.

Then we saw and heard them again. On the highway they had seemed, though intrusive, somehow distanced, almost like video images. Now they were real and close, screaming up the state road in our direction, and I could see the dust rising behind them.

Penn stood up. "I think..." he started to say.

But then the ambulance had turned, too fast, into the entrance to the College, fish-tailing for a second as it braked to enter the oval. The police car made the curve more smoothly. And in another second they had pulled up, in a driveway.

"It's Mott Hall," Penn said, alarm rising in his tone. "Someone at the Conference. My God, what now?"

CHAPTER EIGHT

The Valley that under God's blessing had bloomed as a rose, and from its richness had fed for years the Armies of the Rebellion, that had been a passageway for the advancing Rebel hosts to invade the North and endanger the capital of the nation, whose people were eminently disloyal and bitterly hostile, and who had promoted, as far as possible, every expedition of invasion, must feel the avenging hand of Freedom's arm.

> --Charles King, in James E. Taylor's *Sketchbook*
> of the Civil War

A gurney was being wheeled from the dorm, two uniformed attendants looking over their shoulders and lifting the ends expertly over the curb. A third was holding an IV bag on its pole with one hand, and adjusting an oxygen mask with the other over the face of the limp figure strapped to the bed.

Besides the pulsing red and blue lights, and above the racket of people's voices and the metallic crackling of the police radio, I heard the faint, insistent beeps of electronic medical gear. Will any of us, I wondered irritably, arrive in heaven, or even hell, without those small, unrelenting beep-beeps echoing as the last sounds we heard on earth?

I couldn't make out the face under the mask, but Penn knew immediately from the shape of the head, and the thick, shiny black hair. "Dear God," he croaked, "it's Goode."

I tried to get another look, but the big white doors of the

51

ambulance were clumping shut behind the loaded gurney, and with the siren starting up again, it pulled carefully out of the driveway past the anxious and curious faces of onlookers caught in its headlights.

One police car followed it; two others, which had come in while Penn and I hurried down from the meetinghouse, stayed. Several cops were moving to and fro, mumbling into walkie talkies or scribbling on clipboards.

I glimpsed Rita among the crowd looking out from the front lounge. She was barefoot and barelegged, in a thick tee shirt nightgown, her hair loose, eyes still drowsy. I went over to her, past a local TV newsperson who was pressing one hand against a headset, while murmuring into a foam-topped microphone for a camera a few feet away.

"What happened?"

She shrugged. "Somebody said a fractured skull."

"Did he fall, or what?"

"Nobody seems to know just yet." She leaned toward me. "If you ask me, Friend," she said in a stage whisper, "I suspect foul play."

"Rita!" I heard myself protesting, "how can you say such a thing? At a Quaker gathering."

She shrugged again. "We'll see." She glanced past me. "Looks like the excitement's over, unless there are more casualties up on the boy's side. I hope the guy will be all right, but personally, right now I need my sleep. Tell the cops to turn down their squawk boxes if they come upstairs," she said. Then, stifling a yawn, she waved and wandered toward the hallway.

I wanted to tell her to stop, to wait, to come back and talk. But the truth was, I didn't know what to say. So I looked for Penn, and saw him on the other side of the lounge, huddled with a couple of the evangelical superintendents. They were ashen-faced, and nearby a cluster of half a dozen or so, men and women, sat crowded around a small table, heads bowed and hands tightly clasped in a circle of fervent, whispered prayer.

I began to feel a bit out of place, and Rita was right, things were definitely quieting down. As the adrenalin rush of the past half hour began to fade, fatigue welled up behind in its wake.

Murder Among Friends

It had been a long, tumultuous day, so I headed up the stairs to my room.

Or rather, our room. I had forgotten all about Eddie until I flipped the light switch by the door, and he sat up in his bed, blinking and swearing under his breath.

"Oh--sorry," I mumbled. "Do you want me to turn it off?"

He lay back down and gazed at the ceiling. "No," he said weakly, "I was awake anyway. Who could sleep with all this racket downstairs. What the hell's going on?"

I told him what I had seen, and his eyes widened.

"No shit?" he gasped, sitting up again. "Goode? Jesus, couldn't happen to a nicer guy." He put a hand to his mouth.

"Ooops, did I say that? Don't tell, Bill, or the Overseers will be on my behind in a minute."

I just stared at him, and in a moment the glee faded from his face. "God," he said, "as if there wasn't enough violence in the world already."

As he talked, I was remembering the confrontation in the auditorium. "Where have you been?" I asked. "You weren't at dinner."

"Who could eat with *them* all over the place? I just walked around Winchester. Thought about taking the display down and going home. If I could get the money back for the Lavender Friends Fellowship I *would*. But the small print on the receipt says 'No refunds.'"

He rubbed his eyes and stood up. "Actually," he said with more animation, "Winchester is an interesting place in its way. All the rebel soldiers are buried in the Stonewall Cemetery. Is that camp or what?"

I had to think a minute to catch the double entendre. It was a relief to hear him joking again, even if in bad taste. I began pulling clothes out of my bag and shoved them untidily into the wooden dresser by my bed.

"Don't be so sloppy," he chided, "your clothes will be all rumpled and tacky."

He sighed elaborately, then took a shirt out of my hands, refolded it tenderly and precisely, and placed it carefully in the drawer. "That's better. I've said it before, William, and I'll say it again, because it's still true: You need a wife."

"So, find me one," I shot back. "I've been between girlfriends for a year. And anyway, you need a husband yourself."

"You are such a nag," he pouted. "Are we going to have a fight?"

I threw a pair of socks at him. "That's about as violent as I'm getting, with cops roaming all over the building. Besides, I'm tired. Big day tomorrow, you know."

"You *would* have to mention the future," he grumbled, tossing the socks back. "Who'll give the reverend doctor's big crusade speech?"

"I don't know. But he's got plenty of backups. And we've got our own preachers who'd probably love to fill in, get all that publicity."

"'What you mean we, straight boy?'" he called, as I picked up my toothbrush and headed down the hall to the bathroom.

When I came back he had rolled over toward the wall. The playful mood had passed. His shoulders were hunched and his body looked forlorn and withdrawn. I hit the light and said, "Good night."

He didn't answer for a moment. Then it was only a whisper.

"It sucked down there today, Bill. Big time. I have too many friends dying of AIDS to put up with it. Too many more who've been attacked by punks charged up by his kind of talk. I *am* going home tomorrow. They can keep the goddam money."

"I'll take you to the bus station," I said, in bed myself now.

"Don't bother," he said. "I can walk."

That was bravado, I knew. The display weighed thirty pounds if it did an ounce. He'd take a ride when the time came. I crawled into bed.

After that, silence. Through the half-open window I heard an occasional buzz-pop of a walkie talkie, but the cops were mostly keeping quiet as they made their rounds. Now and then I seemed to hear that premature cricket who had talked at Penn and me by the meetinghouse.

After awhile I thought I could hear Eddie breathing, in the regular and deep rhythm of sleep. But maybe it was really mine.

Murder Among Friends

In my dream there was a sudden bright light. The whole sky blazed white and hot, and something was grabbing at me and shouting.

And then it wasn't my dream, but three cops with flashlights. One of them, I couldn't make out his face, was pulling me out of bed and snarling something about my right to remain silent.

"What the hell is this?" I cried out, and began to struggle. But I was on the floor by now and another cop had my right arm and began to twist it. I stiffened in pain.

"You're under arrest, Mr. Smith," said the cop, with the kind of quiet relish that showed he wanted to find out how far my arm would twist before it broke. For good measure he leaned a knee into my lower back.

"I'm--" I gasped through the pain, "I'm not--"

"I'm the one you want." Eddie's voice was bleak. He sounded tired, sad and resigned all at once. "Here. Let him go."

With evident disappointment, the cop on top of me loosened his pressure, but didn't let me up. "Check their wallets," I heard him say.

The ceiling light went on, and after a few seconds I could focus on the marbled gray and light brown pattern of the linoleum floor. Subdued earth tones, lightly swirled together. The tiles must be relatively new, I guessed, because scuffs and scratches were few, with only a thin film of wax.

You could probably learn a lot about a place, I decided, by analyzing its floor from a distance of about three inches. Right now, though, I felt I had probably learned enough to last, oh, say thirty years or so.

Behind and above me I heard someone fumbling in pants pockets, and indistinct voices. Someone said something, and the cop on top of me let go of my arm. I gasped with relief and started to get up. But his knee still held me down.

Then he grabbed my hair with one hand and pulled my head back. I choked, and started to struggle again, but just as I realized he was holding my drivers license next to my head, he let go. My chin bumped on the linoleum, and I bit my tongue.

"It's him," the cop said glumly, "Leddra." His knee pulled away.

Murder Among Friends

I rolled onto my left side, half under the bed, and curled into something like a fetal position, gasping, fighting a wave of nausea and feeling tears slide down the side of my face.

Being mugged once, ten years ago near Capitol Hill, wasn't this bad. Or if it was, I had repressed the memory. At least there you knew to be scared. Here I had felt safe, even after Goode's mishap. It made the sudden assault that much more shocking and raw.

The nausea passed quickly, and feeling a corner of sheet with my left hand, I rubbed my wet eyes and face. As I slowly pulled myself up, the cops had Eddie facing away from me in his shorts, handcuffed with one of those damned plastic straps. They let him stick his feet into his sneakers, and then they were hustling him through the door. One cop looked over his shoulder at me. He grinned, and one upper tooth was missing.

"Sorry to bother ya, Mr. Leddra," he drawled. "But it's all straightened out now. Better get yaself some rest."

I staggered to the doorway, rubbing my neck. Our room was almost at the end of the hall, and as the cops hustled their quarry toward the central stairs, more heads poked from other doorways. I recognized Horace Burks a few doors down, and then Gus Murray looked out from across the way, hurriedly putting on his thick glasses.

He turned to me. "What was that all about?" he asked.

I wasn't feeling conversational. My tongue, arm and back hurt. "Just a little law and order," I muttered angrily, and turned away without giving him a chance to reply.

The travel alarm on my dresser read 3:52 AM in angular electric red numbers. I clicked off the alarm button and fell into bed.

With the light off, I saw a few fading reflections of red and blue, as a police car pulled out. Rubbing my right arm, I could visualize Eddie in the back seat, hands held behind him by that damned plastic. No doubt the cops would take back roads, and be sure to hit every pothole on the way into town.

A sense of cold helplessness washed over me. Just like that, out of the night, you could be face down on the floor with a knee in your back, or hauled away in handcuffs. For nothing.

Murder Among Friends

I lay on my left side and shivered despite the cloying warmth of the night. Only as I was nearly asleep again, did the thought come to me that this attack hadn't been for nothing. They were looking for Eddie. They wanted him, but for what?

Of course. Ben Goode. They think he attacked him.

And maybe he did, one part of my mind said.

That's crazy, said another. And it was getting ready to defend him.

But the glare of flashlights kept interrupting the conversation, and the words never quite came out.

CHAPTER NINE

"Some of our members not subject to conscription were arrested by military order on account of their known Union sentiments, and held under guard in a loathsome guard-house or in the camp, without a charge against them....All were subject to taunts, threats and reproaches, by a vindictive and unscrupulous soldiery...."

--Report on Civil War Sufferings, Hopewell Meeting

The Winchester Frederick County Adult Detention Center is only a few years old. No doubt the county fathers were very proud of it, and of the local Republican congressman who brought home the millions in federal grants to build it. It was in an industrial park on the north edge of town. The design was modern, low-slung and trapezoidal, all smooth red brick except for a few accents of dark blue here and there. An occasional thin slit of black might have been a window. There were no fences or barbed wire around it, just a widely spaced row of signs saying "No trespassing" in the broad grass fields behind it.

For me, it was hate at first sight. My Toyota bumped across the railroad tracks into the access road, past the packaging plant and the industrial printer and the electronics supply house, and the very sight of the modernistic complex repelled me.

It looked like a school, and was big enough to be a new satellite campus for Valley State. And God knows the Valley--the country--needed new schools. Or health clinics.

Murder Among Friends

But this, I thought angrily, is the true legacy of the Reagan Revolution. New ways to lock up, silence and conceal our failures. And let them fester out of sight. Get your revenge now; our kids will pay later. The dumb, vindictive bastards.

It was probably also a vicious place behind that smug, sound-absorbing brick veneer. Concrete and clanging metal bars and total enclosure. Not to mention all manner of depravity cultivated among its denizens.

I was on my way to find out what went on in there, at least a little bit. Wearing the one suit packed against the chance of just some such unimaginable emergency, I was making, of all things, a pastoral visit. A pre-breakfast phone call to the Clerk of Washington Meeting had quickly got me anointed its prison chaplain, pro tempore.

With a faxed letter of introduction in my coat pocket, Parson Bill was preparing to make a pastoral call on our hapless brother Smith, to comfort his soul, if I could not free his body. The latter of which, at the moment, I had not a clue as to how to do.

"Reverend," a Mr. Dukes had drawled over the phone a half hour earlier, "Your man Smith is headed for some deep and troubled waters." Dukes was Eddie's court-appointed attorney,

Dukes sounded like he might be half-drunk, and it was not yet ten AM. "His fingerprints were in Doctor Goode's room," he said, "and then they found half a torn sheet of paper in his pants pocket when they picked him up. Other half 'the paper was clenched in Goode's hand."

He belched. "'Scuse me. Indigestion. Anyway, reverend, if yy'all are going down there, tell him I'll be along this afternoon, soon's I get some paperwork together. We'll do the best we can for him, hear? But between you and me, I'm afraid he's up against it."

I hung up with a burgeoning case of indigestion myself. Dukes sounded like the kind of fee-sucking courthouse hack who would have you copping a five year plea to settle a traffic ticket.

Inside the main entrance, a woman deputy let me through the big electric barred door after frisking me with an electronic wand, inspecting my letter and writing down my drivers license number on a clipboard. Then I too was inside the jail.

Jail. I refused to reinforce the euphemistic doublethink of its official title, Adult Detention Center.

Not so long ago I had visited a navy base near Newport News. Every building there had signs out in front telling you what went on inside, all the same size, all black lettering on white metal rectangles, all hung in blue painted frames of metal pipe stuck into the grass. "Fleet Operations." "Accounting and Finance." "Communications Center." Stuff like that.

Then on one shady corner stood a sign that read, so help me God, "Confinement and Retraining Facility." You had to look close to see, at the bottom in one inch deadpan letters, "Base Guard House."

So some captain had once had a funny idea, no doubt. And in fact I had laughed when I saw it. My laughter seemed to echo hollowly down the bare hallway as another guard escorted me to the visiting room. A few prisoners passed us in the hallway, silent and watchful in blue jeans and tee shirts.

The deputy opened a door into a room divided by a glass wall, against which stood several cubicles. Each cubicle had a mesh-covered opening just over a counter, and a cushioned stool bolted into the floor on each side. The stool could be raised or lowered by turning the seat, but it didn't come apart, so there was nothing to throw at the glass. It wasn't very private, but what was I expecting?

Two of the cubicles were occupied, on my side by suited men who figured to be lawyers. They were leaning close to the mesh, nodding rapidly and scribbling notes. The figures on the other side were hard to make out.

I sat down at the cubicle farthest from the door, and the lawyers. A minute later Eddie came in. He had on baggy jeans and a tee shirt that read "Wild, Wonderful West Virginia," obviously somebody castoffs. He was unshaven and looked haggard, as if he hadn't slept. But there weren't any obvious bruises or bandages, and no plastic handcuffs.

"Did they beat you up?" My first, reflexive question surprised me a little. But this was, after all, my friend. "Do you need anything?" I said. "A toothbrush? Soap? Something to read--?"

"Look, dickhead," Eddie cut into my babble, "what I *need* is to get out of this place."

I flushed, ashamed of my nervous chatter. "Right. The lawyer said he'll be in by this afternoon."

"Who, Dukes?" Eddie sneered. "Right after he drinks his lunch, no doubt." He rolled his eyes. "It was probably just as well he was shitfaced last night. Couldn't see he'd been stuck with defending a faggot."

"Jesus, Eddie," I began defensively, "lighten up on me a little, can you? I'm new to this too."

"Which reminds me," he said, "how did you get in here?"

I pressed the fax against the glass. He smirked a bit when he read it.

"My chaplain, huh? So, aren't you gonna ask me if I've accepted Jesus as my personal savior? Where's your Bible?"

I snapped my fingers. "Damn, I knew there was something I forgot." I was glad to see him kidding, however bitter the undertone might be.

But he shifted gears again abruptly. "So when did he die?"

"They said on the morning news it was about dawn, but around the dorm they're saying Goode was pretty much DOA when they got him to the hospital. Skull fracture. Blunt instrument."

"Christ," he breathed.

"Look, Eddie..." I began, then faltered.

"You wanna know what really happened, right?. Is it confession time? Are you a priest now, Bill? Ready to absolve me, father? How many Hail Marys do you give out for homicide?"

"Eddie, look....Yes, I'd like to know. And if I remember correctly, I have confidentiality privileges acting as a chaplain. All I know is that Dukes said they found your fingerprints and...." I trailed off again. "Not that I'd ever testify against you," I finished lamely.

Eddie put his head in his hands and shouted at the floor.

"Did you hear what you just said?" Then he looked up, and his eyes had filled. He took a deep, shaky breath. "Okay. Right now I don't know what else to do, and there's nobody else to consult. So bless me father, for I have sinned, I guess."

He took another deep breath. "I went up to Goode's room last night," he said, "sometime around eleven. I saw a list of names and rooms on the registration table when I came back to the dorm. Believe it or not, I wanted to apologize to him for being so melodramatic yesterday afternoon. I was a little excessively fulsome, you might say. So I was going to try to talk to him reasonably. Do the Quaker thing...you know."

I nodded, though it was, in truth, a little hard to feature. The theory of dialogue and reconciliation, even the gospel of it, was one thing; the practice was another. How many times had I walked in on somebody who thought of me and all my kind as abominations and said, "Hey, why don't we talk this over?"

But why not? We supposedly did believe in it. We recommended it to our government all the time.

"I knocked," Eddie continued, "and when there was no answer, I knocked again. The door wasn't latched. It came open a little and the light was on, so I pushed in and found him on the floor."

"On the floor?"

"Yeah, yeah," Eddie said, more intensely. His eyes narrowed as he brought the images back. "He'd already been hit, in the back of the head. There wasn't much blood, but his neck was bent funny and when I touched his hair the skull underneath was all spongy." He shuddered a little.

"You touched him?"

"Yeah, yeah. I don't know why. I was very gentle, though. I mean, he looked so totally, oh I don't know, *vulnerable* there, all my aggression just disappeared. There were papers thrown around the room too, and for some reason I started picking them up and putting them in a neat pile in his briefcase, which was open on the desk. You know how compulsive I am about that anyway, and I must have been in some kind of daze."

I nodded again. He was talking rapidly now, as if he could somehow be free of the memories if only he could get them out of his brain and into words.

"Some of the papers were ripped and wrinkled up. I was

putting them in the wastebasket, when I heard footsteps coming down the hall. That scared me, so I went over and very quietly pushed the door shut, locked it, and turned off the light. Somebody knocked and said, 'Dr. Goode?' But when there was no answer after a minute, they went away. It seemed like a week, though."

He stopped, and looked over his shoulder nervously, at the deputy by the door on his side. "Then I knew I had to get out of there. I waited til the hall had been quiet for a minute, and started to open the door. But then Goode groaned and I jumped, and that made the door bang shut."

He rubbed his hands together, and I saw that his fingers were trembling. "I went over to him again, and bent down the way you would over child having a nightmare. It sounds crazy talking about it, but I leaned over and said, *'Don't worry, it'll be all right. I'll call for a doctor.'* That hadn't occurred to me til right then."

He glanced at the deputy again. "He can't hear," I whispered impatiently. "Go on."

"Okay. Goode kept making sounds, and I realized he wasn't just groaning, he was trying to speak. So I leaned over him and said something like, I don't know, *'It's okay, you can tell me,'* something totally crazy."

Eddie's voice got lower and lower as he talked, and as it did I leaned closer and closer to the glass. When he paused, my forehead clunked against the glass. I jerked back and he snickered.

"Come on," I insisted, "what did he say? Was it about who hit him?"

"I don't know," Eddie murmured, his voice fading again. Then he said, "See the Greek."

"What?" I demanded. "Seed the wheat?"

He shook his head, and spoke louder. *"'Cedar Creek.'* That's all I could make out. I know it was 'Cedar Creek' because he said it twice. Just in a kind of whisper.

"Then it was just more groans again, and they scared me again. I peeked out the door, the hallway was quiet, so I left.

Went to our room and got into bed. You came in maybe a half an hour later. And that's that."

"That's all?"

His expression became defiant. "Yeah. What were you expecting, padre, a real confession? That I hit the guy, killed him? So I could end up here?" He rubbed at his eyes. "Which reminds me. If you wanna do you chaplainly duty and save my soul, find a way to get my body outa here. There's guys back in the block that are already measuring my butthole. But if I'm gonna end up with AIDS, I'm at least gonna have some fun doing it. I've been as kinky as the next queen, but prison rape isn't really my scene."

I nodded one more time, without having any idea of what to do about it. "I suppose there'll be a chance for bail." I said weakly.

"Bail?" he sneered. "With my bank account for collateral? I'll be in here til doomsday."

His eyes shifted, and he seemed to tense up. "Well, not that long," he said. "Remember all the announcements at meeting about vigils to protest capital punishment?"

"Vaguely," I admitted. "I was always too busy to go."

"Me too. But they were all in Virginia. Yeah, they love to fry folks here, done more of it than most other states since it was brought back. And that's what the DA is probably cooking up for me right now, Bill. Murder one, and a visit to Old Sparky. Isn't that a clever nickname?"

His fingers were shaking again, and his voice sank to an urgent whisper. "You gotta get me *outa* here."

He looked up past me, and I saw in pale reflection that the female deputy was at my shoulder. "You all about finished?" she asked.

To be honest, I was a bit relieved at the signal to leave, because I had no idea how to respond to Eddie's vehemence and anxiety. I was as dubious about Mr. Dukes as Eddie was, but had no better ideas, and not much money.

So I nodded to the deputy, and stood up. "I'll be back as soon as I can," I said lamely. "I'll talk with Lem Penn. He'll think of something."

Murder Among Friends

"Penn?" Eddie was incredulous. "Oh, I'll bet he'll think of lots of ideas. Like changing the fuses down at Mecklenburg."

"Mecklenburg?"

"That's where they keep Old Sparky," he said. "One learns so much in this place."

"That's unfair," I protested. "He's not like that at all."

"He isn't?" Eddie shouted. "Then why'd he invite that son of a bitch?"

The deputy was coming up behind Eddie. He turned angrily away from me and stalked off.

Back outside, I was so preoccupied with what Eddie's story about the night before that I missed the turnoff back to the railroad tracks and the main road, and had to pull into a lot in front of a strip of small offices to turn around.

As I pulled the Toyota around, my gaze was drawn to some black wrought iron fencing which enclosed a small square of grass. It seemed out of place in the middle of all these earnest efforts at modern entrepreneurship. Stopping the car at the curb, I rolled down the window and peered out at it.

There was a dark marble marker in it, and a little American flag stuck in the ground. I could tell the flag was a recent addition, by the still-bright colors of the stars and stripes. There were no yellow ribbons on it, though, so it must have been a Pre-Gulf gesture. Looking closer, I saw a sign, hand-lettered on something like a piece of formica, leaning against the stone.

Curiosity piqued by the odd mix of media, I got out, leaned over to the fence and read the sign.

"On this spot Major Jacob Chapin of the 23rd Battalion of Massachusetts volunteers was wounded in action during the Battle of Opequon Creek, September 24, 1864. The Regiment's casualties in the Valley campaign were 57 dead, 43 wounded. Major Chapin placed this monument here in September of 1894."

The stone itself was low, the chiseled letters now all but indecipherable. Around it in the tiny square were a sprinkling of yellow dandelions, white clusters of Queen Anne's Lace, a stand of chicory, its pale lavender blossoms hanging on a single crooked stalk, and a shiny Pepsi Cola can.

I picked up the Pepsi can, got back in the car and drove away. I had been reading about Opequon Creek, or Third Winchester as the Confederates called it, just last night at the library. It was another time when Jubal Early had come close to whipping Phil Sheridan, running him out of the Valley, and spoiling Lincoln's bid for reelection. He was turned back in the nick of time by men like the late Captain Chapin, who obviously still had his admirers more than a century later.

They had chaplains in their units then too, I thought. What did they say to those of the 57 dead they managed to reach before their end?

I wondered whether, forty years from now, I might be coming back to add another furtive, unsigned memorial to whatever was left inside the wrought iron fencing.

A lot of damn good that would do.

CHAPTER TEN

While John Scott...was preaching with unusual power the Gospel of Peace, the noise of battle was heard without, sometimes so loud as to almost drown the voice of the preacher. The terrible shock caused by the discharge of cannon shook to its very foundations the stone structure in which they sat. But the gospel message flowed on without interruption and the congregation remained quiet until the end.

--Quarterly Meeting, Sixth Month, 1863, Hopewell Meeting

I found Penn in, where else, a committee meeting. Back in the auditorium of Woolman Hall, up on the stage, the same group was around the tables. A local TV station van was parked out front, and several media types were hanging around in the foyer, carrying camera equipment or notebooks, idly browsing the exhibits and looking bored.

The press. Just what we needed. No wonder the heat seemed to be on Penn when I pushed through the door and into the auditorium.

Gus Murray was speaking as I took a seat at the table, in a calm, almost businesslike tone. "Dr. Brewer and I met with several committee members over breakfast," he said, "and we agreed that Dr. Brewer and Superintendent Burks should step in and make a joint keynote address tonight. Superintendent Burks will eulogize Dr. Goode, and Doctor Brewer will introduce the Crusade for Family Values."

67

Penn looked uncertain. Something was bothering him. And to my surprise, Rita then spoke up. "I wonder if we should be going right ahead with this," she said. "Isn't this something we should consider as a whole committee?" She looked toward Penn as if for support.

Atta girl, I thought. I could sense she shared my liberal Quaker's instinctive mistrust of self-appointed committees of pastors.

Horace Burks could sense it too. "But we're considering it *now,"* he insisted. His long face was drawn, and I felt some sympathy for him. "Can't you see, Lem," he went on, "the conference is now to be his first memorial. At least this opening day."

Gus Murray chimed in. "Doctor Goode is now a martyr, and we can't avoid paying him the respect his sacrifice deserves."

Tommie Lee Brewer kept up the pressure. "The shocking circumstances of Dr. Goode's death, and the identity of his killer, say to me that there was more involved here than some personal grudge, or a robbery."

He paused for effect. "Yes, *more,"* he declared. "This attack was *Satan's* work." He raised a hand as if to ward off a blow. "And Satan's goal is not only to strike down Dr. Goode, but to *destroy* his ministry at its most crucial moment. But we're *not* going to give in. We're going to *strike back."*

He glanced around, blinking, as if surprised not to be hearing cheers from a packed house. But the empty auditorium seats merely stared blankly back at him. The only response was a raised hand.

Mine.

Penn nodded in my direction.

"If the clerk please," I said, "this sounds an awful lot like a rush to judgment to me. I've just been to visit Eddie Smith, and for the record he denies attacking *Doctor* Goode." I almost choked on the title. "Don't we still believe in innocent until proven guilty?"

"I think Bill Leddra has a good point," said a grey-haired man from Baltimore. "We ought to be careful about taking sides on something that's going to be in court, where a man's life is at stake."

Burks replied bitterly. "One man's life was already at stake, if I recall correctly."

"And how sadly typical," Murray put in, "that the first response of some is to defend the criminal. Where's the concern for the victims of this crime? Dr. Goode was not the only one. He was giving leadership to a national movement that will touch millions of people's lives. I don't see how we can abandon those good people and their hopes."

Now, finally, Penn spoke for himself. "Of course you won't abandon them," he said agreeably. "Yet I think we need to remember that this conference has its own agenda, our own Quaker family business, so to speak. And I am not comfortable with having that lost in the understandable shock and grief we feel at what has happened here."

One of the volunteers from the registration table came in with a note, and handed it to Penn. He put on his glasses, read it slowly, then took off the glasses, and frowned at them, stretching the silence in order to think about what he had read.

"Our friends from the press have just passed on an interesting report," he said. "Dr. Goode's family has set his funeral for Thursday, at the church in Harrisonburg. According to this, the Vice President has agreed to attend."

The Vice President. Penn's news changed the whole atmosphere. Burks and Murray leaned toward each other and whispered urgently. Then Murray turned to his right to confer with Brewer. Finally he looked toward Penn again.

"I think you have a point, Mr. Penn," he conceded. "There is something to be said for letting the observances by Dr. Goode's family and his church take their course unhindered."

Right, I thought, and with the Vice President on hand you'll get plenty of free political publicity anyway.

Penn relaxed a little, but he moved to make sure the opening did not slip away. "Then I propose we postpone the opening of the conference for three days, until Friday," he said. "That will give time for the funeral, and we can still have a couple of days of fellowship with those Friends who can stay that long. We'll

69

end as planned on First Day. I regret that will mean a foreshortening of the actual conference time, but under the extremely unusual situation we find ourselves in, I don't see how it can be helped."

"But what about those of us who are already here?" Rita asked. "What are we supposed to do until Friday?"

Penn didn't miss a beat. "I suggest you take advantage of the superior opportunities for sightseeing in the region." He gestured in my direction. "Our Friend William Leddra can tell you about the many Civil War sites in the Valley, can't you Bill?"

I bowed slightly; for this I was brought into the world, or into this corner of it at any rate.

"For those who prefer more urban attractions," Penn continued, "Washington is less than two hours' drive. Both areas, you will find, have many Quaker historical sites of considerable interest. And in either case," he pointed out, "such excursions should provide many opportunities for fellowship among Friends from different backgrounds. That will fulfill at least one part of our original agenda."

He faced Rita and spread his hands consolingly. "I realize this may not be exactly what you came for. But under the circumstances--"

"I approve of the Clerk's suggestion," the gray-haired man from Baltimore solemnly.

Heads nodded, and several others repeated the phrase, "I approve," Rita among them. There wasn't exactly enthusiasm in the response; but they could see the practical logic of Penn's suggestion.

"Can we hear the minute?" Penn asked the Recording Clerk, a woman from Philadelphia with white hair and large, unstylish glasses, who had been writing steadily throughout the session. She put down her pen, raised the notepad and adjusted her glasses.

"'Friends considered the impact of the extraordinary events of the last 24 hours on the plans for the opening of the Conference,'" she intoned. "'We agreed that it was best to postpone the formal opening of the Conference until Sixth Day, and asked those Friends already here to make use of the many opportunities in the area for sightseeing and fellowship until then.'"

More nodding of heads and murmurs of approval. It should, I thought ruefully, always be this easy to reach unity in a Quaker business session.

"Very Good," Penn said, and turned to details of how to make the changed plans known and where to find more tourist information. As these details were discussed, Brewer and Murray shifted impatiently in their seats, obviously anxious to get out of there and make the most hay out of Goode's memorials.

I was itchy too. If Eddie had told me the truth about his visit to Goode's room, then he shouldn't be in jail, and I should be figuring some way to get him out. To do that, I'd have to find some proof of his innocence. How to do that?

But in one part of my mind, doubts still nagged. What if Eddie *had* killed Goode, and made up the story about finding him, to pour in the credulous ear of an amateur chaplain? Lord knows I'd fall for such a tale easily enough.

Hell, I already had. The notion of Eddie as a murderer didn't really fit the rest of my knowledge of him. So I might have doubts, but I felt obliged to act as if I believed him, because basically I did.

I only half-heard when Penn told us to settle into silent worship to conclude the meeting. And as hands were folded, eyes closed and breathing deepened, an idea came.

When Penn shook hands with the recording clerk to break the meeting, I hurried down the steps and around the stage to intercept Brewer coming down his side. "Uh, *Doctor* Brewer," I said as he stepped down to the floor, (still choking a little on the"Doctor") "could I ask you something?"

"Certainly, Bill," he boomed heartily, as if we had been pals for decades. "What can I do for ya?"

"It may sound a little strange," I said nervously, "but can you tell me if the words 'Cedar Creek,' meant anything special to *Doctor"*--another gagging sensation--"Goode?"

Brewer smiled a broad professional smile. "Well, that's easy enough," he answered. "Cedar Creek's where he was born.

Practically right at the battlefield. House is still there, too. Right across from Good Shepherd Church."

Murray, who had been listening, interrupted. "The place ought to be made a memorial, don't you think, Tommie Lee?" But he sounded less interested in that idea than in preventing Brewer from getting caught up in a distracting conversation.

"We should talk about that on the way to Harrisonburg," Murray went on, hurrying Brewer past me and up the aisle. "It will be hard for Mrs. Goode to think of such things right now, but someone has to begin looking ahead."

They swept out the door, but I cared less about Murray's cutting me off than about what Brewer had said: Goode was born near Cedar Creek. This was fascinating, especially to a Civil War buff. But what did it have to do with his dying words?

Brewer and Murray were not at lunch, just as I had expected. Seeing Penn by himself at a small corner table in the cafeteria, I carried my tray of salad over to join him. He was picking at a plate of salad, and his expression was distant. He gave off vibes of wanting to be alone, but that was too bad; I was on a mission.

"Lem, sorry to barge in, but I have a lot to tell you." I recounted my conversation with Eddie at the jail, and what Brewer had added.

Penn's detachment quickly dissipated. The story intrigued him as much as it did me. "But where can thee go with it?" he wondered.

"I'm not sure myself," I admitted, "but something tells me there must be a connection between Cedar Creek and whatever really happened to Goode."

"Thee's assuming that Smith is telling the truth."

I threw up my hands. "What else should I do? He's my friend. I've never known him to be violent before. He doesn't fit the profile of a murderer." At least, I added silently, I don't think he does.

Penn was musing again. "However, most murderers only kill once," he said, "in a moment of extreme passion or distress. Only a comparatively few plan out their crimes or kill more than one victim. Of course, those are the ones we read about. And Smith was certainly feeling passionate yesterday."

"Okay," I conceded, "so maybe he could fit the moment-of-passion profile. But I'm not convinced."

"Yet if it wasn't him," Penn continued, looking thoughtful, "who else could it have been? Who are thy other suspects?"

I shrugged. "I don't know. Security isn't exactly tight here. Anybody could have walked into the dorm."

"That's true," he said. "But unlikely."

"No more unlikely than what *did* happen," I insisted. "How many other murders have there been at the College? Or at Quaker conferences you attended? How many reporters are waiting to talk to you about it?"

This last remark unsettled him, I could tell. The local reporters who showed up last night had not asked him many questions. But chances were they would get around to him, as the conference organizer, before the story dropped off their priority list.

The idea of being on television did not appeal to Penn, I knew. This was not a matter of modesty or shyness. Rather, the image of Quakers as a quiet, peaceful group--however antiquated or overstated--was important to him. He understood its practical value from the years in the Middle East; he also knew that discretion and a low profile were the best preservers of this image.

There were certain ambassadors in Washington, friends of his, who would find the sight of Lemuel Penn on the small screen in connection with a sensational murder fascinating grist for cocktail party chatter, but disqualifying for service as a discreet, informal intermediary.

"I'd like to avoid the press if at all possible," Penn murmured. "Goode being killed is bad enough, but press attention could completely undermine the atmosphere we need for the work of the conference."

He sighed. "I wish there was some way to get away from them."

A thought struck me. "Say, why don't you clear out for awhile? Suppose--suppose we went down to Cedar Creek and

73

nosed around a bit about Goode. Maybe there's something in his background that would give us some new light on him and all this."

Penn brightened. "That's a good idea. I doubt if there's anything down there, but it wouldn't hurt to have a change of scene."

"And to be out of the clutches of the media," I added.

He grinned, stood and picked up his tray. "Except thine," he said.

"Aw, c'mon, let's go," I demurred. "I don't really count."

He paused before heading to the dishroom window. "Is thee sure?" he asked.

CHAPTER ELEVEN

"There may be members of this catholic Church not only among all the several sorts of Christians, but also among pagans, Turks and Jews. They are men and women of integrity and simplicity of heart. They may be blind in their understanding of some things, and perhaps burdened with the superstitions and ceremonies of the sects in which they have been collected. Yet they are upright in their hearts before the Lord, aiming and endeavoring to be delivered from iniquity, and loving to follow righteousness."

--Friend Robert Barclay, *Apology for the True Christian Divinity*, 1676

Penn surprised me by bringing a battered leather briefcase when he climbed into my car. "What's that for?" I asked.

He clicked open the lock on the worn flap and pulled the top open. "I thought thee might enjoy a little light reading on the way," he said, and pulled a hefty paperback from its maw.

I gave the cover a quick sidelong glance. *"Rebuilding God's Divided House,"* I read aloud. "What's that? A manual for meeting house refurbishing?"

Penn raised it a little higher so I could see the author. "Of course," I said sardonically. "'By Reverend Ben Goode, D.D.' I should have known."

"His autobiography," Penn said evenly. "Brewer sent me a copy last week, so I could prepare a fitting introduction for the great man. He said Random House paid Goode half a million

75

dollars for the rights."

"Christ," I groaned, thinking of my own stillborn efforts as a book author.

"Now, now," Penn chided, "it's very interesting in its way, though I've only had time to skim it. The title is a play on Jesus' saying, 'A House divided against itself cannot stand,' which is found in all three Synoptic gospels."

"And a play on Lincoln," I added, "who used it in his speeches against slavery."

"Of course," Penn replied. "But it's more candid than thee might expect."

He started paging through it. "Says he was an only child, born in a big old house at 324 Ramseur Street, on the edge of Middletown. Shabby genteel origins, though by his time more shabby than genteel. His great grandfather, Israel P. Goode, was at the Virginia Military Institute, planned to be a lawyer, and fought with the VMI cadets at New Market in June 1864. After that he left school and took up with Jubal Early's troops. Fought at Cedar Creek--"

"He did!" I exclaimed. "There it is again."

"Yeah, and then his regiment was sent to join the defense of Petersburg. He was full of devotion to the Confederate cause to the end, Goode says. Poor fellow nearly starved to death that winter, and was never quite right after Appomattox."

"Sounds like too many Vietnam veterans," I commented.

"Or like too many veterans of most any war," Penn said grimly, and gazed out the window for a moment. Then he started turning pages again. "Anyway, the family scraped along, rented out rooms, farmed some, the usual. The house passed down to Goode's mother, and by the time Benjamin was born, they were ready for another try at VMI. Father died when he was ten, though, and his mother scraped to send him there, class of '59."

He raised the book again, and I looked away from the road just long enough to glimpse a photo of a youth in the brass-buttoned cadet getup.

"But it seems he wasn't cut out to be a soldier," Penn went on, "except in God's army--and that wasn't clear for awhile. He dropped out of VMI after a year, kicked around awhile. Even says he was a bit of a hell-raiser, a great trial to his long-suffering mother."

"No doubt," I said. "Best thing I've heard about him so far."

"Didn't last," Penn continued, fast-forwarding through the pages. "By Chapter Seven he's saved, and made his mother proud by deciding to go back to school. This time he went to the Chickamauga Bible Baptist Seminary in Chattanooga, Tennessee."

We were just about out of Winchester, now, passing through Kernstown, a narrow rind of suburb famous mainly for two more major battles, in the first of which Stonewall Jackson was defeated, but only momentarily. Except for the large historical marker, the site, like all the others around the city, was now built up, home to laundromats and ranch-style bungalows.

The Quaker side of me said this development was good: beating the late haunts of swords into the domain of plowshares, or their technological descendants.

But the other side of me said this was a shame; another hunk of our most vivid and formative history wiped away, as if we could proceed better without knowing about it, which both sides of me agreed we couldn't.

On this score, it appeared the late Rev. Goode and I might have seen eye to eye. A disconcerting thought.

"Goode came back to Middletown," Penn was saying now, "on fire for the Lord, and anxious, as all hungry young Baptist preachers are, to start a church of his own. But something went wrong--his text is rather vague on the point--and it didn't work out. So he moved down to Harrisonburg and was assistant pastor at First Valley Baptist for a year."

"Just a year?" I asked. "What happened?"

"The usual," Penn said, with mild sarcasm. "He had the itch to be in business for himself. He doesn't put it that way, of course, but that's a big part of it. Evangelistic religion, whatever other good it might do, is always and everywhere an arena for the American entrepreneurial impulse."

"So he started a church?" I asked. "How do you do that, anyway? Weren't there plenty of churches in Harrisonburg already?"

Murder Among Friends

"Sure," Penn said, "and not just Baptists. It's a stronghold for Mennonites, too, college and all. But church loyalties are brittle among evangelicals, and besides, the Valley was a growing place in the sixties. So in Goode's world there are always plenty of lost sheep needing to be gathered, not to mention some which can be rustled from nearby flocks."

He raised the book again, and my quick glance took in a picture of a young woman, smiling.

"In his case, though, the real spur was personal tragedy. He lost his first wife and a new baby."

"That's awful. How?"

"Car wreck. He blamed himself, and says it almost killed him with grief. But he finally pulled himself together by deciding to build her a fitting memorial."

"A church, right?"

"Right. Evidently, in the small print, his temple is actually called the Wanda Lynn Goode Memorial."

"Wanda Lynn," I said. "It had to be."

"Don't be a Yankee snob," Penn chided. "Anyway, it says here that in December 1961, Goode took the last of his savings, bought a shoebox full of gospel tracts and rented an old skating rink north of the city. Then on New Years Day, 1962, he put on his one good suit and sturdy black shoes, walked into town and started knocking on doors."

Penn flipped a couple of pages, then read from the text:

""Good morning, Mrs. Jones," I would say cheerfully, taking off my hat to show special respect, "it's all right, I assure you I'm not selling anything," It was usually women who were at home, busy with laundry and cleaning, or shabby with age and loneliness. They always had a guarded look when they opened the door, but generally relaxed when they heard I wasn't selling anything. I gave them a tract, told them my name and that I was holding services that Sunday, and invited them to come.

"'If they said they went to such and such a church, I just said, "That's wonderful, ma'am, God bless you," and

*left, still smiling. But if they didn't mention another church,
I repeated the invitation, and then left, with an even bigger
smile.   It was important to keep moving, but before I
knocked on the next door, I wrote down the address.'"*

Penn closed the book. "He kept that up, door to door, forty
hours a week, all over Rockingham County, for over a year. Says
he wore out three pairs of shoes, lost twenty pounds, and got
bitten twice by unchristian dogs. But by New Years Day 1963,
The Good Life Baptist Temple had outgrown the skating rink,
moved to a school auditorium, and was breaking ground for its
original temple. Dr. Goode then traded in his walking shoes for
a radio show--"

"I know," I said, "'The Good Life Bible Hour'. I've heard it
many times." With more bravado than aptitude, I crooned the
opening lines of the show's signature hymn:

"*"With Saving grace Jesus set me free,*
"*His cross brought the good life home to me...'"*

"I forget the rest," I said. "But it's fun to listen to sometimes.
At least until he starts ranting and raving about godless secular
humanists and the liberal-gay-pornographic-abortion-mill-New-
Age-satanic-cult-Anti-christ-feminist   conspiracy.   Whatever
happened to the good old Communists on his laundry list, for
pete sake? They seem rather tame compared to us liberals, at
least in his description."

"Oh, he did his share of red-baiting," Penn replied. "I can
remember some of that myself. Though if there were ever any
communists in the Valley, outside of one or two who took a
wrong turn on their way to Gastonia or Harlan County, it's news
to me. But he was always a great salesman. His Temple is the
biggest church in the Valley now, six thousand members
according to the book, but that was a couple years ago.

I whistled. "Sounds more like a fan club than a church to
me."

"You might say that. Until the late seventies, Goode was the
most popular preacher in this end of Virginia, and was itching to
go national. But Jerry Falwell and Pat Robertson got out ahead
of him, at least for awhile. Now, though, with the Moral

Majority gone and Robertson busy running for president or kingmaker or whatever, Goode is--*was*--just about to hit his stride in the big leagues."

"With the Crusade for Family Values as his big push."

Penn nodded ruefully. "'Course, in the early days, in place of real Communists there was always the civil rights movement."

"A segregationist," I said. "It figures."

We were nearing the Lord Fairfax Community College, cresting a knoll where the marker stood noting the end of Sheridan's famous ride, on the northern outskirts of Middletown. From here the land gently sloped down, to where in the southern distance the bulk of Massanutten loomed, dark and angular.

A ragged phalanx of thick clouds was passing over it in grey procession, uncertain yet whether to become thunderstorms to wash eastward over Manassas, Fairfax and perhaps Washington. I the meantime, slanting columns of light and shadow streamed from their serrated edges and played over the green landscape below.

In that moment, at that spot, the Valley was breathtakingly beautiful. No wonder it had been thought worth fighting over, I reflected.

Penn was used to such vistas. "I think Ramseur Street is a few blocks after the light," he said.

It was, and 324 was almost at the end of it, which was only four blocks west of the highway. The white clapboard house stood empty and boarded up on a large overgrown lot, across the street from a small cinder block church. Beyond it, the street became a county road which veered off through fields thick with tall green corn.

We tried the rusty gate at the foot of the broken sidewalk up to a wide front porch painted a peeling grey. One end of its roof listed visibly. The gate didn't open.

The swinging buzz of a weedeater started up behind us. Penn turned toward the sound, but I examined the house more closely. It was two stories, with a New England style cupola and a widow's walk, Yankee features that looked utterly incongruous in this Old South stronghold. One of the window panes was empty and open.

Murder Among Friends

When I leaned to comment on the odd architecture to Penn, I realized he wasn't beside me.

He had crossed the street, where an elderly black man in khaki work clothes was carefully trimming the grass at the edge of the sidewalk. Behind them was a low cinderblock church, painted white from the foundation to its skinny, cross-tipped steeple. The hand-painted sign above its door read: Good Shepherd CME Church.

Penn had already shaken hands and was talking when I got there. The black man was shaking his head, and clicked off the weedeater.

"'Sa shame, sir" I heard him saying when the noise died away, "the way they let that house run down." He shook his large grey head again. "And it's awful the way they killed him, sir. Lord have mercy, ain't anybody safe today?"

Penn turned to me. "Bill, meet Reverend Phillips. He's the pastor here." I introduced myself and extended my hand. Phillips took it firmly.

"How long has it been empty?" I asked, gesturing over my shoulder.

Phillips removed a vintage fedora, tugged a large handkerchief from his pocket, and wiped his forehead. "Been more than ten years 'so, since old Miz Goode died. They was talk about rentin' it out, but didn't nobody want it. Too big for one family, too small for a hotel. And Rev. Goode was too busy down in Harrisonburg." He shook his head again. "Ain't it awful what they done to him?"

We nodded solemnly. Then Phillips said, "You all want some lemonade? I could use some myself, workin' in this sun."

I was thirsty too, and he led us around the west side of the church, the side which faced the fields beyond. A large garden ran halfway down the length of the church, soaking up all the sunlight that leaked between the clouds. I could see orange and red tomatoes dangling among its green stalks, and a quartet of tall yellow-rimmed sunflowers yearning toward the sun from the columns. Two sparrows darted away from a sunflowers' big seedy bullseye as we passed.

Not far from us a fence marked the border of the rolling

81

cornfields, and a half a mile further was the line of trees that I
recognized as following Cedar Creek. The battle, I realized, had
raged all around here. Goode was born right in the middle of it.

Not far from the rear of the church, next to a large gravel
parking area stood a weathered-looking housetrailer. Phillips
ushered us in through a small parlor which was dominated by a
large fading photo of smiling newlyweds, the man a younger
version of himself. The silence in the room, and a patina of dust
on the old furniture, led me to conclude that he was a widower.

He motioned us toward a small kitchen table while he
reached into a humming refrigerator and brought out a plastic
carton of pale yellow liquid with a Seven Eleven label. It was
ersatz and overly sweet, but I sipped gratefully, feeling the glass
grow sweaty and slick under my fingers.

I put down the glass and blurted out a question which had
been growing in me ever since I noticed the church. "What was
it like living across the street from someone like Dr. Goode.
Wasn't he a segregationist?"

Phillips smiled tolerantly, and scratched a stubbly chin.

"Well," he said, "wasn't so long ago they was all
segregationiss' around here." He chuckled quietly. "Yes sir. Lot
of folks still are, but they know better'n to say so out loud." He
chuckled again, and took another pull of lemonade.

"But wasn't Goode on the bandwagon to close public schools
in Virginia to avoid desegregation?" Penn asked. "Part of 'massive
resistance'?"

Phillips nodded solemnly. "Sure. But he was just a pup then,
and it never got very far in this county."

Penn wasn't mollified. "But later didn't he put up one of
those 'Martin Luther King at Communist Training School'
billboards outside his Temple, right by the highway? I'm sure I
saw it there myself. Shameful thing it was."

"You right about that," Phillips agreed. "I saw it too. But
that was Harrisonburg, and it's a long way away for most of us."

He proffered the carton again, and refilled my glass. "No,"
he said, "the only time we had any trouble with Doctor Goode
was right at the beginning, just after we'd started building the
church here. And that didn't last all that long."

"What was it about?" I pressed.

Phillips put his glass down, empty. "Money, son. Money and land. He had the money, and we had the land."

"I don't quite follow you," I said.

But Penn did. "He wanted thy land?"

"Right again, sir," Phillips said, his smile broadening into a grin. "All twenty-five acres of it. He had the idea of starting his church right here, across the street from the house, so his mamma could walk to service. Had forty, fifty folks with him too. But we had the land, bought it fair and square the year before. Or I should say, started to buy it. We had a mortgage on it, and for awhile it looked like we might not be able to keep it up."

"What happened?" I said.

"Combination of hard times and what they callin' nowadays hard ball," Phillips answered. His grin faded with the memory. "A few of our folks got laid off at the plant, and then a few more got mysteriously fired, and we began to come up short. 'Fore long we was almost three months behind on the mortgage, and about to be fo'closed."

"And meanwhile," Penn guessed, "Goode came to see you."

"He did, sir. Him and some 'his church folks. One of 'em was a vice president of the Middletown Bank, 'gave us the mortgage. They was ready to buy the property and pay it all off for us."

"But you said no," I suggested.

Phillips's eyes were old and deep, rimmed in white and red. They rolled toward me. "Not exactly," he said. "We was just about to tell him yes, 'cause we didn't know what else to do. And then one mornin' I found a envelope in the mailbox outside, and in it was twenty one hundred dollar bills. No address, nothin' but a little note, with the words cut from a newspaper: *'For the love of Jesus--John 13:35.'* The three months' mortgage was nineteen hundred and sickty five dollars."

"Where did it come from?" Penn was intent.

But Phillips just shrugged. "'Couldn't prove it by me. I figured an angel musta left it." He paused, and a hint of shrewdness came into his expression. "Or maybe it was some liberal white folk up at the college."

"Valley State?"

"Thass right. They was some NAACP members up there then, I knew some of 'em. They was usually pretty quiet about it, since they wanted to keep they jobs. But they coulda heard about us and passed the hat. That was my guess anyway."

"You think they'd care enough about a church to do that?" I asked.

"It could have been," Penn mused. "There were dozens of black churches bombed and burned down further south in those years. Or maybe it was some of the Valley Mennonites. They have churches around here, that they'd do things quiet like that."

Phillips nodded agreement. "Matthew Chapter Six, Verse Three," he quoted: *"'When you give alms, let not your left hand know what your right hand is doing.'"*

"So you paid up the mortgage and Goode backed off?" I said.

"Thass about it," Phillips answered. "The factory started hirin' again and we was able to keep it up. And it was only a few months later that Miz Goode had a stroke, and was never out of bed again. That kinda took the wind out of Doctor Goode's sails, it seemed to me. Few months after, he took a job down to Harrisonburg. Then he lost his wife, and pretty soon started up his temple there."

"And the rest," I said, "is history."

Phillips had that sly expression again. "He didn't like our beatin' 'im, no sir. But I guess it didn't do him no harm, now, did it. Once he got his Temple going, he plum forgot about us."

"And his own house, it looks like," Penn murmured.

Phillips nodded, pursing his lips.

"Something bothers me about this," I said. "He was a real anti-civil rights crusader in those days. How could he just let a black group beat him like that?"

"Well now, after all we wasn't civil rights agitators from outa town," Phillips explained patiently. "Most our people been 'round here as long as his family--some of 'em longer."

Phillips scratched his thinning grey hair. "And there's something else you need to understand about Doctor Goode,"

Phillips said finally. "He didn't really hate colored folks as much as it sounded. Lotta that stuff was for show. He found it kept folks coming to church, and he had to keep the folks coming. After all, he had mortgages to pay too."

He paused a moment, sizing us up, considering. His eyes narrowed. "Maybe you should look into that," he said finally.

"That's a good idea," Penn said. "Does thee know which bank?"

Phillips frowned and rose slowly from his chair. "Lemme see," he said, and shuffled into the living room, returning with a shoebox full of receipts. "He sent us a donation a few years ago, when we put on a new roof."

"A donation?" I asked.

"It figures," Penn said. "His book says he finally saw that segregation was a sin, and he's repented of it. The Temple is now integrated--barely, and mainly in the choir."

Phillips was studying a receipt. "I reckon Doctor Goode was about as good a Christian as he knew how to be," he said. "Rockingham Trust was his bank."

Penn suddenly brightened. "I know the executive vice president there, Bernie Carruthers," he exclaimed. "We were in business school at Charlottesville together, class of '49. Does thee have a phone, Reverend Phillips?"

The minister pointed toward the living room.

Penn was back in a few moments, rubbing his hands. "Bill, I think we'd better be on our way. Thank thee for thy hospitality, Reverend."

Phillips solemnly shook our hands. "My pleasure," he said. "It gets pretty quiet out here sometimes in the middle of the week, since my wife passed. If you're back this way of a Sabbath morning, yall'd be welcome at service."

"I hope we can do that," Penn said, and moved toward the door.

Back in the car, he announced, "Carruthers said he'd be glad to talk to me on the quiet, if we can get down there today. He expects to be too busy after that."

I started the engine. "Let's go."

Back at Highway 11, I turned right, toward where Cedar

Creek ran under us, less than a mile south. We could pick up the interstate at Strasburg for a run to Harrisonburg. But first, I slowed to take a look at the largest battlefield marker, which was just south of a boarded up store and gas station. Behind the marker, amid broad rolling fields, sat Belle Grove Mansion.

The unofficial center of what memories are maintained of that huge and bloody fight, Belle Grove is a stately old seat of grey stone with four tall brick chimneys, one on each corner of its dark gray roof. Here was where Early's commandoes expected--and failed--to capture Phil Sheridan on the morning of their brilliant surprise attack.

Nowadays Valley dowagers conduct tours above, through the quiet, high-ceilinged rooms. Picnic tables sit out back and a gift shop specializing in fabric arts occupies the cellar, next to the reconstructed dirt-floor kitchen. Once upon a time numerous slaves sweated over pots hung in the elaborate brick kitchen fireplace, and scores more labored in its fields.

As we crossed the bridge over Cedar Creek, I wondered how many of Reverend Phillips's ancestors had been among them.

CHAPTER TWELVE

There lives a people in the Valley of Virginia, that are not
hard to bring to the Army. While there they are obedient to
their officers. Nor is it difficult to have them take aim, but
it is impossible to get them to take correct aim. I, therefore,
think it better to leave them at their homes that they may
produce supplies for the Army.

--Stonewall Jackson, quoted in H.A. Brunk, *Mennonites
in Virginia*

But Bernie Carruthers, who had evidently been so cordial to
Penn over the phone, was a different person when we met us an
hour later, not in his office but in the wide, old-fashioned lobby
of the Rockingham Trust. With bright red suspenders snaking
their way around his white-shirted belly, and a matching scarlet
four-in-hand tie hanging limp under his thickening neck, he was
a picture of late middle-aged preppy rectitude. His round face
was stiff, and he barely nodded to me as he pulled Penn aside
for a muffled consultation.

I was already feeling a little spooked. Given the county's
heavy density of Mennonites and Amish, supposedly similar to
Quakers in their pacifist views, I realized as we pulled into
Harrisonburg that I had been expecting to find the city somewhat
exempted from the wave of war fever generated by Desert Storm.

I couldn't have been more wrong. The courthouse, which sits
in a square smack in the middle of town, had a pillared entrance
on each of its four sides. And every pillar, on every side, was

87

festooned with a wide yellow ribbon--as was every tree trunk and lamppost, and most of the parking meters, on the entire square.

The extent of the adornment was shocking, and I thought I'd seen as much yellow ribbon as there was to see.   Where, I wondered, were the children of Menno Simons now?

Then I recalled that Mennonites are quietist, separatist peace people, unlike Friends, who had been sticking their noses into public policy for 340 years.   And the Rockingham plain folks, who had lived in the Valley for two centuries, doubtless knew much better than I when to keep their opinions quietly and separately to themselves.

So I wasn't surprised when Carruthers seemed to look a little askance at me.   While hardly a hippy, I did have a beard, had shed my chaplain's suit, and probably exuded antiwar sentiment like halitosis.   Well, up thine, Bernie, I thought, cooling my heels.

But Penn, who returned in a few moments and gestured for me to follow him, deflated my sense of being a player in this little skit.   "Somebody got to him while we were on the way down," he said as the car started up again.   "He was told there may be some problems with some of the Temple's accounts, may even be some legal actions.   So he has to keep quiet.   And nobody gets to see anything without a subpoena."

"He didn't say who called?"

Penn shook his head.   "Turn left here," he said, pointing. The sign said North Main, US 11.

Two miles up, as the suburbs thinned into a scattering of houses among open fields, we rounded a curve and he pointed. "The Temple," he said simply.

The complex occupied a ridge east of the highway.   The Temple itself was big and octagonal, with milky white triangular windows several stories high and an immense parking lot all around.   The effect was clearly meant to give the impression of soaring effortlessly toward heaven, perhaps like souls snatched away in the Rapture just before the Great Tribulation hit.

On either side, sprawled along the ridge for a quarter mile or so, were lower buildings, a mix of red brick and cinder block, the mishmash of architecture approximating that of an obscure state college.   A half-finished building sat nearest us, with dusty dump trucks and pickups parked around it and hard-hatted construction workers busy in its exposed insides.

A sign in front of the construction site read, "Our Foreign Missionary Training Center--Bringing the Gospel to the World's Unreached Peoples."   Next to it was a two-story fundraising thermometer, with the red part most of the way up.

Behind that sign were others, a veritable parade of billboards along the edge of the campus.   One urged us to attend one of their several Sunday services.   Behind that came an invitation to complete our unplanned pregnancy at the Wanda Lynn Samaritan Home, because *"Abortion Is The American Holocaust."*   And next was a call to send the kid to their Christian Summer Camp program for the disadvantaged.

The climax was a series of billboards warning of the perils of drugs, pornography and homosexuality that lie in wait for the little ones outside the sacred gates, and how sending them to the Temple Christian Schools and College would keep our children pure and upright.

"I guess he doesn't like to leave much to your imagination," I said, as we passed the first billboard.

"Communication is what all this is built on," Penn replied. "He sends out fundraising letters every week to one or another of his constituency lists.   Gotta keep the wheels turning, and the pot boiling.   There's a lot of mortgage money to be repaid here."

We passed the main entrance, a wide drive which divided around a guard station, then emptied into the main Temple's vast parking lot.   As usual, yellow ribbons hung here and there, but not as many as around the courthouse.   And people on scaffolds were hanging black bunting over the Temple's main doors.

"Quite a spread," I admitted grudgingly. "He sure must know how to raise money."

"Yes," Penn agreed.   His tone was thoughtful. "But I have to give him credit where it's due.   He's done more than just build a big church, college and broadcasting center.   The summer camps have helped a lot of poor kids, even a few black ones. The adoption center is the best kind of anti-abortion witness, if you ask me.   And he even sent a lot of relief supplies to Ethiopia. Our Friend Phillips may be right; he did his bit, by his lights."

89

At the north end of the campus a huge radio tower loomed over the rest of the compound, red lights blinking atop the satellite dishes at its peak. The dishes pointed north and south, up and down the Valley. A billboard on the high fence around its base exhorted us to listen to WVCR-105FM, *"Your Full-Power Valley Christian Station, Where Christ is Preached and the Lord is Praised."*

"Hmmm, I said, as the campus receded behind us. "Let's see what's on the Valley Christian Station."

The radio flicked on. I was expecting the usual menu of such outlets: fervid preaching, pleas for money, or the uniquely odious nouveau middleroad gospel music that seemed designed to prove that you could get low-cal pancake syrup out of a synthesizer.

Instead, we heard the cries of an evidently unruly crowd, behind a breathless announcer who was actually speaking live and minus a script. "While we're waiting for the Commonwealth's Attorney to come out of the Judicial Center, let's run the tape again of the announcement an hour ago that set off pandemonium here in Winchester."

The crowd noise faded. Then another voice came, in strident mid-sentence. "--We are *not* going to sit back and allow another gay man to be *railroaded* by a kangaroo court controlled by the forces of homophobia," he cried, and there were shouts of approval.

"What is this?" I wondered.

"Hush," Penn scolded, leaning forward to hear better.

I turned the volume up.

"Fundamentalists like Ben Goode have been promoting hatred against lesbians and gays for *years*," the harangue continued.

"Their campaigns have fueled an increase in attacks on our people *all over* this country. And whoever killed Ben Goode, that merchant of hate was *reaping* what he had *sown."* More shouts.

"But *now* they want to keep this hatred growing by making a *scapegoat* out of a gay man who swears he's *innocent.* And the repressive courts of Virginia, which is Goode's home state, and a state which *loves* to use the electric chair, are *happy* to go along." Loud boos and shouts, of "No, No!"

"You're *damn* right, no!" the speaker shouted back. "And The Queer Commandos are here to say it's time to *fight back.* We are everywhere, and we're in Winchester to see to it that our brother Eddie Smith gets *justice!"*

More cheers.

"The Queer Commandos," I breathed. "Oh, my God."

CHAPTER THIRTEEN

And wider still those billows of war
Thundered along the horizon's bar;
And louder yet into Winchester rolled
The roar of that red sea uncontrolled,
Making the blood of the listener cold....

--Thomas Buchanan Read, *Sheridan's Ride*

Then the reporter was back. "That was Brent Edwards, leader of the militant homosexual rights group, Queer Commandos, speaking here an hour ago. Edwards announced that the group had posted bond of $100,000 for the accused killer of Dr. Ben Goode, and would hire flamboyant celebrity lawyer Arnie Wolfowitz to defend him. He also announced that the Queer Commandos were planning a mass demonstration by militant homosexuals in Winchester this weekend, in support of the defendant Edward Smith and gay rights generally."

Penn slumped back against the seat. "It's starting," he whispered. "We were too late."

"What's starting?" I asked.

"Shhhh," he hissed. "Listen." A new, florid voice was on the air.

It was familiar. "Brewer!" I said. "I thought he was down here."

"--We returned the *moment* we learned about the ungodly invasion of this peaceful Christian city by an army of *perverts,"*

92

Brewer was declaring passionately. "And we could *not* let the sacred memory of that hero, now struck down in *God's* service, be besmirched and *dragged* through the slime without reply. So if the *gauntlet* is to be thrown down *here*, in the *Valley* that was his beloved home, we say *here* and *now* that we shall pick it up."

There were faint boos at this, I noticed, and no cheers. "He must not have had time to organize a crowd," I said. "The Queer Commandos must still be around."

"He'll have his turn," Penn observed.

"Winchester was the scene of *many* battles in America's *first* civil war," Brewer was declaiming grandly. He was in full throat, preaching past the catcalls to a larger, not yet gathered audience. "Historians tell us this city changed hands more than *seventy* times between the Union and Confederate forces. Thousands of soldiers of that war, known and unknown, found their final resting places only a few short *blocks* from where we stand."

His voice dropped to a husky whisper. "And last evening, our *dear* brother, to whom the memory of these men was so precious, became a full *member* of their ranks."

I groaned as Brewer paused, reverently. "That was a *tragic* time," he resumed. "But it was also a time of *glory*, a time of *devotion*, and a time of *sacrifice*.   So if there is to be yet *another* battle of Winchester, I am saying to you today that we must make it *another* time of glory, *another* time of devotion, *another* time when its true citizen heroes must be ready to bear *whatever* sacrifices may be called for to assure that, *this* time, the forces of God will prevail!"

A weak round of applause came through the speaker. Someone was rallying to this sermon, if only a few passersby drawn to his half-recognized baritone.

"I'm calling on all the *true* Christian people of the Shenandoah Valley," Brewer climaxed, "and Christians from throughout Virginia and the entire region, to *join* us this weekend in a rally for *God* and the American Family. We'll pay tribute to the memory of that *great* man of God, Dr. Ben Goode,

93

and rededicate ourselves to the *work* for which he lived, and for which he has now given his *life.*"

Again the tepid clapping, then a moment of dead air, before the reporter realized that Brewer had finished. "Reverend Brewer," he called out, "can you tell us the time and place for the rally, sir?"

Another voice answered. Cooler, less musical than Brewer's, it too was familiar. "Doctor Brewer hasn't been able to pin that down yet," Gus Murray said, "but we expect to have it settled before the day is over. We hope to hold it in the stadium at Valley State College."

Penn sat straight up. "The *College?*" he sputtered. "That carpetbagger. Over my dead body!"

"I guess a few thousand Baptists would be something of a distraction for an All-Friends Conference," I deadpanned.

"As if it weren't distracted enough already," Penn sighed.

Murray was warming to the microphone, his tone more professorial, almost pedantic after Brewer's fervor. "This fiasco shows only too well the ultimately disastrous consequences of the Enlightenment Project of unfettered individualism," he intoned.

"What's he talking about?" I asked. Penn only shrugged.

"These homosexuals," he went on, "are like other special interest groups of deviants today, demanding their so-called rights, regardless of the communal imperatives of two thousand years of Judeo-Christian morality and culture. And as we see here today, the common norms of civility that make the public square a safe place for authentically democratic, reasoned discourse are cast aside as soon as they fail to serve their agenda. The conflict between their obsession with rights and our determination to uphold traditional, objective values is irreducible, and as far as I can see, irreconcilable."

"If I hadn't earned a masters degree," Penn said drily, "I don't think I'd understand a word he's saying."

"I gather it means he doesn't like the Queer Commandos," I concluded.

"I don't much like them either," Penn said. "We don't need a

mass march of blatant homosexuals this weekend any more than
we need a swarm of fundamentalists." He shook his head. "What
next?"

"I don't know," I said, "but at least it means Eddie will have
a decent chance to defend himself. That court-appointed lawyer
Dukes was a loser for sure. He'd cop Eddie a plea for a new
wire on the electric chair."

Penn was suddenly fierce. "Don't talk to me about Smith,"
he said. "I'm not at all sure he's innocent, and anyway he didn't
have to take this kind of help. I didn't think a Quaker would be
part of an bunch like those Queer commandos. Their habit of
disruption and abuse is hardly Friendly, and often not even
arguably nonviolent."

"It surprises me too," I said. "But he doesn't have the money
for a real defense lawyer, and he seemed pretty desperate this
morning. I guess I really can't blame him for taking help where
he can get it. That jail was a creepy place."

We were nearing New Market now. A nondescript hamlet
today, without even a decent truckstop to draw business off the
Interstate, it holds a secure place in the mythology of the Lost
Cause. Here in May, 1864 a bunch of teenaged VMI cadets
force-marched sixty miles from Lexington to join the ragged
troops under General John Breckenridge, the traitorous former
Vice President of the United States. Together they ran the
Yankees and their feckless General Franz Sigel off a broad field
along the North Fork of the Shenandoah.

The Union got its revenge soon enough, thrusting south to
Lexington in June and burning VMI to the ground. But the
Institute is inordinately proud of the New Market skirmish,
maintaining a big battlefield park and one of the largest and
gaudiest Civil War museums in the state, grandiloquently called
the Hall of Valor.

As was usually the case, the Confederates' New Market
engagement was a tactical victory and a strategic defeat. It was
one more heavy straw that helped break the backs of those two
lumbering but dangerous camels, Lincoln and Grant, moving
them to loose the scourge of Sheridan upon their beloved Valley
before that sanguinary summer's end.

"Can we pick up I-81 here?" Penn asked. "I need to get back to Winchester, to see if I can talk Fred Harrison into keeping Brewer's rally out of the stadium and off the campus."

"I'm ready," I said, turning into the ramp where US11 crossed beneath the interstate. "I want to know how deep Eddie's gotten himself in with these Queer Commando people."

To the east the crest of Massanutten ran along beside us, darkly green with its national forest covering, as we left the slower lanes of the Valley Pike and accelerated past sixty. Nearer the highway the fields were rolling and lovely, peppered with tiny fir trees and salted with white barns. Before and above us, though, the haze loomed and thickened, a mix of blue and grey.

On the radio, the Commonwealth's attorney was now expostulating, in reply to the reporter's query that, "Yes, we believe the bail was set too low. My staff is reviewing our options now, and if we think the evidence warrants it, we will seek to have bail revoked, in order to protect our community."

So Eddie might need his new lawyer sooner than he figured.

CHAPTER FOURTEEN

Eddie turned up where I least expected him, in our room. He was packing, and he wasn't alone. He and a somewhat younger man were talking animatedly as Eddie stuffed clothes in his bag. The other was jogger and health club lean, with a short, carefully sculpted haircut, tight jeans a white tee shirt and brown leather vest, a full mustache and one large earring. The Marlboro Man in mufti, I thought.

They both looked up with slightly startled expressions when I came in, as if I'd barged in on a conspiracy, or the beginnings of a tryst.

"Karl Russell," said the newcomer, and his grip was sixty pushups firm.

"He's the brains behind the Queer Commandos," Eddie boasted. "Brent Edwards is just a mouthpiece." He sounded like a teenybopper who'd just been adopted as a mascot by the Grateful Dead.

It had been a long day, and I didn't feel like mincing words. "Great," I said sarcastically, sitting down on my bed. "I'm glad you're out of jail, Eddie, but did you really have to turn this whole thing into a media circus?"

He wasn't ready to apologize. "Look," he said forcefully, "the Queer Commandos may not be your ideal of a quiet Quaker committee, William. But before you get too righteous about it, let me fill you in on a thing or two I didn't get to mention this morning."

He knew I hate to be called William. He squatted on the edge of his bed and leaned toward me. Some of the intensity I had seen through the glass was coming back into his face.

Murder Among Friends

"I spent a very long night as a guest of the commonwealth," he said, "and I wasn't kidding about the prison rape part. There were at least two dudes twice my size who were already planning to fight it out over who would get the first shift in my cell if I'd stayed in there another night. And they weren't coming to hear about the Inner Light or the Friends Peace Testimony."

Russell was leaning against the dresser, arms and ankles crossed in a James Dean pose. He snickered quietly, and I glared at him.

"It was these same guys who were talking about Old Sparky," Eddie said. "They told me I didn't have to worry about AIDS, because I'd get fried before I got sick."

He stood up abruptly. "Maybe I just scare easily," he blurted, "but when I heard that bail was a hundred grand, I about fainted. So when Karl passed me a note through Dukes, offering to post the bond and hire Arnie Wolfowitz for me, sorry, but I didn't even notice that he had an earring. Though he did have a suit on at the time."

"I hate wearing 'em," Russell said, sardonically. "I much prefer leather. But you gotta play the role, especially here in Dixie. Besides--" he abruptly dropped the cinematic pose and sat on the bed next to Eddie--"this could be a tremendous opening for us."

He lifted his right hand with the fingers touching, as if he was holding a piece of paper in them. "Look," he said intently, "Eddie says you're a friend, so I'll level with you. We've been gathering a file on this Doctor Goode for years, and there's tons of shady stuff in it. But he was slick; there was never any smoking gun, and he got away with preaching his hate and homophobia all across the country for all those years. But now, with the media play this thing is sure to get, we can bring it all out, blow his image all to hell, bam!" The raised hand jerked, as if yanking the pin from a grenade.

Eddie watched Russell's gesture admiringly. But I was skeptical. "I just spent all day trying to find out about Goode's background myself," I said, "and I didn't turn up much. Sure, he knew how to separate rednecks from their money. And he didn't like gays or liberals. Twenty years ago he was for segregation.

Big deal. But--"

I paused, recalling Bernie Carruthers, but I was unwilling to talk about our wild goose chase to Rockingham Trust just yet.

"But what?" Eddie asked.

I dodged. "But what," I said, "makes you think you can turn him into another Bakker or Swaggart?"

"Plenty," Russell snapped. "Follow the money, for one thing. His building program at the Temple is bigger than his budgets. So where did all the loans come from?"

This struck a chord. Now that I thought of it, the way the Temple campus was spreading across the ridge did look haphazard, hurried, almost headlong. The sprawl bespoke big bucks in play, and Russell was right: with big churches and big money, there was almost always big trouble sooner or later.

But my skepticism lingered. "Suppose you're right," I said to Russell. "What difference does that make to Eddie? Goode is dead, and who cares about all that now?"

Russell's hand jerked up again, this time with the index finger pointing toward the ceiling. "But that's just the point," he exclaimed. "This stuff is all raw material for leads on who else could have killed him."

Now Eddie raised both hands, palms toward me in supplication. "Bill, all the basics are there: Money, sex and power. With all this sleaze, Goode had to have rivals and enemies."

"More than that," Russell said, standing up again. "There was also plenty of opportunity." He moved to the door, opened it a few inches, and peered furtively out. "Was there any security in this dorm that night?"

"Security?" I stammered.

"See?" Eddie said triumphantly. "Who thinks about security at a Quaker conference? Especially here, in bucolic Winchester? The dorm wasn't locked. A lot of the rooms weren't locked. Goode's room wasn't locked. I can testify to that."

"You better not," Russell warned.

Now I snickered. "Are you trying to tell me you think some hit squad snuck in here and bopped him and then melted away into the night? Who were they, Mosby's Rangers reincarnated?"

Russell shrugged. "Who knows? A Quaker conference might make a great target of opportunity for somebody, especially if they knew there were folks around who would make perfect suspects."

"Like for instance," Eddie said, "a loud-mouthed faggot who had screamed at Goode the same day."

"But who would have known about that," I protested, "except for the people here? Do you think one of us--?"

"Careful how you use that word, breeder boy," Eddie interrupted. "There are quite a few people here who are not 'us' as far as I'm concerned."

"You really think somebody at the Conference--?" I repeated, but left the thought hanging unfinished.

"Who knows?" Eddie echoed. "Personally, I think it was somebody on Goode's side, maybe somebody close. Brewer. Murray."

"Get outa here," I said. "He was their meal ticket, their claim to fame. Without him, who'll remember them a month from now?"

I thought for a moment. "If you want an inside conspiracy, try somebody like Horace Burks. Lem told me he went to seminary with Goode. Maybe there was some old hidden rivalry, a secret grudge. Or what about Lyndon Coffin? Maybe under his plaid jacket he's just pretending to be an evangelical, and really hated Goode's guts."

This all seemed so far-fetched that I didn't know myself where real speculation left off and sarcasm began. But I couldn't deny that it was getting interesting.

"So you're going to sniff out another suspect, the real killer," I said, half mockingly. "You and how many other amateur detectives?"

Now Eddie leaned toward me again. "Just one, to start with," he said quietly. His index finger came up, pointing. "You."

Then he opened his hand and put it gently on mine.

It felt a little strange, but I didn't draw back; the years in men's group had taught me better than that. What *was* strange was the note of plaintive appeal in it. Eddie's hand felt as if it was grasping a rope to keep from falling off a cliff.

100

His face became grave, almost funereal. "I need you to help me, Bill," he said quietly. "Life and death, remember?"

"Yeah," Russell drawled. "Eddie told me you have some investigative experience.   And off the record, contrary to the bravado of our press conference this morning, putting up pretty boy's bail here just about cleaned out the Queer Commando checking account. Arnie Wolfowitz is doing the courtroom gig pro bono. But we're gonna need some free gumshoe too."

I rolled my eyes toward the ceiling. "Christ," I said to Eddie, "you told him about *that?*"

CHAPTER FIFTEEN

"Likewise, how often the Jews murmured against Moses and Aaron, and what destruction came upon them in the wilderness...and therefore take heed of murmuring and rebelling against the Lord and his Spirit, but in all things learn to be content...."

--George Fox, *Epistle # 394*, 1684

If I have avoided mentioning my own professional background thus far, it is not by accident. When I go to Quaker conferences, part of my agenda is to leave my worldly identity behind:

I don't read the papers. I don't watch the news. I minimize talk of politics, and otherwise sedulously ignore what's happening Out There.

I especially resent it when outside news barges into our little subculture. Take Ollie North, for example. When he faced off against Congress in the summer of '87, it wasn't bad enough that he tore up the law and Constitution, bragged about it in front of God and everybody, and then went on to beat the rap.

Even worse, his solo act came on right in the middle of our Potomac Yearly Meeting sessions. We might as well have called them off; even the most spiritually-minded Friends couldn't resist following the crowds into the TV lounges and plugging into the whole disgraceful show. It was a prime example of backsliding into what George Fox called the "vain world" that we were supposed to be rising above.

Murder Among Friends

Partly my isolationism is a matter of preference; these assemblies are fun for me, or I wouldn't be there. And partly it's theology: They're a kind of sabbath, freeing up a small chunk of our time from the ordinary, to focus on the life of the spirit in our small and often beleaguered faith community. Then there's sociology: They are the only chances we get to be in the majority--to live, however briefly, in a Quaker neighborhood.

But on a more mundane level, they also provide a respite, a break, from my job. That goes especially for the part about ignoring the news, too much of which comes from Washington. I need such breaks more than many, because Washington news is my business.

Not, alas, the network news, or *The Washington Post, The New Republic* or any other such highfalutin rag. Though I admit to having sent resumes to most such at various times, and articles too, on spec.

So, yes, I earn my bread churning out copy in the nation's capital. And hence, George Will, David Broder and I are technically colleagues; but if you don't recall my face or byline, relax; your memory is not prematurely fading.

The truth is, I'm a member of Washington's unsung battalions of third tier scriveners, the trade press. While Woodward and Bernstein become legends and make movie deals; McLaughlin and Pat Buchanan bluster for seven figures on the tube and the op-ed page; through it all, the legions of us lesser hacks labor on, innocent of glamour, undistracted by renown, unsullied by riches.

Instead, we track the endless twists, turns and mind-numbing eddies of the myriad policy processes which grind on, ceaseless as the sea, outside the mass media spotlight in scores of forums--or fora as they are called in the trade--all over Power City.

There is plenty of such work. Almost every federal department, commission, administration, agency, office, council, authority, bureau, board, service, tribunal, committee and court has one or more dedicated media satellites, some coming out seven days a week. Our product serves the equally specialized bands of lawyers, lobbyists, academics and other professionals who hover around each federal agency like flies over fresh cowpies. For whom the information we provide can open the way to institutional advantage, career advancement, and, of course, big money. Thus they cheerfully pay our employers' exorbitant subscription prices, or, more commonly, cheerfully bill them in turn to *their* clients.

I labor in one of the most obscure of these fields, to wit, maritime policy. My work weeks are spent keeping up with such hot issues as the future of the 4701 Loan Guarantee program; the progress of regulatory reform of international shipping cartels; the fate of the Jones Act and the coastal trade; and the quarrels over shipping rates and routes that give the Federal Maritime Commission a reason for being.

If thine eyes have not glazed over yet, Friend, thee has more stamina than I.

In truth it takes several hundred network reporters working full-time to maintain the illusion that federal legislating and adjudicating are exciting processes. For the rest of us, the ability to stay awake in a hearing room is a crucial professional skill.

When, for instance, was the last time you heard the president declaiming on the strategic importance of the coastal trade to the fate of the Republic as the videotape whirred and a hedge of camera shutters rustled and clicked?

You say you can't recall?   Neither can I.

This explains why, though I have visited many of the prestige news locations around This Town, I am not an habitue of the Rose Garden.

Still, our field has its place in the capitol's grand scheme: Congress obscurely but regularly doles out billions of your tax dollars for the agencies and programs we cover. And with that much money being served up, all the usual species of Potomac porcines gather round to get their snouts in the trough.

Further, if they can't get the snouts in one way, they'll get them in another. The maritime industry is notorious on the Hill and around town for its high level of corruption. A long and not otherwise distinguished list of members of the House Merchant Marine Committee has gained fame by climaxing their congressional careers with tours in such federal retirement centers as Allenwood and Danbury.

For their part, the maritime unions, especially the eastern longshoremen, are in many places no more than licensed Mob subsidiaries.   But they make campaign contributions at a per capita rate thirty times that of the ordinary union stiff, so their wages continue to be fatly subsidized, and the process goes on.

All of which, in my corner of this little universe, means that, to maintain any sense of professional self-respect--not to mention credibility with the 2500 subscribers who pony up $795 per year each--the *Maritime Legislative and Regulatory Bulletin*, or MLRB as we call it, must occasionally get out there and spade up a bit of the dirt, too.

As one of MLRB's veteran staff reporters, I've done my share: Back at the turn of the '80s, when the Abscam case ensnared a number of maritime-connected Members, I managed to come up with a few items on the ways some of them tried to launder their suitcases full of cash from the FBI men posing as Arab sheiks.   That was actually exciting, and made the job seem like fun for a couple of weeks or so.

My biggest coup, though, was blowing the whistle in '83 on a Texas House member's cozy scheme to slip thirty five million into a rivers and harbor bill for another, utterly unnecessary set of docks in Galveston harbor.

That one was a genuine scoop; uncovering it was fun, and revealing it sank the scheme.   It also, in one stroke, saved the taxpayers several hundred times my annual salary.

Though I am regretfully obliged to acknowledge, for the sake of Truth as Quakers say, that it was only after the *Wall Street Journal* pilfered the story and ran their own version of it, without crediting the source--maintaining one of our profession's oldest traditions--that the plan really came a cropper.

But do I complain? No more often than the sun comes up. In between times, I drown my sorrows in work, then seek diversion or transcendence.

Since I'm a natural puritan, drink, drugs and organized decadence don't fill these bills. And, as pointed out earlier, I am currently between girlfriends, or whatever the hell the politically correct term is nowadays. Thus, what diversion I find comes largely in learning about and reexamining the Civil War. And a sense of transcendence, when it happens, generally arises at meeting or, yes, even in Quaker conferences.

Which brings me back to my chagrin that Eddie had evidently been telling Karl Russell, doubtless with some degree of exaggeration, about my exploits as an investigative journalist. It was not just the presumed embroidery, up to which I might have to live; there was also a sense of intrusion about it, an encroachment by these worldly pursuits onto the sacred turf of my sabbath time.

I had come to Winchester to consider the future of a Society, about which no trade paper to my knowledge gave a tinker's dam, and perhaps to be useful to this convocation by providing a respectable diversion to some of my co-religionists. It was a simple mission but a meaningful one: Like the Zen master said, before enlightenment one hews wood and draws water, ditto afterward; or words to that effect. And there was no room in this modest scenario for the labor of following leads, making endless phone calls, tracking through documents, pursuing interviews and fitting pieces of information together; no room, in short, for work.

But when Russell spoke of this, and I turned to glower at Eddie, the appeal in his eyes made clear in a flash that there was no avoiding it. After all, there hadn't been room in my plans for Dr. Ben Goode, either--alive, or, especially, dead. And I had already journeyed to Middletown, then to Harrisonburg doing nothing other than digging for leads on him.

The only question, and it nagged at me even as I knew I was going to ignore it for now, was that I might just as easily be about to help a murderer get away with his crime as helping to catch one.

"Okay, Eddie," I sighed, "I'll do what I can. But remember I have to be back at work next Monday morning. And I may have to take time out for a local history tour at two."

Eddie looked relieved. "No problem," he said. "It shouldn't take that long."

Behind him, I could see in Russell's expression that he knew better. "So where is this fat file you have on him?" I asked.

"At my apartment," Russell replied, "in Arlington."

"Which is good," Eddie said, "because I'm not supposed to leave the state."

"I'll need my computer and rolodex," I said. "They're at home, too. East Capitol Hill. We better get started."

Eddie turned to his bag again, talking rapidly to Russell. I stepped out of the room, heading to the bathroom, for a pre-road leak.

I pushed through the door. Steam was rising from the shower room, and Gus Murray was at the sink, wet hair slicked down, a towel around his middle, and one side of his face lathered white. His glasses lay on the edge of the sink, beside the can of shaving cream.

"Not exactly a normal day," he said mildly, raising a Bic to his white cheek.

"You got that right," I said, heading for the urinal. "And more to come."

"Ummm," he responded, guiding the blade carefully around the point of his chin. The razor swished in the sink. "You gonna march with your friend on Saturday?"

The abrupt coolness of the query put me on guard. I shook off the drips and zipped my fly. "Haven't thought that far ahead," I answered, honestly. "You'll be at the stadium, I suppose?"

He nodded slightly, squinting at the mirror to maneuver the razor without his glasses. "I won't be on the podium," he said after the stroke. "I'll be doing media arrangements. There'll be hordes of 'em. Probably one for every deviant marcher." He smirked. "Invading quiet Winchester like Sheridan's army."

"And you're going to be Jubal Early?" I said, edging into sarcasm.

Murray was cool. "No," he parried, "just think of me as Captain Jed Hotchkiss, the mapmaker who showed Early where to counterattack."

"So Brewer gets to be the General?" I said.

"Yep. Except," the look had become arch, "Doctor Brewer won't be Early. Early was brave, but in the end he was a loser."

"Of course," I was simpering myself. "I should have guessed. He gets to be Stonewall Jackson."

"That's it. The Valley Campaign will rise again."

I was about to ask if he was going to suck lemons, too, as Jackson did. But suddenly I tired of the conceit; something about it was nagging at me. "Do you really believe all this stuff about a new civil war?"

"What do you think?" he retorted. "In our culture we've now got two incompatible worldviews, with contradictory definitions of humanity, fundamentally opposed understandings of morality and community. And like your hero--and mine--Honest Abe said, 'A house divided against itself cannot stand.'"

The Bic made one last long stroke. "I'm all for civil debate and democratic processes," he went on. "But there are some struggles you can't escape, or compromise. Then it was slavery. Now it's abortion and the family. In such a context, liberal talk of tolerance and pluralism is just an obtuse way of saying 'be reasonable, do it our way, and let the gays and the abortionists take over.'"

He sighed. "I've been in denial about it like everyone else. But I see now that last night was as inevitable as Harper's Ferry in 1859. Oh, it didn't have to happen here. It didn't have to be Dr. Goode. But it was coming."

He picked up his glasses and rinsed them under the faucet. "One side's gonna win the right to shape America, and through it much of the world, and the other side will lose."

He put on the glasses. "Bottom line. Like it or not, it's a zero-sum game."

I didn't buy it. "Does it really have to be either/or?" I objected. "It seems to me there are a lot more than two sides to most important questions, and a lot more than two groups in society. Why can't we just muddle through, to some ambiguous and untidy set of compromises we can't imagine yet?"

Murray wiped at his chin with a corner of the towel. "It's a nice thought," he said. "What I'd expect of a Quaker--and I mean that as a compliment, at least in an ultimate, theological sense. But where's the compromise position for the preborn child when its mother goes into an abortion clinic? How is that baby supposed to tolerate what's about to happen?"

He noticed a spot near the base of his right nostril that had escaped the blade. But when he applied the razor, it slipped a bit.

"Damn," he swore, as a bright crimson line trickled down to his full upper lip. He swiped at it with the towel, but the red kept coming, and he stood there with the towel pressed to his nose. The cut made him more implacable.

"Same with the family," he said. "It's the best--no, the only--way to reliably produce healthy, law-abiding children, and then responsible adults. It's not one option among others, like one boutique among dozens in the grand lifestyle shopping mall. Civilization depends on it."

"Bottom line again, I suppose," I said.

He lifted the towel gingerly, and the bleeding had stopped. "You live in DC, don't you?" he said, pulling out the clincher. "You should see the proof of that every day."

I just grunted, refusing to rise to the bait. Families are fine; but Washington's many pathologies looked to me like better proof of a society reaping the whirlwind sown of its own racism. But it takes me half an hour just to get warmed up on an that.

Hell, I thought, for that matter, DC locks up people, mainly young black men, at a faster rate than any other American city, and it hasn't helped do anything except train more older black male criminals. Then there's the haunting, multiracial legion of homeless people wandering its streets, prattling, pissing and panhandling--they've been one of its few growth industries in the Reagan-Bush years. I take every one of them as a prophetic sign of judgment on that blighted decade, and those who have fattened on it.

But this tirade was internal; I had no energy to get into it here. There was something desolating about the vision Murray was laying out. Especially with the evidence of Goode's death on his side. Yet as it sank in, my sense of historical parallels felt scrambled. He might be comparing Goode's murder to Harper's Ferry, and that made some sense. Yet he was the one who sounded like John Brown to me.

I took another, oblique track. "Do you think Goode can really

serve as the symbolic martyr in this apocalyptic struggle?" I
asked. "Isn't there something archetypally self-destructive about
these big-time evangelists? You know, Bakker and Swaggart, and
Oral Roberts? It seems like only a matter of time before some
bimbo, or even a bimbo boy, turns up in their beds. Or the bank
account turns up mysteriously empty. Or both."

Murray's face showed distaste; he clearly didn't appreciate
the comparisons. "Goode is no Swaggart," he said vehemently.
"Was no Swaggart," he corrected more quietly. "But I suppose
you're going to help those Queer Commandos try to wreck his
good name."

"I'm not interested in wrecking anybody's good name," I said.
"But I do want to help my friend, who may be innocent."

"I doubt that." Murray was rubbing some aftershave on his
cheek. He grimaced when it reached the cut. The odor was
acrid and alcoholic. "As for Goode, look all you want. Sure, he
was human, but you won't find any bimbos, male or female. He
was no Jim Bakker."

Then he paused, adjusted his glasses, and regarded himself
in the mirror. "Of course," he said thoughtfully, "there was that
business with the radio tower...."

"The what?" I asked quickly.

The door banged open and Eddie looked in.

"Hey, come on!" he called. "What's the matter? You
constipated or something?" Then he noticed Gus.

Murray's face had gone rigid. "Get out of here," he spat. I
wasn't sure whether he meant just Eddie, or both of us. But
Eddie quickly retreated, and I turned toward the door.

"They never found anything on Stonewall Jackson either,"
Murray called after me. "He lived clean, he fought clean, he died
clean. But even if you *do* find something, it won't make any
difference. It's too late for that."

The bathroom door banged behind me, and I had the cold
feeling he was right.

CHAPTER SIXTEEN

Still sprung from those swift hoofs, thundering South,
The dust, like smoke from the cannon's mouth;
Or the trail of a comet, sweeping faster and faster,
Foreboding to traitors the doom of disaster.
The heart of the steed and the heart of the master
Were beating, like prisoners assaulting their walls,
Impatient to be where the battle-field calls....

--Thomas Buchanan Read, *Sheridan's Ride*

We headed for Washington in Russell's car, a sleek white
Camry. As he drove, Russell laid out the elements of his case
against Goode:

"Some of his fundraising was really sleazy, maybe even
illegal. And we know of a former secretary that sued him for
sex harassment. There were mass layoffs of the workers in his
Moral Majority affiliate when the money suddenly 'disappeared.'
And there's probably more, once we get into it."

"Sounds promising," I agreed. "Let me look over your files
tonight and then dig into it tomorrow."

"Check," Russell said. "Let's talk over dinner at my place, and
go from there."

Eddie looked excited, boyish. "Go for it, homeboy," he urged.
"Can't I sneak over the bridge and watch? Do a little
hacking for you?"

"Don't try it," I said. "Assume the state troopers are watching,
which they probably are."

He glanced up at the rear view mirror. "Come to think of it," he said nervously, "there's a grey chevy van that's been behind us ever since we left Winchester."

I looked. The van was nondescript and a good distance back. Nothing obvious. The mark of a good tail; or a touch of paranoia.

Karl shrugged. "Let 'em follow. We're clean."

"Anyway," I resumed, "if I have questions I'll call you. I work better on my own, at least at this stage."

Russell's condo was in a building not far from the Netherlands Carillon at the western edge of Arlington National Cemetery. I arrived promptly at six,, and as soon as the door opened I smelled something good cooking.

The place was arranged in a martial arts/Zen motif: off-white walls, bare except for a couple of framed parchment certificates calligraphed in Japanese. A portrait of some Zen master, wearing a loose black outfit and an inscrutable expression, sat on a little side table, an unlit candle before it and a small bonsai tree off to one side. Mats on the floor, and minimalist wooden chairs that were nonetheless very comfortable.

The one item that looked out of place was the laptop computer on the dining room table; it was a 486, the latest model, with numerous bells and whistles, and probably had enough memory to hold the entire Library of Congress. Eddie was hunched over it, intent on a screen whose colors flashed and shifted.

I leaned over his shoulder to see better; he was playing Tetris.

Russell, whom I was soon calling Karl, also looked out of place, because he met me wearing a flouncy flowered apron. Noting my confused glance, he spoke huskily. "Underneath my militant Queer Commando exterior," he breathed, "I'm just another sweet southern belle, suh."

"Frankly, my dear," I recovered quickly, "I don't give a damn."

His accent was *faux*, but he also turned out to be a good cook, serving us up a pasta primavera that was more substantial than nouvelle stuff, yet still tangy and intriguing. Plus whole wheat french bread, followed by tofutti with fresh fruit topping. And, respecting my teetotaler inhibitions, sparkling apple cider. From the Shenandoah Valley, the foil label said; a nice touch.

Unfortunately, dinner was all I had to look forward to. The papers in my briefcase, after ten hours of concentrated effort, boiled down to a tale of drawing blanks, touring blind alleys, and climbing mountains that turned out to be molehills.

"Goode was bombastic," I reported, "and he pushed the envelope in some of his fundraising pitches--well, maybe a lot of them. You've heard the refrain: 'This ministry is under Satan's *direct* attack, and will fold in two weeks, unless *you* help God make us a miracle and raise us a million dollars in the next ten days'--that sort of thing. 'Emergencies' that he and his direct mail consultant carefully planned a year or more ahead."

"Really?" Eddie seemed shocked.

"That's the fundraising biz," I said. "But not all of his emergencies weren't planned in advance. Remember when the Korean Airlines jet was shot down near Russia?"

"KAL 007," Karl murmured. "I still think it was really on a CIA mission."

"Maybe. Anyway, Goode had an emergency letter out about that in less than two weeks. It was really quite a feat--from a standing start, he wrote it, printed a million copies and got them in the mail, all in probably less than 96 hours."

"The flight must have meant a lot to him," Eddie mused. "Did he have family, or missionaries on it?"

"That's the thing," I said. "Near as I could tell, he had no connection with it whatever. The Congressman who was on the flight, the real far right-winger, what was his name?"

"Larry McDonald," Karl recalled. "Georgia. Certified John Bircher."

"Right. Turns out Goode hated his guts," I said. "Some arcane conservative blood feud. But that meant nothing when the plane went down. It was a big Cold War Communist outrage, and Goode jumped on it. The letter probably pulled in millions. A brilliant stroke, if you look at it purely from the technical standpoint."

113

"Technical standpoint?" Eddie snapped. "How cold-blooded can you get?"

"Pretty cold," I said. "You should see how many letters he wrote about AIDS. But none of this," I sighed, "is illegal in the slightest. In fact, unfortunately for us, that's standard operating procedure in the direct mail fundraising business. Liberal groups do the same thing, just not usually as well. It's tacky, even ghoulish, but I didn't find anything that was really over the line. And," I concluded, "that's the good news."

Karl leaned back and munched on a hunk of the french bread. "So what's the bad news?"

"Try this," I said. "His house is large, but it's no grand mansion. His salary is $89,000 per year. Nice, but no fortune, even adding in an equal amount in executive perks and travel. Peanuts compared to Jim and Tammy's playhouses and slush funds. Evidently most of the money he raises goes into the Temple campus. He's making the church and the schools into his personal monuments."

"Hmmmmmm," Eddie grunted.

"And speaking of Tammy," I went on, "Charlotte--that's the second Mrs. Goode, is plain, quiet, and low in profile. Two kids, boy and a girl. Mid-twenties by now."

Eddie perked up. "The *second* Mrs. Goode?" he asked, eyebrows raised.

"Relax. First one died young. Wanda Lynn, her name was. Charlotte doesn't preach or make records, and if her mascara ever runs, it does so in private. Which is not to say she's unimportant in the Temple operations," I added quickly, "because by all reports she's one of his closest advisers."

"Christ," Karl said. "he would have to be happily married."

I shrugged. "Who knows how happy it is," I said. "But the public front is seamless. Was seamless."

"What about the secretary?" Eddie wondered.

"I was getting to that," I said. "Helen McNamara. But she wasn't actually his secretary. That's Eleanor Mabry, and she's seventy-two, formerly a missionary to Burundi, and to judge from the photos that my fax turned up, as plain as grits."

"So who--" Karl began; I cut him off.

114

"Helen McNamara was secretary to the Temple's board of
deacons; she worked in the executive offices, across from Mabry.
And she *did* sue.   The case was titled *Helen McNamara vs
Benjamin Goode*, *et al*, which is what gave most reporters the
idea that he was the harasser, because they didn't read any
further.   But that was just legalese.   The guy she actually
fingered was a former Temple vice president, Not Goode.   Name
was Torrance."

I opened a file folder. "It took some digging, but I found
local clips of her testimony," I said. "That was my coup for the
day.   Rather a short-lived one.   She testified that Goode put up
with Torrance's behavior, but never bothered her himself."

"What came of the suit?" Russell asked.

"After three days of testimony, the Temple settled," I said.
"Paid her an undisclosed sum, admitted no wrongdoing.   A few
months later, Torrance left the Temple.   Said he was heading for
a foreign missions job somewhere."

"Probably Burundi," Eddie giggled.

"You have a filthy mind, suh," Russell's version of Dixie
indignation was better than his housewife.

"Anyway," I said, "McNamara might be lying, but that's her
story, she's stuck to it, and it's no smoking gun.   And of course
she's kept quiet since they paid her off."

"Not much," Russell acknowledged. "Goode covered his ass
real well there.   But what about the broadcast tower?"

"That may be the only item left on your list with any
potential," I said. "And it's fishy alright.   Blown up mysteriously
in the fall of '85.   Goode made barrels of money with emergency
fund appeals after it was destroyed.   Then it later came out that
the tower was 100 per cent insured, so the rebuilding really
didn't cost him a dime."

"Now that sounds like fraud to me," Eddie said.

"It did to me too," I said.   Reaching for another folder, I
pulled out a faded xerox of a newspaper clipping. "The
Richmond papers smelled something and followed it for awhile.
But he was too slick for them.   There was small print in his
letters that said the donations would go for rebuilding the tower

'or for other crucial ministry projects.' So he had an out."

Eddie scanned the sheet. "This says the Temple's revenues were down in 1984 and early 1985, but they broke records by the end of '85. How timely for him."

Karl was sifting through other clippings. "Did they ever arrest anybody for this?" he asked. "We never found any sign of it."

"I didn't either. So I guess not."

"That's not right," Karl said. "Something smells here, for sure."

"Who would know why there were never any charges?" Eddie asked. "The sheriff?"

Karl looked up from a clipping. "That'll be Wilbur Byrd Hanson. Says here he's a distant relative of old Senator Harry Byrd. The Byrd machine ran the state from the Valley for decades."

Karl pushed back from the table. "This is too much of nothin'," he complained. "We need some new leads. We should get to that sheriff. If he's out of office now, he might talk more freely."

Now Eddie was up. "I'll call him," he declared boldly. "Right now. Why not?"

He stood and strode to the wall, scooped a cordless phone from its holder and started pressing buttons. As he waited for a response he came and took our plates to the kitchen, scrunching up one shoulder to hold the phone in position.

"I just couldn't *live* without mah cordless, suh," he breathed at us, sounding more authentic than Karl. From the kitchen we heard him murmuring into it as plates and forks clinked into the dishwasher.

Eddie returned, looking frustrated. "The guy retired three years ago, moved into the hills. County won't give out his home number, and it isn't listed."

"I wonder if they bought him too," I said. "But how do we find the guy? I don't have many maritime sources out in the Valley."

Karl, however, was not deterred. "This," he said grandly, "calls for the help of the FBI."

"Sure," I said, "no doubt they looked into it, but--"

Karl had picked up a small electronic address book, and was scrolling through some numbers. "I mean the Fairy Bureau of Information, silly," he said. "Here," he took the phone from Eddie, "Let's try this." He punched some numbers.

Then: "Hello, Eastern Mennonite College Library? Archivist's office please. Hello, Ernie, Karl here. Yeah. *Yeah.* Still got those chin whiskers? You sweet *thang.* Say, I need a favor."

He told him what we wanted, bantered a bit more, and hung up.

"Never thought a broad-brim hat could look sexy 'til I ran into him," he mused. "Country boys, I love 'em." Looking over at me he added, in a stage whisper, "We are everywhere."

Five minutes later the phone rang, and Ernie had what we needed: a phone number and directions.

"He's up in Fort Valley," Karl said. "Ernie says it's God's country."

"Where's that?" Eddie asked.

"Massanutten," I said. "It looks like it's one big long mountain on the eastern side of the Valley. But really it's two, close together. Fort Valley runs between them for forty miles or so, from south of Front Royal down to about New Market. George Washington was thinking about hiding his army there after the winter at Valley Forge, if the revolution hadn't starting going his way. It's cozy, quiet, almost unknown."

"Okay, know-it-all," Karl said, extending the arm with the phone, "since you know where it is, you can call the dude."

"Me?" I protested. "What do I say?"

"Hey," Eddie said, "remember what George Fox said."

"What was that?"

"When all else fails, Friend, thee should tell the truth."

Karl handed me a slip of paper with a number on it. "It may not be much," he said. "But right now it's all we got."

I punched in the number.

CHAPTER SEVENTEEN

As toilsome I wandered Virginia's woods...
I mark'd at the foot of a tree the grave of a soldier;
Mortally wounded he and buried on the retreat...
The halt of a mid-day hour, when up! no time to lose--yet
    this sign left,
On a tablet scrawl'd and nail'd by the tree by the grave,
Bold, cautious, true, and my loving comrade.

     --Walt Whitman, **Drum-Taps,** 1865

We picked up state highway 55 just north of Front Royal, below the mountains and almost within sight of the confluence of the North and South Forks of the Shenandoah River. Then we headed west, parallelling the North Fork, headed toward Strasburg. We were looking for Waterlick, which is really only a sign at an intersection, and Route 678, which heads south from there, up into the mountains and their thick stands of the George Washington National Forest.

We had just got on to 55 when Eddie announced, "I think they're following us again."

"Who?" I asked.

"You know," Eddie said. "Whoever. This time it's a yellow van. It was behind us on I-66, and it's still there."

I leaned to glimpse the rear view mirror. The van was as nondescript as the one yesterday, and who could say? I shrugged.

Gray sheets of morning fog were curling around the crest of Massanutten on our left when we saw the Waterlick sign and made the turn. In a moment the fog was just a grey ceiling, somewhere above the enclosing treetops, and we were swerving this way and that along the road that followed the bends of Passage Creek.

Eddie was still peering out the back. "So?" Karl asked indifferently.

"The van kept going," Eddie replied.

"So, relax," Karl said. "We're legal. We're going to see a cop, for chrissake."

No one was interested when I pointed to a roadside marker. "That's the trail up to Signal Knob. It's where Gordon got his view of Sheridan before--"

"I know," Karl snapped. "I've been up there. Can't see much usually. Too smoggy."

"Where do we pick up the road to the sheriff's place?" Eddie asked. He was scanning a map.

"Just south of Detrick," I said, "on the right. 'Bout ten miles."

It was only after several miles of climbing curves that we emerged from the tree cover to glimpse stretches of fields, their shades of green still dusted with dew, sloping into the mountains on either side. Houses were few, but looked agriculturally substantial.

There were no towns. At one crossroads a white house trailer with faded red and blue horizontal stripes bore a Post Office sign: Fort Valley, Virginia 22554. Across the road was a tidy Brethren church.

"It's so quiet," Eddie said. He sounded a little awed.

"Kinda spooks you, eh, city boy?" Karl needled.

"You don't look exactly hayseed yourself," I challenged. "Or do the Queer Commandos have a farm team?"

"Try forty miles west of Wheeling," he said. "My family thought of St. Clairsville, Ohio as a big city. I milked cows, shoveled manure. It was college at Ohio State that corrupted me."

"Speaking of which," Eddie said, "did you really have to wear that leather vest?"

"What, you're afraid he'll arrest us?" Karl retorted.

"No, but if we look too weird, maybe he won't talk to us."

"I doubt it," Karl said. "Weirdness was his business, and we're coming in voluntarily. Besides, if I get the feeling I'm making him nervous, I'll take a walk." He grinned. "And besides, I did leave my nose ring at home, so cut me a little slack."

"Here's Detrick," Eddie said, noting a small sign. A gas station and another Brethren church were its highlights.

"I'll bet these woods were full of Christian pacifists on the run back then," I said. "What a life. Hiding from two armies, and god knows how many groups of general outlaws. I hope they liked eating squirrel."

"And possum," Karl said. "Don't forget possum."

"I wonder if it was as gross as sushi," I said. "Anytime now we should see 2263 going off to the left."

"Here it is," Karl said, and made gravel fly as he turned into it.

The narrow road took us through one of the shimmering fields, then climbed steeply around a spur of the mountain and into the forest again. After a mile or so, we saw a mailbox with the name Hanson in block letters.

Karl pulled into the gravel drive. It wound for an eighth of a mile before opening into a wide clearing where a large A-frame cabin stood, framed by a tree-covered hillside. A deck spanned the front of the cabin, and a mud-spattered Ford pickup was parked next to it. An old man was sitting in a rocking chair on the deck, smoking a pipe and watching our arrival without any evident interest. A blackhandled aluminum cane leaned against the chair, catching the sunlight when the chair rocked back.

"We're here," Karl murmured redundantly.

"What was it the guy said to you?" Eddie sounded cautious.

"He said to come if we wanted to," I repeated. "He wasn't going anywhere. Not exactly enthusiastic. But not hostile either."

Hanson pulled a pipe from his mouth and raised it to us as we approached the deck, but stayed seated. He was a big man, yet an unmistakably weakened one. His hair was thin and white, carefully combed; the brown eyes were large and clear. His face was lined, with a hint of grey in the skin. A checkered wool blanket covered his lap and legs.

"Had a stroke in May," he said, without preamble. "Slowed me down a bit."

His grip was still firm, though, as he acknowledged our introductions.

"Beautiful view you have here," I said, politely.

But Hanson was uninterested in pleasantries. He sucked on the pipe, which was unlit, and said, "You all wanted to know about Doctor Goode."

His directness surprised me, but his tone was not brusque. I got the sense that here was a man who understood he had no time to waste.

"You all reporters?" Hanson asked. "A lotta reporters was nosing around on him 'fore I retired. You're the first ones since then. How'd you get my number?"

Karl grinned. "A friend," he said. I could tell he liked him.

Hanson squinted up at Russell, his gaze lingering on the leather vest. "A friend, eh?" He pulled on the pipe. "I reckon your friends make it their business to know where the cops are."

Karl was still grinning. "You got that right, sheriff," he said.

"Well, I can figure what you're after," Hanson said. "Dr. Goode's hardly even cold, not in the ground yet, but here come the buzzards to peck out his gizzard."

"Now, sheriff," Karl bantered, "we're just trying to get at the truth."

Hanson looked away, into the distance toward Massanutten's western crest. "Then you came to the right place," he said. "I don't give a damn where the chips fall now." He reached under the blanket and pulled out a tin of Prince Albert.

Watching his old, thick fingers stuff the tobacco into the bowl of the pipe, I felt a familiar sense of anticipation. You work on a story for days, maybe for weeks, and get nowhere. You know there's more to it than what you've been able to find, but all the main players are shining it on, and you can't break through the hype.

Then, either by luck or as the karmic payoff for your persistence, you come across somebody who knows, who really knows, and wants to talk. Retirees are good candidates. Or ex-players with scores to settle. You have to account for their biases, of course, but more often than not, they give you what you need to finally pry the story open.

Then you come back at the principals with information they didn't want you to have, but which this time they can't ignore. Now you're cooking, and with another break or two, plus more persistence, you can blow the thing sky-high.

It's what happened with my big expose of the Galveston harbor scam.   A staffer for the House Merchant Marine Committee got fired when he refused to go along with the deal. I heard about his sudden departure, and on a hunch dug up his home number by cross-checking area phone directories. He met me in a parking lot near Tyson's Corner, carrying his grudge and copies of all the right documents.

Hanson put away the tobacco and retrieved a blue plastic lighter from under the blanket. Its yellow flame bent down into the bowl, and the tobacco glowed orange. Pungent smoke billowed from his mouth.

Then he said, "I'm happy to talk about Dr. Goode. I've watched preachers come and go in the Valley for forty-five years, ever since I first pinned on a deputy's badge." He chuckled, then coughed. "Hell, they're one of our major exports. Seen lots of 'em mess up, too. Busted several, and run a dozen more out of Rockingham County."

"For what?" I asked anxiously.

Hanson paused and gazed toward the mountain again. "I expect we'll see a deer soon," he remarked, as if he hadn't heard me. "They like to snack on my corn in the morning. Can't even try to stop 'em now."

He looked back at me. "The usual stuff," he said. "Money, sex and power, that's about all there is. Some were stealin' money, others tried to steal whole churches away from their denominations or other pastors. And some were messin' around. Baptist preachers seem to go for the deacons' wives."

He squinted at me. "Though there was a couple who were after the deacons, or their sons."

I colored in spite of myself, but he was now eyeing Karl. "Mr. Russell," he said, "I'm not so sure I'd trust you around any young Baptist deacons."

"Not to worry, sheriff," Karl said. "I'm a strict Catholic myself."

Hanson sniffed. "I'll bet," he said. "Now as to Pastor Goode, it's fair to say he was no saint. He put on a good show, and milked his people like a pro." He paused again, and pursed his lips.

"But as far as I could see," the sheriff went on, "he didn't keep all that much of it for himself. It mostly went right back into this area. Oh, there were the missionaries to Borneo, and some food shipments to Africa. But they didn't amount to much. Mainly he put it into building: The temple. The college. The radio and TV studios. All that. He made a lotta work for folks in Rockingham and Shenandoah counties."

He scratched his stubbly chin meditatively. "These days," he said after a minute, "that's a downright Christian thing to do, if you ask me."

The brown eyes came to rest again on Karl. "And if to collect the money to make that work he needed to talk trash about a lotta limpwrists and bureaucrats in Washington, well, that never bothered folks around here much. Includin' me."

"No deacons' wives?" I asked, my hopes fading.

He shook his head, the pipe glowing.

"Or young deacons?" Karl added boldly.

The sheriff snorted. "If he'd had, I'd of heard about it sure. And we'd of sent him off someplace where they enjoy that sort of thing. Fire Island. Or Dupont Circle."

Karl was ready to reply, but Hanson took the pipe from his mouth, put a finger to his lips, then pointed past him with the pipe stem. I turned and saw a tawny doe and her spotted fawn ambling out of the woods, nibbling at the grass and bushes, and headed for a stand of corn that, once I noticed it, did look pretty well picked over.

We all watched silently, scarcely breathing, as the deer slowly grazed their way along the edge of the clearing. At one point I was sure the doe looked right at us, and wiggled her supple velvet ears in our direction, but she gave no sign of noticing us. Finally, they passed out of view behind the cabin.

123

Hanson clamped his teeth on the pipe, but it was out. "Goode wasn't as innocent as all that," he said reflectively, fumbling for the lighter. "But he wasn't so far away either. Too bad there's too many of 'em."

"Too many of what?" I asked.

"The deer," he said. "Had to give up on my corn patch in the back; couldn't keep 'em out of it. They're way overpopulated in Virginia."

"Like preachers," Karl drawled.

Hanson nodded slowly, and raised a thick salt and pepper eyebrow. "No surplus of real Christians, though."

I was beginning to feel desperate. There was only one card left in our hand. "What about the broadcast tower?" I said.

Hanson snorted again. "I figured you'd get to that eventually," he said. "Half a dozen reporters been down sniffin' around that one. *Washington Post, Wall Street Journal.* I forget the others."

His head turned toward Karl. "What paper'd you say you was with?"

While Russell was clearing his throat, I stammered, "Er, I'm free-lance," adding hastily, "but I've done stuff for *The New York Times*, and they might be interested in this too."

(This was not entirely a falsehood. I once had a letter to the editor printed in the *Times*, on the benefits of cutting maritime subsidies.   And I honestly did think the paper would be interested in the radio tower story, if we could break it....)

Hanson was now scrutinizing me, as smoke rose from his mouth. "Well, that would be a helluva story," he said, "and I wish you luck. The other fellas all seemed to think it'd be easy enough to figger out, at first. They thought us redneck cops down here were either too stupid to crack it, or were in on it somehow. Yeah, they were sure their Pulitzer Prize was here just waiting to be picked up."

He gave a hollow chuckle. "But they never found nothin'. Which didn't surprise me, because I looked into it for months, and I never found nothin' either."

He knocked ashes from the pipe, and opened the tin of

tobacco again.

"Except for one thing," he continued. "It was a professional quality job. Plastic explosive, the kind those terrorists use. Not a lot of it--the blast wasn't all that loud. But the charges were very carefully placed, in just the right spots on all four of the legs, and the cables."

The plastic lighter flamed again. "Then, Bang!" Hanson said, emitting a grey cloud. "Down it went, three o-clock in the morning, and the switches and transformers with it. Nobody hurt--the charges were timed so it fell away from the nearest building. Mighty considerate of whoever it was. The blast only broke a few windows around. Nice and clean."

A surgical strike, I thought.

Hanson puffed contentedly, and gazed out over the valley again. "Yep. Top quality job, start to finish."

"And not a clue as to who it was," I said forlornly.

He shook his head firmly.

In which case, I thought, there was nothing to do but voice the suspicion that, above all, had brought us here. "Suppose he did it *himself*," I suggested tentatively. "You know, for the public relations. The fundraising." It sounded a bit inane here, but it had to be raised.

Hanson swiveled in my direction. "You think that never occurred to *me?*" he snapped.

I felt my face flush again. Karl came to my rescue. "Goode was first on your list, right?"

"Him and his cronies," Hanson said. "Bet your behind they were. Don't have to work for *The New York Times* to add two and two."

Now both hands came up from the blanket, in the most animated gesture he had yet made. "Hell, the way he milked it, I checked 'em all out. Goode, Brewer, the deacons. Quietly, of course. Gotta be discreet when you're tailin' men of God in their own hometown."

The hands opened, empty, and he shook his head again. "But nothin' added up. Goode and Brewer both been preachers all their lives. Prob'ly couldn't light a roman candle without blowing

125

their noses off. Most of the deacons were veterans, but half of those were clerks, and the rest were infantry. Shooting and guns, yeh, they knew 'em. Grenades, maybe even mortars. But fancy explosives? Nah."

He squinted one eye, and gestured again. "'Course, they coulda contracted for it. But that's a tricky business too, and chances are it woulda left a trail. But that never turned up either. So I had to consider other possibilities."

"Like who?" Karl asked.

Hanson rubbed his chain again, and squinted toward the trees. "Yeh," he echoed. "Like who?" He jabbed the air with the pipe stem for emphasis. "I figger there's three main groups that can do this kinda work: The Mob. The CIA. And the military."

His held up his free hand with three fingers extended, tapping each in turn with the pipe.

"Now, the Mob is a long way off. DC and Baltimore and Virginia Beach. 'Bout as close as it gets to us is the race track up in Charles Town. Sure, Goode talked a lot about law and order, but by that he mainly meant keepin' the colored quiet. No, far as I can tell, Goode never crossed the Mob. So that's one."

With a final tap, one finger folded up.

"As for the CIA--why, Goode was the biggest fan the Contras and all that Reagan stuff ever had. Raised money for 'em, had Ollie North preach at the Temple, the whole nine yards. Far as he was concerned, all of it was for Christ and they were just missionaries in disguise, with guns. So if the CIA was gonna come down here, it'd be to give him a medal."

Another tap, and a second finger folded.

"Same with the military; he loved Desert Storm. Thought Saddam Hussein was the Antichrist Himself, and Iraq was the curtain raiser to Armageddon. Yes, sir. So that makes the Pentagon boys pretty unlikely suspects."

One more tap, and the last finger folded into a weathered fist. "So if it wasn't one of those three, my guess is it musta been a freelance job, done by somebody who'd been *in* one of these other three and trained in demolition."

Now he turned back to Karl, and sized him up again.

126

"Frankly, Mr. Russell," he drawled, "I finally decided it was most likely one o' your fellows."

Karl didn't even blink. "Naw, sheriff," he rejoined pleasantly, "we were all too busy chasin' them young deacons."

Hanson stared at him, and I thought for a second he was going to take offense. He squinted and muttered, "I thought you said you were a Catholic."

"Right," Karl responded. "Actually, I was cruising the seminaries."

"There aren't any Catholic seminaries in the Valley," Hanson said evenly.

"Then I guess that gives me an iron-clad alibi," Karl said.

"Think so?" Hanson bit down on his pipe, and I realized he was stifling a grin. He was enjoying this repartee.

"Maybe it does," he said after a moment. "But then that leaves the case stuck in the unsolved file. And I still think--" he paused and knocked ashes loose again,"--that Goode was mainly clean. Now, his sidekick Tommie Lee, there's the one you should check out. He ran the building program, while Goode raised the money. I never got anything on him, but my insides tell me he's slick."

"Would he know about how to contract for the tower bombing?" I asked.

Hanson's only response was a shrug.

"What about Gus Murray?" I asked.

"Don't know him, really," Hanson replied. "Seen him once or twice down there. Doesn't wear polyester and uses a lotta big words. I understand he's from DC, so naturally I wouldn't trust him. Figgered maybe he was working undercover."

"You mean," Eddie spoke up, "like for the FBI?"

Now Hanson couldn't hide the grin, or his tobacco-stained teeth. "Nah," he drawled. "I figgered it was for *The Washington Post*. Be just like them."

"Yeah," I agreed heartily. "It would."

Back on Highway 678, the sun was high over Fort Valley. The fog had dissipated, the dew had vanished, and in the harsher light of full day, some of the vale's air of secluded romance had faded too. Road dust dulled the shrubbery, and beer cans labels flashed out at us now and then. At King's Crossing we headed west on 675, through the gap toward Edinburg and I-81.

After a mile or so, Eddie turned from the dark green mountainside rushing past and said to me, "Let's see. If I heard right back there, Goode was a raving homophobe, an enthusiastic warmonger, a cynical racist and a con man. But except for that, he was a good Christian and downright decent fella."

"Well," I responded, "when you're talking TV preachers, I guess you can't set your standards too high."

But the wisecrack felt strained. Eddie stroked his chin, and turned back out the window. "It's a pretty place," he mused, "and the sheriff is quite a guy. But where does it all leave us? Do we know anything more than we did? Anything useful?"

"I'm not sure," I admitted. Then more truthfully, "I don't think so. Except that maybe we should start digging into Brewer and his background."

"Do we have time for that?" Eddie wondered. "Do I have time for it?"

"I don't know," I said. "But on the other hand, an unsolved case is one which doesn't eliminate any possibilities. So it's still possible that Goode somehow set up the bombing himself. But I'm not sure at this point where we go next. We're getting short on leads.   What do you think, Karl?"

I realized then that Russell had been silent since we left the sheriff's place. He was gripping the wheel steadily and staring ahead at the road.

"Hello," Eddie called. "Earth to Karl. What's your take on all this?"

Karl sighed. "I think we can forget about it," he said quietly. "The sheriff is way ahead of us."

"What do you mean?" Eddie asked.

"The way the bombing was done," he said tiredly. "So carefully and professionally. It matches exactly what a guy in Washington, one of our early Queer Commandos, told me a year ago. At the time, I thought he was bullshitting or hallucinating. But he was an ex-Navy Seal, and they have the training."

"Jesus," Eddie said. "Who was it?"

Karl glanced away from the road momentarily, and there was pain in his eyes.

"Does it matter?" he said quietly. "The guy died of AIDS a month later."

CHAPTER EIGHTEEN

The neighing troop, the flashing blade,
The bugler's stirring blast,
The charge, the dreadful cannonade,
The din and shout are past.

--Verse on a plaque in the Winchester National
Cemetery

"We need gas," Karl said. We had passed Edinburg and were headed north again on 81. "And I should call home and check my messages."

"Try Tom's Brook," I said. "Next exit. There must be a truck stop."

"Ah, truck stops," Russell said, his mood lightening. "What's your pleasure, gentlemen?" he asked. "Shall we look for a new one, the kind with bright primary colors and all the latest phony Canadian mineral water? Or perhaps something a bit more venerable? Someplace indigenous, the true habitat of the carnivorous *Valiensis Redofneckus?* A screen door, dark inside, with headache powders and a big jug of pickled pig's feet on the counter, next to the shotgun shells. They're an endangered species, you know."

Eddie was rolling his eyes. "Suit yourself," he said. "Just so it doesn't have segregated johns, and their Klan robes are put away."

Karl peered ahead. "Aha," he cried, pointing. "I think I see the telltale blue X not far ahead now. Yes! 'The Stars and Bars Truck Depot and Gift Shop,'" he read. "What else could it be?

130

Gentlemen, we're in luck."

"That's your opinion," Eddie growled.

The Stars and Bars was unique, certainly, though there were no pig's feet in sight. As a truck stop it was no great shakes, one line of pumps and an undistinguished convenience store array of chips, soda, with a big rack of rock 'n roll, abridged techno-thrillers and Louis L'Amour westerns on tape.

But the adjoining gift shop was a find: It specialized, not in Confederate gimcracks, but in Elvis memorabilia. I wandered through the doorway while Karl pumped the gas.

Once inside, the King grinned at you from all directions, young and old, on trading cards, playing cards, postcards, towels, thimbles, pens and posters, to name but a few. A tape of one of his more sober Las Vegas performances played in the background; the man himself flickered on a video screen next to a display of movie and concert tapes. The only exceptions to the theme were a couple of counters in the far corner, which were a private chapel dedicated to Hank Williams, Jr.

Here the spirit of Dixie was stirring a bit. A large Confederate flag hung in the corner, bearing the younger singer's profile and the legend, *"If the South Would'a Won the War, We'd of Had it Made."* Nearby, a stack of jigger glasses sported a drawing of a rebel soldier with folded arms declaring, *"Lee surrendered. I didn't."*

This furtively insurrectionary display reminded me that Tom's Brook was the site of yet another prominent Valley Civil War engagement. On October 9, 1864, several of Early units ran into Custer and the Union cavalry near here. The result was predictable: Early's men, tired, hungry and short on weapons, got whipped by the golden-haired warrior of Little Big Horn. Maybe that's why there was no mention of the battle among the gewgaws on these shelves.

Eddie came in from the men's room a few moments moment later. "Jesus," I hard him say, taking in the scene. Nervous as he was, Eddie appreciated quality kitsch when he saw it.

A young blonde in a Hank Williams Jr. sweatshirt perched on a stool behind the counter. She smiled vaguely at us, but her mind was focussed between her walkman headphones.

My attention was caught by a display of Elvis refrigerator magnets, which had iridescent plastic frames. Suddenly I felt I *had* to have one.

Ah, but which? There were two designs, an older and a younger version. As I considered the options, I heard Karl came in to pay for the gas and ask the blond where the pay phone was.

What sort of statement did I want my fridge to be making? This was a tough question. The young Elvis was handsomer and had that irresistibly lopsided grin. But his was also a face from the retro fifties, when places like this did have segregated restrooms; the innocence we saw in him was ersatz and culpable.

The older Elvis had figured that out, and had become the kind of seasoned, cynical pro who delivered the goods to the packed Las Vegas crowds every time. But he was also an overweight junkie, and even in the glittering white jumpsuit, the aura of decay and death was almost palpable.

History is a terrible burden, I was thinking, when a local stuck his head in the door. "Hey," he called, "can y'all move the Camry, so's I can get some gas?"

"I'll get the keys," Eddie volunteered, and I gladly returned to the agony of indecision. A magnet in each hand, I was still undecided but leaning toward the older Elvis when Karl tapped my shoulder.

"Trouble," he murmured. "Arnie Wolfowitz called. The judge revoked Eddie's bail last night, and wants him to show up by tomorrow noon."

The vision of My refrigerator door faded. "Why?" I asked.

"The Commonwealth's attorney says he has new evidence."

"Like what?"

"He said he has the murder weapon."

I could feel my eyes widening. "Omigod," I breathed. "Did you tell him?"

"Not yet," Karl said. "I thought he'd be in here."

As soon as he said it, our eyes met and recognized the same thought in each other's expression. We headed for the door.

"Hey," called the blond. "Y'all gonna pay for them magnets?"

Flustered, I slowed to drop them on the counter and followed Karl out into the sunlight. He had a fist raised and was shouting.

"Shit! Eddie! Come *back* here, goddammit! Eddie, you *stupid* ass!"

His white Camry, trailing a faint haze of gravel dust, was just rounding onto the ramp up to the interstate.

"Oh, for Christ's sake," Karl groaned. "There goes a goddam fool."

"Or maybe a killer on the loose," I said.

"Don't say that!" Karl shouted angrily, waving away my doubts. He turned back toward the shop. "C'mon, I gotta call someplace to find another car. You have a credit card? Mine are all in my bag, in the trunk. Along with the computer." He shook his head. "Christ," he said, "he could get a long way on my cards."

"How'd he find out?" I wondered.

Russell was already back at the counter, getting change for the phone. "Here," he said, holding up a copy of the *Shenandoah News* from a rack beside it. *"Bail Revoked In Goode Slaying"* read the headline. He dropped it and went for the phone.

I walked to the counter and picked up the paper. Then I noticed the Elvis magnets lying beside it, the frames throwing off little circles of rainbow colors.

The blond had taken off her headphones, and was staring at me with an alarmed expression. Was she starting to get the drift of my conversation with Karl? Had she finally recognized Eddie's face from TV or somewhere?

To divert her, I snatched up one of the magnets. "I'll take this one," I said, reaching for my wallet.

It wasn't til I got back outside, and stood listening to Karl shouting into the pay phone to the lawyers, that I thought to look at my purchase.

It was the old Elvis. In the white jumpsuit, with the aura of death all around him.

CHAPTER NINETEEN

A picket line of Queer Commandos was shuffling and chanting along Cameron Street in front of the Judicial Center in Winchester. Lavender T-shirts and baseball caps, studded leather and close-cropped hair were the looks. Two men, gaunt with the ravages of AIDS, stumbled along on crutches. The signs read *"No More Victims," "We're Here, We're Queer, Get Used to It," "Gay is Good(e)"*, and suchlike.

"All *right!"* Karl hooted, "The brothers are here!" He honked the horn on the '82 Sentra that was the only car for rent in Strasburg, Virginia that afternoon, and stuck a fist out to wave at the line.

He was so into his gestures of solidarity that he didn't notice a pickup truck behind us speed up and pull around on our left side. As it squealed past, two missiles flew out of its window and splattered onto the Sentra's hood and windshield.

We both jumped and Karl hit the brakes. The pickup raced off, a rebel yell fading in its wake. By the time I unbuckled my seatbelt and caught my breath, the car was stopped and Karl was examining the hood.

"No big deal," he said when I climbed out. "Just flower pots." He fingered a small stalk and root cluster that was caught in a windshield wiper. "I think I recognize the leaves. Pansies."

We got back in and drove away, with the wipers and washer spray going."Pansies," I repeated.

"Yeah, he said, raising an eyebrow. "Some rednecks in Winchester must think they've got a sense of humor. Aren't we lucky."

Murder   Among   Friends

We passed the aging apple processing plants, with their tall stacks of battered grey pallets piled all along the block across the street. When we reached the corner where Cameron angled into Highway 11, he turned to me. "Sure you wanna go back to the college? Looks like there's more action downtown."

"Nah," I said, "that's your department. I need to get back and find Penn. He should hear about Eddie from me rather than the press, or he'll think I helped him escape. Besides, God knows what's happened to the Conference since we left."

"I thought everything was on hold til Friday," Karl said.

"That was the theory," I agreed. "But events are moving rather fast, as I think you've noticed, and show no sign of slowing down. I need to check in and catch up, maybe help Penn think about how to deal with Eddie's disappearance."

We passed markers noting key moments in Second and Third Winchester. They were barely visible amid the surrounding commercial clutter. I sighed. "I hope to God the state cops don't find him before he decides to turn himself in," I said. "They'll shoot first and claim he was resisting arrest."

"I don't think they'll find him," Karl said. "The West Virginia border is only a few miles west of Tom's Brook, and if he has even half a brain, that's where he headed."

"But won't they be sending out alerts to look for your car?" I wondered.

"Not if it isn't reported stolen," Karl said. The eyebrow arched again. "And it isn't."

I considered this a moment. "But how long can you protect him?" I asked. "Come noon tomorrow, won't all kinds of cops be wanting to know what you did with him after you bailed him out?"

Karl shrugged. "That's one for the lawyers," he said. "Arnie Wolfowitz can stall them for awhile. I'll see him at the Holiday Inn tonight for a powwow. Three more busloads of Commandos are comin' in tomorrow, at least." He grinned. "We can keep a lot of state cops busy watching us right here."

When Karl dropped me off at Valley State, I headed for Woolman Hall; might as well see if there was a committee meeting I could join.

In the wide foyer, I saw at once that the display for the *American Friend* magazine and publishing house was back up where Eddie's had been, with the jacket for *Quakerism and Biblical Truth* again in center stage.   And a peek through the double doors to the auditorium disclosed that there was in fact a committee meeting going on up on the stage.

The faces were familiar, and I was surprised to see Gus Murray among them.   The talk was desultory, though, and they had clearly been there awhile.   There was a feeling of spent force in the air, as if I had missed some fireworks.

I slipped into a vacant seat next to Rita.   A pencil and notepad were lying on the table, and I scribbled her a note:

"What's Murray doing here?" I wrote.   *"I thought he was busy handling the press coverage for the funeral tomorrow in Harrisonburg."*

She frowned down at my handwriting, then wrote a reply and passed it back. *"He's setting up the Temple rally at the college on Saturday.   Or trying to."*

Oh, God, I thought, remembering the scene downtown. Spare us that much.

Penn breathed heavily and spoke. "I don't see that we're going to get any farther this afternoon," he declared.   His lined face looked drawn and tired. "So I believe we should close with a few moments of silence, and the subcommittee will meet over dinner in the faculty room."

When the silence ended and chairs began scraping, I leaned toward Rita. "What subcommittee?" I whispered.

"On the rally," she whispered back. "It's not clear whether it's going to happen on the campus.   Penn is fighting it, but Murray is insisting."

"I hope Lem keeps it up," I said.   There was a tap on my shoulder.

It was Penn. "Good to have thee back, William," he said. "Can I see thee for a moment?"

"Sure."   I followed him back to the clerk's seat, beginning to worry about what he might be wanting to ask.

Murder Among Friends

Penn sat down heavily and picked up a sheet of paper. "William," he said, "it's time for thee to do a bit of the work thee promised to do for us."

"The work--?" I started, then stopped, confused for a moment.

"A civil war history tour," Penn said, adding wryly, "remember?"

I grinned sheepishly. "Oh, that. Whatever you want, Lem."

"Well," he said, "the tour is to be whatever *thee* wants, and can show Friends between now and dusk. A College bus is ready when thee is, and I've arranged for bag suppers from the cafeteria. Just finish it up at the meetinghouse; they can walk back from there."

I hesitated. Local history had been rather low on my agenda over the past day or so, and I wasn't sure I could focus on it enough to talk coherently or for very long.

Penn saw me faltering. "William," he said more quietly, "I know thee's worried about thy friend. But the Friends who have stayed here are getting rather antsy. They need some organized diversion. We need--I need thy help."

I nodded. "Sure," I said without conviction, "no problem." Then I added, "But there's something I need from you too, if you know it."

His eyebrows rose. "Yes?"

I too a deep breath, and scanned the stage. The last of the committee members were halfway up the aisle to the auditorium doors. Leaning toward him, I spoke in a confidentially, "Can you tell me anything about what they found. The police, I mean." I started to stammer. "You, you know, about--"

His curt nod stopped me. "Yes," he said quietly, "I can. They had it in a clear plastic evidence bag, and spoke with me about it later. It was a sawed-off baseball bat. They found it under his mattress. Goode's blood and hair were ground into the end."

"Omigod," I croaked, my mouth suddenly dry. "I remember. He showed it to me. It was signed by Roberto Clemente. He called it his homophobia deflector."

"I'm sorry," Penn said. "I know he's thy friend."

"Yes," I forced out. "And I guess he's also a killer."

CHAPTER TWENTY

"We deem it our religious duty to take no part in [this war]; and to abstain from every act that would give aid to its prosecution."

--Declaration of Virginia Half-Yearly Meeting of Friends, Ninth Month, 1861:

"Very many Friends love thee with all their hearts, for thy brave efforts on behalf of the poor oppressed...we openly approve thy intentions, though many Friends would not think it right to take up arms."

--Letter to John Brown from Friend Elizabeth Buffum, Providence Rhode Island, Eleventh Month, 1859

As the tour started, I felt like a sleepwalker. I told the bus driver to take us through Winchester, coming in on National Avenue from the east. There we passed the tiny, block-square National Cemetery, its austere white headstones in their silent ranks surrounded by a waist-high grey stone parapet. I pointed out that just across Woodstock Lane behind it was Stonewall Cemetery, where several thousand Confederates were buried, under parallel lines of dark grey markers.

From there we turned north several blocks, giving the Judicial Center a wide berth to avoid getting caught up in any modern history that might still be unfolding there. I was heading for Upper Loudoun Street, and the house that was Stonewall Jackson's headquarters for several months in 1861 and 1862. There we stopped and trooped through the shrine to this Confederate demigod.

Having already heard the spiel by the old ladies who led the house tour, I stood back and watched the Quakers trying to hide their amazement and growing disgust for the sanctuary and its onetime inhabitant.

Not many of us Friends are conscious of it, but devotion to the Union cause in the war is practically bred into American Quakerism, such that even converts like me absorb it with the macaroni and cheese at every meeting potluck. After all, Quakers re-tell the well-worn stories of our exploits on the Underground Railroad at every opportunity. Friends provided the troops for many of the first Republican cadres, back when Lincoln was just an ex-Congressman and the party a marginal, extremist sect. Quaker settlers streamed into "Bleeding Kansas" in the 1850s to help snatch the territory from the greedy hands of the "Slave Power" when it became a state. Old John Brown, with his Pottawatomie massacre of slavery supporters there in 1856, was too violent for Quaker tastes, but they knew where he was coming from.

The same in 1859, when Brown raided Harper's Ferry, less than an hour away from here, hoping to spark a slave rebellion. The Quaker elders recoiled from his rash use of "carnal weapons," but there were many among the rank and file who sympathized with him more than they dared to admit, even to themselves.

In fact, one of the three wounded men pulled out of Brown's last stronghold in the Harper's Ferry firehouse, and hung with him later at Charles Town, was Edwin Coppock, a Quaker from Iowa. Coppock's brother Barclay, another member of Brown's band, managed to escape.

This sympathy flowered after Fort Sumter, when many a Quaker lad--all too many, if you asked Lem Penn--threw over the Peace Testimony to join the Union Army and its real war against slavery. By the time Lee met Grant at Appomattox, Quakers,

139

whether in the army or out of it, saw the extinction of the peculiar institution, as perhaps the Society of Friends' crowning achievement. The means may have been regrettably "sanguinary," but the end they accomplished had been Quakerism's primary public goal for at least six generations.

No wonder, I thought, Quakers came South in a steady stream during Reconstruction, especially the women for whom Valley State was begun, to redeem this darkened and blooded land for the forces of Light and Liberty.

And now here, in tourist motley, was a busload of the natural and adopted heirs to this crusade. Some were pudgy in baggy madras shorts and knit shirts. Others sported beards, leftwing slogans on their tee shirts, or tiny feminist battleaxes on silver chains. They were shuffling through rooms hallowed to the memory of a man whose brilliance in the use of "carnal weapons" could well, if his span had not been cut short by friendly fire at Chancellorsville, have foiled their forebears' generations of effort and preserved slavery until this very day.

If few of these visitors could recount many details of Quaker abolitionist history, that didn't alter their reaction to this display, which was immediate and visceral. They worked hard, and with considerable success, at masking it behind polite and carefully neutral comments.

But I saw through them like a glass of water: This old, reverently-preserved house; all the shelves of artifacts behind the glass panes; the florid pictures and framed documents, sepia with age in their gold leaf frames; everything that all of it stood for, made these Quakers sick.

This was something, I also realized, on which this fractious bunch seemed, for the moment at least, in complete, if unspoken agreement: Lyndon Coffin, a point and shoot Kodak dangling below his pumping adams apple, had been diverted momentarily from his anxiety about the heresies of the National Council of Churches. He looked just as appalled as Rita and her humanist-pagan colleagues from New England.

When we left, no one spoke about it until we were back on the bus, heading south again. But I heard muffled gasps when I pointed to the white-columned building where Phil Sheridan had made his headquarters. They could see that it was not a museum, but a combination real estate office and antique shop, with a garish plaster apple, six feet tall and painted bright red, behind the picket fence around its small front yard.

They could also see, as we passed down the block, the rundown neighborhood market with an unpainted wooden bench out front, on which sat two old white men, waiting, perhaps, for a city bus.

The men were thin and red-faced. Suspenders held their faded khaki work pants up to where white socks stopped and pink calf began. One wore an old seed cap; the other, peering up at us through thick, dark-framed glasses, seemed to be missing a big chunk of his jaw; his left cheek sank into his neck in a flash of smooth pink.

He spat a dark wad on the sidewalk as we passed, and I figured throat cancer.

I wanted to stop the bus and point them out. I wanted all of us to see, and understand, that this was another part--the living part--of the legacy which we had just seen pickled in the house on Loudoun Street.

Go anywhere in the Real South, I wanted to say, away from the malls and the new housing developments and the military bases and the historic sites, and this is what you'll find: a thick layer of pinched white desperation and want, generations old, haunting the region and the nation like our national ghost. These men, I wanted to say, are as much a monument to the reality of the Civil War as anything you will see in a guidebook or a historic park. Remember them whenever you get caught up in the mystique of that extended orgy of slaughter.

But I didn't say anything. The two old men slid from view, and soon enough we were passing the site of the battle of Kernstown, and then on our way down the Valley Pike to Belle Grove.

There we got out again. But the mansion, pale and peaceful amid the rolling green fields, had a very different feel from Jackson's headquarters. After all, it had just been caught in the middle of a big battle; otherwise, it had always been no more than the seat of a large farm spread. There was little war memorabilia in its stately, high-ceilinged rooms.

Besides, the late afternoon sun gave everything a gilded, serene look, and with bags of sandwiches and chips in hand, we streamed gratefully toward the picnic tables in the back. As we ate, blue-grey clouds rolled over us from West Virginia. They dropped rain on Strasburg, but merely stirred and cooled the air for us.

From there, we took the bypass back north around the west side, while I told about Rebecca Wright, Winchester's famous Quaker spy. She sent a message to Sheridan wrapped in foil and stuck in an old freedman's hollow tooth, passing on information about Early's troop strength just before Third Winchester in September, 1864.

Sheridan almost blew it anyway, but his bacon was saved by the timely charge of General George Crook, aided by a spectacular cavalry charge by none other than George Armstrong Custer, who was just then achieving his reputation as a hellatious warrior. That was the battle, I remembered, which produced the little marble marker I had found by the new jail when I went to visit Eddie.

Eddie. Where the hell was he?

No time for that now.

As we turned into the gravel driveway up to the Opequon Creek Meetinghouse, I was just wrapping up the tale of Rebecca Wright, how news of her espionage leaked out a few years after the war, when Sheridan sent her a big gold watch as a memento. Word got out about it, and the good southern folk of Occupied Winchester promptly ran her out of town.

But not to worry, I assured Friends: Wright ended up with a husband and a government sinecure in Washington, where she died happy, by all accounts, many years later.

The Quakes were eating it up. So to wrap up the tour, I assembled them on the porch and talked about how while Winchester was changing hands 75 times or so during the war, the meetinghouse had been often caught in the crossfire, and had also been used as a neutral hospital and burying ground.

There were reports of ghosts here, I said, especially on summer evenings like this one, I said, rustling through the trees around the cemetery. Then I turned them loose to look over the tombstones in the dusk before making their way down the hill across the campus to the dorms.

As the group broke up, I noticed Fred Harrison and Gus Murray standing off to one side, apparently listening. Harrison came toward me, hand extended.

"I heard your tour was going to finish up here," he explained, "and wanted to see how it went. We'll want to do tours from our Center too."

He glanced around. "Looks like a bunch of satisfied customers," he commented. "You must do well as a tour guide."

"I'm interested in my subject," I said. "Enthusiasm will cover many of the gaps in my knowledge, at least when I'm dealing with amateurs."

Harrison nodded knowingly. "That was a good story about the meetinghouse," he said. "I hadn't heard about the ghosts before."

"To tell the truth," I confessed, "I made that part up. It's the right time of day for it."

He grinned. "Young man, you could go far in this business," he joshed.

I am just reaching the age where to be called "young man" has ceased to feel patronizing and is beginning to sound like a compliment. I grinned appreciatively, we turned and strolled through the gate into the cemetery. Harrison stooped and touched a weathered headstone, streaked darkly with lichens. "'Mahlon Evans,'" he read, "'1768-1829. Steadfast for the Truth.' He was clerk when the big fight with the Hicksites came, you know. They threw him out on his ear."

"Yeah," I said, "Lem told me about it the other night. So much history here. I find it fascinating."

Harrison stroked the rough surface of the granite. "History," he repeated quietly. "Ben Goode was fascinated by it too."

"What?" I was surprised.

"Oh, yes," Harrison said firmly. "I've heard it was one of his private obsessions. He would have been interested in our Civil War museum project. Very interested, I think. In fact, I had an appointment to talk with him about it the day he was, um,

143

attacked."

"Uh, right." I recalled Harrison had mentioned it when we met by the library, but I had figured, good salesman that he was, he was just glomming onto every possible prospect that came within range. This information was very intriguing. It would fit with what Lem had read to me of Goode's heritage. What else didn't I know about this dead man? "How did it go?" I asked. "Did he like your plan?"

Harrison straightened up and brushed lichen dust from his fingers. "I didn't see him. Reverend Brewer called that morning and cancelled the appointment. Said something urgent had come up."

"Too bad."

I heard a step behind us and turned to see Murray approaching. "I thought you were handling press for the funeral," I said, not exactly warmly.

He shrugged it off. "That's all ready. The Temple staff is very efficient. My job this afternoon was to get brother Harrison here to host our rally on Saturday."

I shot a quick look at the president. Had he weakened since this afternoon? He was gazing off in the distance, maybe hunting for ghosts. His head shook slightly.

"But Fred here says it's no dice," Murray sighed, "so I've got to get back to Harrisonburg. I'll pester him again after that."

I was relieved. Lem Penn must have made the better case, and made it stick. "Hey," I asked Murray, "was Goode really a Civil War buff? Fred was just telling me about that."

Murray waved a deprecatory hand. "Yeah," he said, "he was, but it wasn't really that big a deal. He had some old family things, and he'd collected a little more. He was hoping to have them kept in a display case somewhere, with his name on it. Maybe here. That's about all."

Harrison turned abruptly. "But I think he would have done *more* to help us if I could have explained the project to him," he said.

There was a new intensity to his voice; the smooth academic salesman's tone was gone. "I talked with the president of the Chamber of Commerce just today," he went on, "and he agrees now that it's the best economic development idea around right now. Especially since Cedar Creek is closing down."

"Cedar Creek?" I asked.

"Right," Harrison said. "Cedar Creek Industries. They're shutting down their gypsum plant near Kernstown. Three hundred fifty more jobs gone by next month. Biggest plant closing in the Valley this year, but it won't be the last."

"Jesus," I said, my mind racing. "I hadn't heard."

CHAPTER TWENTY-ONE

On fame's eternal camping ground,
Their silent tents are spread,
And glory guards with solemn round
The bivouac of the dead.

> --Verse on a plaque in the Winchester National
> Cemetery, and on the Monument to the
> Confederate Unknowns, Stonewall Cemetery,
> Winchester

The Vice President's black limousine slipped silently up the horseshoe driveway to the Good Life Baptist Temple's main entrance. As it slowed, stony-faced Secret Service men fanned out on either side, watchful even in this obviously friendly crowd.

A receiving line waited at the curb. I recognized Tommie Lee Brewer at the curb, and thought I spotted Gus Murray a few heads down from him.

The limo's big door swung open, and a heavily veiled woman stepped out.

"Mrs. Goode," Karl murmured.

The scene was on the big set in his room at the Holiday Inn, live on WVCR-TV, your Valley Christian station. A laptop computer lay on the unmade bed, along with two pizza boxes and a rumpled bag from Taco Bell. Russell faced the screen, standing with one leg drawn up in a triangle against the other in what I guessed was some kind of Tai Chi exercise, a sheaf of papers stuck under one arm.

With the camera following, Mrs. Goode leaned to accept a ritual hug from Brewer. Then the unmistakable, glossy blond head of the Vice President emerged from the car, and Charlotte Goode slid from view as the camera moved him to center screen. As he began handshaking his way down the receiving line, the crowd closed in and some of them started to applaud.

The clapping was soundless, though; Russell had the audio all the way down. He strode away from the tube and handed me some papers from his bundle.

"The police report," he said. "Arnie Wolfowitz got a copy." He flipped a page. "This is a xerox of the pieces of the paper that was found in Eddie's pants pocket and in Goode's hand. No date, no signature."

I tried to start reading it, but he rushed on, pointing again. "See the dark line there in the corner? There must have been a staple there, holding a second sheet. But what was that? Where was it?"

I looked at the paper again. The sheet had been torn and crumpled, and the text was hard to read. But I managed to make out a heading: *"FOR IMMEDIATE RELEASE."*

It was a press release about the kickoff of the Crusade for Family Values. *"'...announced a nationwide campaign to roll back the tide of pornography, militant homosexuality, abortion and moral decline that is threatening American culture today,'"* I read aloud. *"''Let the word go forth,'"* Dr. Goode declared....'"

I quickly scanned the rest, and gave it back to Karl. "This is just boilerplate. What's the big deal?"

Russell was watching the television again. "Don't know," came over his shoulder.

The Vice President was shaking hands and exchanging soundless pieties with Brewer. "The president of the College told me something interesting last night," I said.

"Yeah?" Russell didn't turn.

"He's pushing a scheme for a big Civil War history center on the campus, and he says Goode was interested. Goode agreed to talk to him about it last Monday. But Brewer canceled the appointment."

"Why?"

"Harrison--that's the president--said Brewer didn't explain."

"You think it means something?"

I shrugged. "Maybe. I don't know."

Russell pirouetted and handed me several more sheets of paper. "See if anything in here rings a bell."

They were entries from *Who's Who In Religion*, the 1985 edition, on Goode and Brewer. I read Brewer's sheet.

"Let's see...born in eastern Kentucky, high school in Beckley, West Virginia. Two years at college in Huntington....Worked in construction and contracting in Beckley and Raleigh County. Contracting?"

Russell, still watching the screen, nodded.

"...Served two terms in the legislature, on the Public Works Committee. Right place for a contractor. Then he entered Chickamauga Bible Baptist Seminary in Chattanooga, Tennessee."

"Goode's alma mater," Russell said.

I checked the dates. "But several years later. Churches in Beckley and Lynchburg, before joining Goode as chief operating officer for the Temple."

"A politician," Karl said scornfully. "Doesn't it figure?"

"So why didn't he stay in West Virginia and run for governor, or Congress? He must have really got religion."

"Or something."

On the screen the huge Temple choir, in robes of satiny blue and white, was pantomiming a hymn. The camera panned away from them to follow Brewer, Charlotte Goode and the Vice President coming slowly down the center aisle toward the big round platform, which was almost covered in bouquets of flowers.

"The call of the Lord is not easily resisted," Karl mocked. "And sometimes He has help." He faced me long enough to thrust another sheet in my direction. "This just came over Wolfowitz's fax this morning."

Murder Among Friends

A fuzzy copy of a news clipping. The West Virginia *Daily Gazette;* I couldn't make out the date. The headline was "12 Indicted in Influence-Peddling Scandal." I skimmed it.

"Par for the course in West Virginia politics," Karl commented.

"And lots of other states too," I objected. "But I don't see Brewer listed here."

Karl came over with a second sheet. "That's right. But the followup explains why. He *was* a target of the investigation. But when the grand jury got around to him, some key documents turned up missing, and there wasn't enough evidence. Nice break for him. He announced his retirement from politics about two weeks later. You smell a deal?"

Something was bothering me. "Okay, so he's got a shady past. But his brand of ministry is full of redeemed sinners. Chuck Colson, all that. How does any of this make him a suspect as Goode's killer? The Temple was his ticket to the stars. Looks to me like it still is. Couldn't he expect to take it over some day?"

"Not necessarily. Goode has a son, remember? Randall."

"Vaguely." I thought back over the material I had turned up in Washington. "Mid-twenties, I think."

Russell nodded. "That's him a couple seats to the right of the Vice President."

Once pointed out, the resemblance was obvious. A shorter, pudgier version of the late paterfamilias.

"He just enrolled at Chickamauga Seminary last year. And he's done an internship at the Temple already. Wait--" he reached for the audio button. "The veep is gonna talk. Let's hear a bit of it.

The familiar boyish face was doing its best to look solemn. "My friends," the familiar boyish voice began, "let us pray."

Two thousand heads bowed in unison, and Russell flipped the button again. "That's enough," he sneered. "I won't listen to piety from an American university graduate who can't spell potato."

I couldn't help picking up the refrain. "Yeah, I said, no

149

wonder the Japanese are whipping our butts."

"Right," Karl echoed. "Have you noticed that *sushi* spells the same singular and plural? No extra letters to remember. It's not fair, I say; an obvious nontariff barrier."

He touched the channel button, blinking over to CNN.

Now there was a street scene. I recognized the Judicial Center. The camera panned back to show a noisy picket line on the sidewalk in front: men in tee shirts, earrings and bright lavender baseball caps. The Queer Commandos.

The picket line receded into a visual sidebar to a woman reporter. "Meanwhile," she said, "at a nearby church, Christian activists are preparing to launch their own protest."

Karl shouted at the screen. "They are *not* the only kind of **Christians**, lady." Still on one leg, he scratched his bottom. "Hell, half the queers I know go to church."

"Or meeting," I added.

The sidebar switched to a church basement, where a collared minister was praying over a squad of well-dressed men and women. Signs leaned against the wall behind him: *"Family Rights Ever, Gay Rights NEVER!"* they blared.

The screen suddenly winked into black. "Enough of this," Russell said. He checked his watch. "Twenty more minutes, and Eddie Smith officially becomes a fugitive. He'll need all the help he can get." He reached under a pillow, and retrieved a lavender baseball cap.

"Speaking of Eddie," I said, "have you heard anything from him? Or about him?"

Karl shook his head. "It's the question they're all asking, but not a word. I hope he's taking good care of my computer."

He adjusted the baseball cap. *"And* my car."

He moved toward the door. I hesitated.

"You coming?" he asked, pushing into the daylight.

I raised my hands irresolutely.

"Come on," he coaxed. "You can be our Quaker peacemaker."

I let my hands drop. "Fat chance," I said. But the barb had sunk in. "Still, I don't suppose I can miss it." I followed him out.

Murder Among Friends

At the Judicial Center, the situation seemed well in hand. The opposing picket lines were now in place: Gays on the east side of Cameron, and Temple Christians on the west, in front of City Hall and along the back of the old Frederick County Courthouse. The gays were chanting, the Christians were singing. Both sides had signs. Several clusters of TV cameras and photographers were scattered around the perimeter.

Security was heavy. A double line of police and state troopers stood motionless in the street between the marchers, a line facing each way. Barricades and black-and-whites with flashing lights blocked off the one-way street a block south. Paddy wagons and prison buses were parked in the lot at the Judicial Center, awaiting the call.

Groups of people were watching from behind yellow police lines tape at both ends of the street, on both sides. I joined a knot of people watching the tableau from the steps of the Chamber of Commerce building just below the Judicial Center. When I elbowed my way to a good viewing spot, I was pleased to find myself between Rita and Lyndon Coffin. The superintendent was complete with straw hat, flip-lens sunglasses, bermuda shorts, and camera.

A mischievous impulse came over me. I tapped Coffin's shoulder.

"Seen anything like this in Richmond, Indiana yet, Lyndon?" I teased.

He was not amused. "Good thing the police are out in force," he said grimly. "This could get violent any minute." He brought the camera to one eye, squinted, and clicked the button.

"Well if it does," I said, half-serious now, "it'll be up to us to stop it, right?"

He looked toward me quizzically, the camera still raised. *"Us?"* he queried.

"Sure," I said. "You, me and Rita. We're the only Quakers in sight. The nonviolent conflict resolution specialists. Right, Rita?"

She smiled and gave me a thumbs up. "I'm ready," she said simply. I noticed she had on a long-sleeved dark shirt and pants, and sturdy shoes. Her braid was wound into a tight coil above the back of her neck. She had come here ready for action.

Coffin's camera clicked again. "I think that's a job better left to the authorities," he said from behind the viewfinder.

I wasn't ready to let him off the hook. "But Jesus said, 'Blessed are the peacemakers,'" I quoted. "That's Matthew Five, verse Nine. Sermon on the Mount."

"I'm familiar with it," he said evenly.

A bullhorn's metallic squawk stopped me. Karl Russell had mounted a folding chair at the center of the Queer Commandos line. "Eddie Smith is now officially a fugitive from Virginia justice," he announced.

"*No!*" someone shouted from the line. "He's a fugitive from Virginia *injustice!*" There were scattered cheers, and Russell raised a hand to quiet them.

"That's right," he agreed. "But even without being here, Eddie Smith is making gay history in this oppressive state. He's showing that we queers are not gonna put up with a homophobic legal system that victimizes gays and lesbians any more."

More cheers. "In fact," he went on, "In *fact*, I believe Winchester could become as important in American gay history as the 'Sixty-Nine riots in Greenwich Village. As important as Stonewall. They even have the same name in Winchester: *Stonewall.* The Stonewall Cemetery is only a few blocks east of here."

Someone called out, "Let's go liberate Stonewall!" and there were shouts of approval.

Russell's free hand was up again. "We can do that best from right here," he began.

But the shouts were now a chant: "*Stonewall, Stonewall, Stonewall!*" And from the end of the line nearest us, someone yelled, "Come on--it's this way!"

Then the picket line began to sag and bend, and in a moment several of the Commandos had broken away to head in our direction, toward Boscawen Street. They were chanting "*Stonewall, Stonewall!*" loud enough to make Russell's bullhorn unintelligible.

Across Cameron, the Temple Christians' line had halted in place when the chanting began, and I could see its leaders

huddling and watching the Commandoes with alarmed
expressions. And the sergeants in the police lines were muttering
into their walkie-talkies.

More of the Commandos were heading towards us now,
clearly aiming to turn east on Boscawen and make for the Mount
Hebron Cemetery, of which Stonewall was a large section,
complete with a tall Confederate monument.

A squad of police moved from the center of the street to the
sidewalk to head off the insurgents. But the Commandos were
fast and lithe: they slipped around them and began pushing
through the ranks of onlookers.

Among the Temple folk, the enormity of the desecration that
was about to be wreaked on their local shrine suddenly seemed
to sink in. Someone started shouting, "Go *home*, go *home!*"
and then it too was a chant. Around me, onlookers took it up.
"Go *home*, go *home*, go *home!*"

All at once it became a chorus, and when the Commandos
pushed their way near us, people were pushing back.

Then things began to happen very fast. I caught a glimpse
of some of the Christian picketers dropping their signs and their
discipline and running into the street toward us. The police were
mostly facing our side now, and let them past. Scuffles were
intensifying, as was angry shouting.

Behind me came the crash of a rock through the window of
the Chamber of Commerce building, then another. And a few
feet to my right, a knot of Commandos was being held off by
some teenagers, kids with whitening faces, balled fists, and a mix
of fear and loathing in their eyes. *"Get the hell away from
here! Get out of here!"* they were shouting.

"Stonewall, Stonewall!" came the answering chant, and the
spot was at the breaking point.

I found myself shouting in Lyndon Coffin's ear. "Link arms
with me! Come on, if we can get between them, maybe we can
be a buffer, head this off. Come on!"

On my left, I felt Rita's arm slide into mine. I glanced
sidelong at her. Her face was pale, but set. She nodded.

I grabbed Coffin's arm; the camera went flying. I pulled him

153

toward the spot where the shouting was loudest and the pushing and shoving seemed most intense.

Then we were there, being buffeted by the pressure from both sides, and unheard amid the din of competing curses. Rita was pressed against me by the crush of contending flesh. "Push back this way," I shouted at Coffin, motioning toward the Commandos. I figured there was more chance they had some training and might be more likely to return to some semblance of discipline.

"Go back!" I bellowed at them. "You don't have to start a riot! Somebody else will just get killed! It's not worth it!"

Coffin and Rita were echoing me, and then a louder voice weighed in.   It was Russell, his bullhorn gripped in a white-knuckled grip, shoving his way toward us. "Come back!" he called. "We can make our statement here! Don't give the cops a chance to make more of us victims! Come *back!*"

And, for a moment, it was working. The buffeting stopped. Some of them, maybe on both sides, had retreated a foot or two. I could feel that Rita was able to move again.   There was space. The Commandos were listening, if not to us, at least to Karl.

Then the police moved in. From across the Judicial Center parking lot a line of them waded into the crowd, their riot helmets with visors up, billy clubs chest high, and shoving as they came. Commandos stumbled forward again, pressing the three of us against the townies, who pushed back in turn.

Then I made my mistake. The open space was too tempting: I let go of Rita's and Coffin's arms and moved into it, toward the police. Raising both hands, I started to shout at them: *"Wait! They're going back!* Don't push any more, give them some *room!* You don't have to--"

But then a cop was right in my face, grinning under his upturned visor, and I could see he had an upper tooth missing.

What I didn't see was his billy club coming at my head. It hit, I cried out as sparks blinded me, and I didn't even feel the sidewalk.

But I did notice, in the second before I blacked out, that up close, the concrete didn't look a bit like linoleum.

154

CHAPTER TWENTY-TWO

First there was a jolting, the murmur of voices, screaming sounds, and a sense of being paralyzed. My mind refocussed just long enough to note I was in an ambulance, strapped to a gurney, then everything faded out.

When I opened my eyes again, it was quiet, and a nurse with milk chocolate skin and large friendly eyes was leaning over me. Her hand was soft and warm on my brow. "You wakin' up now, honey?" she asked quietly. "You all right. Just a little knock upside the head."

My arms didn't feel strapped down anymore. I touched the right side of my forehead. It hurt, a lot. "Where--?"

The nurse watched me grimace. "Valley State College Infirmary," she answered sweetly. "Here, that bump bothering you? Take this."

While soft, her hands were strong. She helped me sit up enough to swallow a pill and sip some water. Then she lowered me gently and said, "You just rest now. You gonna be fine."

She padded quietly away, and I lay listening to my slow breathing, and began to drift. Bright colors and indistinct, swiftly-moving figures swirled around me. Again I felt a warm hand softly stroking my left cheek.

Then she was back, after five minutes or five hours I couldn't tell which, with a thermometer. I probed the cool glass with my tongue, and noticed that there were late-day shadows slanting across the white ceiling.

When she pulled it out, I asked, "Anybody else hurt?"

She was still peering at the thermometer. "I don't think so,"

155

she said. "Praise Jesus." Her eyes shifted from the thermometer to my left. "But she can tell you better than me."

"She--?" My head hurt as I turned it.

Rita was there, sitting by the bed. Her grey eyes were large, concerned, and lovely. Her braid was down, hanging over her right shoulder. She reached out for my cheek again, her touch cool and tender.

Even with the pain, I felt an overwhelming urge to kiss her fingers. I tried, but couldn't reach. She smiled and moved them to my lips.

"You okay?" I mumbled thickly.

She beamed. "Fine," she said. "That cop took a swing at me too, but I ducked."

"What about--?"

"Nobody else was hurt. A lot of pushing and shoving is all. Some of the Commandos got arrested. A few of the Christians too. It's all over now. For the moment."

The nurse swam back into view. "Well, it looks like you're normal," she said. "Thick head you got. I expect--"

A phone rang. Close, probably beside the bed. Rita picked it up and listened. "Yes, all right, just a minute," she said. Laying the phone down, she pressed a button and the head of the bed began whirring and rising. "It's your father," she whispered.

"My-my father?" I stuttered, wondering if I was hallucinating again. My father died two years ago.

I took the phone from her gingerly, as if it was dangerous, and spoke tentatively. "Hello?"

"Say, 'Hi, Dad,'" a voice commanded.

"What?"

"Say, *'Hi, Dad,'*" it repeated.

My eyes opened wide. It was Eddie!

"Ed--uh, Hi, Dad."

"That's better. Now say, 'Oh, I'll be okay.' Then listen."

"I, oh, uh, I'll be okay, I guess. But how are you?" I smirked uncertainly up at Rita, who was smiling back at this touching familial scene.

Then I listened.

156

CHAPTER TWENTY-THREE

My mind was suddenly clearing up. I motioned to Rita apologetically, and she moved discreetly away. "Jesus, Eddie," I whispered, "where the hell *are* you? Are you--?"

"Never mind where," Eddie answered. "And right now I'm probably doing better than you."

"How did you find me?"

He chuckled. "Hey, buddy, you're a *star*. I saw the whole thing live on your Valley Christian station. They even cut away from the funeral to catch the action. It'll be the 700 Club for you next; and an evangelistic video after that. You're gonna need an agent, buddy."

"Hell, it's just a knock on the head." As I spoke I sat up in the bed. My head felt much clearer now, and the pain from the lump, while still very much there, was receding into the background. "Goddam cops. I think the one that hit me was the same one who was in our room Tuesday. There was no need for it, either. We had the two lines moving apart. It was practically all over. I was gonna be an honest-to-god peacemaker."

Eddie chuckled.

"Hey, punk," I shot back, "we Quakers have our ambitions too. Which reminds me, what about Lyndon Coffin?"

"Who, the preacher with you? No problem. Jesus was watching over him, and he just waltzed out of their way."

"What about Karl?"

"Nah, he's fast on his feet, too. I saw 'em take a swing or two at 'im, but they missed. I think you got the martyr merit badge all to yourself, buddy."

"To hell with that," I said. "If I can get up and walk, which is not yet clear, I'll be fine. What are you gonna do?"

"Me?" Eddie said, "I'm gonna beat this rap, is what. Life underground is the pits, even with Karl's American Express card. Nice of him to leave it in the trunk. But I feel as paranoid as Abbie Hoffman already. I've been on the phone a lot today, though. Karl's computer and his FBI gadget were in the trunk too."

"Karl's pretty pissed about the car," I said. Pushing the sheets back as I spoke, I tried swinging my legs over the side of the bed. Everything seemed to work.

"Tell him not to worry," Eddie said. "He'll get it back. Tonight, in fact."

"Where?" I was standing now. A wave of giddiness came, and passed. Rita moved toward me. I fumbled behind me for the bed and sat back down.

"Cedar Creek battlefield," Eddie was saying. "After dark. Say, ten o-clock."

"Cedar Creek?" I laughed. "What kind of stunt is that? Abbie Hoffman, *hell!* Now you think you're the ghost of Jubal Early, back to chase Phil Sheridan out of town again. That Valley fog's got into your brain."

"Hey," he countered, "take my word for it, you can't figure this whole mess out without it. Just be there, okay? I--shit!" The connection was broken.

I hung up the phone, and suddenly felt out of breath. My head hurt again, and I lay back down on the bed for a moment.

It seemed like just a moment, anyway. But then someone was tugging at my arm. I looked over, expecting Rita.

Gus Murray. Dark suit, correct tie and all. I frowned, but he was ready. Sitting down on the edge of the bed, he pumped my limp palm. "I just wanted to shake your hand," he said warmly. "I saw the tape of what--what you did, um, tried to do. It was brave, just what you'd expect of a true Quaker."

Something about his tone made me wish I was a Presbyterian. I glanced at Rita, and she was looking at him quizzically.

"Why--?" I began.

He didn't let me finish. "As soon as we heard about the--incident--Dr. Brewer asked me to come up. See about getting our people out of jail. And to make sure our rally for Saturday was still on track." He smiled, a thin, self-satisfied smile. "Actually, the phones haven't stopped ringing since then."

"How many were arrested?" I asked.

"Only a dozen or so Christians. I'm not sure how many of the Commandos. I think they're out now."

"Anybody in your group hurt?"

"Some people shook up. A few windows broken. That's all. But it was touch and go for awhile. You were the only real casualty." He forced a grin. "The cameras were on you the whole time, Bill. You could be a star."

I looked away. Just what Eddie had said. But it sounded better from him.

"Er, have you heard anything from Eddie Smith?"

Reading my mind, you bastard? I shook my head, not looking at him. "Nothing," I whispered, more weakly than I felt. "I-I'm tired."

"Right." He stood up, not wanting to weary the patient, and anyway it was now clear he wasn't going to get any information out of me. "Um, once again," he said, "what you did took real courage. And I'm grateful for the example. I'll keep you in my prayers." He nodded to Rita and left.

I listened to his black shoes click away in the hall, then sat back up, feeling now as if I was fully alert. I realized my clothes were on a chair at the foot of the bed. I reached for my shirt and started putting it on.

Folded sheets of paper fell out of the pocket. I leaned to pick them up, but Rita was there first. Another flash of giddiness came, but passed more quickly. Straightening up, I unfolded the papers.

They were the entries from *Who's Who In Religion* Karl had given me that morning. I laid them on the table while I dressed, then picked up the sheets. Having read the one on Brewer, I looked now at Goode's.

Most of it was familiar, repeating what Lem Penn had told

me on our way to Middletown. But one entry stopped me:

"'m. Wanda Lynn Lucretia Burks, Whittier California, July 23, 1957. (d. August 7, 1959.)'"

The cryptic code letter "m." meant married, I knew, as "d." stood for died.

Wanda Lynn Lucretia *Burks?* Whittier, California? The seat of the Evangelical Friends Church--Western Region, Horace Burks, Superintendent?

An eerie feeling came over me, like the giddiness, but from a different source. I grabbed for the phone, and punched 411.

"Bill, what is it?" Rita asked.

A mechanical lady interrupted to tell me I had to dial nine first, and as I cursed her I heard the nurse coming back. "You ain't gettin' ready to leave us, are you?" she asked softly. "You ought to stay and get yourself a good night's rest."

I gestured vaguely at her and pressed the operator for the number of the Winchester Holiday Inn. Tapping in the digits, I muttered something to Rita about having to go to a meeting that wouldn't wait. She shook her head, and the look in her large eyes was gently reproving.

The phone in Karl's room rang a dozen times. Then the hotel operator was back, asking in a well-trained voice if I wanted to leave a message.

You bet your ass, I thought. I gave the Infirmary number and told him to call at once, emergency.

"I can have him paged, for an emergency," the operator offered.

"Do it!" I shouted, and hung up. I sat down, and put on my shoes. There were only fleeting hints of giddiness as I leaned to pick them up.

The phone rang again as I was tying the second knot. I grabbed it.

"Bill!" Karl sounded anxious. "I've been worried. What's happening?"

"Never mind that!" I shouted back. "You've got to come get me. I've heard from Eddie. He wants to meet us tonight."

Rita's eyes widened, and Karl was suddenly guarded. "Christ, don't say anything more about it on the phone. I'll be there in half an hour."

"*Hurry,*" I urged. I picked up the *Who's Who* entry. "I just found something else that may mean we've been on a wild goose chase all along."

"Save it," he barked. "Not on the phone. Look, the lawyers are here. Gotta go." He hung up abruptly.

Leaning back in the chair, I felt my mind click into its professional mode. Think investigative reporting. Think hustle. Who will know about Wanda Lynn Burks Goode?

Someone at the Conference. Yes...but they're all scattered. And besides, anyone who knew might be in on it, or would blab to someone who was.

So forget that. Somebody would know down at the Temple; I checked my watch: 6:37. But their offices will be closed by now too.

Then where can I get information like that at this hour? Libraries will be closing in Harrisonburg, at least the specialized archival and genealogical collections.

But wait--it was three hours earlier on the West Coast, places will still be open there.

But who to call? And what to say? "*Hello, would you please help me find out if maybe your sainted superintendent could be tied in with a murderer, or maybe even be a murderer himself? Yes, I'll hold while you check.*"

Not.

I rubbed my hands. The wheels were turning; I knew the sensation from a thousand forays around Washington. Then the strategy fell into place.

It took a couple tries at information to get the area code for Whittier California: 310. But a minute later and a phone was ringing in an office there.

A woman answered. She sounded young, born-again and sanctified. "Evangelical Friends Church Western region, this is Missy, how may I *help* you?"

I tried to sound southern. "Yes, ma'am," I said, "I'm calling from Winchester, Virginia, and I'm doing some urgent

161

genealogical research for a law office, and I hope you all can give me some information. There's been a bequest made heah in Virginia, and the will specifies that the funds are to go to the foreign missions work of the church where a Wanda Lynn Lucretia Burks worshipped with her family as a child."

I heard the sharp intake of breath when she heard the words "missions" and a synonym for "money" spoken in such close proximity. If I knew my born-agains, that should get their attention quicker than anything but the Rapture itself.

"I believe you're in luck, Mr., uh--"

"Er, Smith," I said. "Edward Smith." Eddie wouldn't mind lending me his name for a moment.

"Well, Mr. Smith, our archives aren't kept here in our office, they're in the library at Pacific Christian College. But the Clerk of our Records Committee happens to be here this afternoon. If you can wait a minute, I'll go get her. She's related to the Burks on her mother's side, and I'm sure she knows all about them.

I glanced up to see Rita regarding me with an astonished expression. *"What* are you up to?" she whispered.

"Catching a killer, I hope," I said.

Missy was back. "Sir, I think she's just down the hall in our lounge, but there's no extension there. Let me see if I can find her."

I grinned to myself. My head still ached, I was pushing middle age, Eddie Smith was wanted for murder and Lem Penn's All-Friends Conference was a shambles. But I hadn't lost the touch. And Rita was there.

"Yes," I said eagerly, "I'll hold while you check...."

162

CHAPTER TWENTY-FOUR

But there is a road from Winchester town,
A good, broad highway, leading down;
And there, through the flash of the morning light,
A steed as black as the steeds of night
Was seen to pass as with eagle flight.
As if he knew the terrible need,
He stretched away with the utmost speed;
Hills rose and fell,--but his heart was gay,
With Sheridan fifteen miles away.

--Thomas Buchanan Read, Sheridan's Ride

The only trouble with Eddie's pick of the Cedar Creek battlefield for a rendezvous was that there really isn't such a place. A big marker stands about a half mile south of Middletown, but the battle raged from there all the way around and through the hamlet to a knoll well to its north, more than a mile away, near the Community College.

Eddie probably didn't know that. But I did, and it made the knot on my forehead throb. Now Karl knew it too, and he didn't like it either.

Karl drove, watching the roadside for cars that resembled his white Camry, and listened distractedly as I tried to explain my discovery.

"Wanda Lynn Burks Goode. There has to be a connection.

She's plastered all over the Temple complex, but minus the maiden name. She was Horace's younger sister, much loved. Horace introduced Goode to her, and evidently it was love at first sight. They courted all through seminary and were married at Burks's home church, South Whittier Friends. Horace was best man."

"So?" Russell was impatient. We were passing the community college on our left, east of the Valley Pike, and there were mostly fields along the other side, no place to park, no place to hide.

"Then she was killed," I went on. "She and their baby, boy I think. Goode was driving. The rumor in Whittier was he might have backslid to his hellion days, just that once, and been drinking. Blamed himself anyway. But the point is that maybe Horace Burks blamed him too. It could be the secret grudge."

"Could be," Karl admitted, "but it's sheer speculation. Not even good speculation at that."

"Maybe," I admitted. "But at least it's a new lead. And think of it this way: Burks lobbied Goode to come to the Conference. He stayed close to him while he was here. And he had a dorm room on the same floor as Eddie and me. So he had as much opportunity to kill him as Eddie. More."

We were through Middletown now, and the battlefield sign was just ahead. Behind it, across a wide dark field, I could make out the pale profile of Belle Grove.

"Nothin', dammit," Karl grumbled. He turned in at the road to Belle Grove, backed out and headed the Sentra north.

"Well, shouldn't we at least do some research on Burks?" I persisted.

"Yeah, sure." Karl's heart wasn't in it, though.

He cruised slowly back toward Middletown. We passed some kind of electronics plant, set back from the Pike on the east side, with nothing in the driveway. A gas station. Scattered houses. A little strip of stores on the left, closed up. A For Sale sign, bearing a limp yellow ribbon like an old bow tie, stood in front of what had been a combination laundromat and a homegrown version of a Seven-Eleven.

"There," Karl hissed. But instead of braking, he speeded up.

"What are we doing?" I asked. "Did you see something?"

He nodded, and pulled a U at the next gas station. "I want to see if we're being followed," he said.

When the closed up stores came in sight again, he pulled into a gravel driveway at one end which ran behind them and out the other end. A rusted dumpster showed in the headlights. Beyond it, at the other end, was the white rear end of a car.

"That's it," he said. "I'd know my baby anywhere."

Karl backed and turned around, so our car faced the road. We crunched our way to the Camry and looked in. A big white folder lay on the front seat.

Karl produced a spare key from his wallet, and unlocked the door. Pulling a flashlight from the glove box, he ripped the envelope open.

The papers were hard to read. Fuzzy faxed copies of what appeared to be real estate records. "Where did this stuff come from?" I wondered.

"Puff the magic faxmodem," Karl murmured. "Ain't modern technology grand?"

"It'd be grander if you'd get a new cartridge for your printer," I griped. "I can't make this stuff out."

I riffled through the sheaf. As we read, a few cars went by, going fast, and whenever headlights appeared in the distance we reflexively stepped back away from the Pike. The text remained inscrutable, though I was able to make out the name TLB Properties in several places.

Then on one sheet a corporate title turned up listed in larger, darker print. I looked closer. It was a corporate charter for-I sucked in my breath. "Cedar Creek Development Corporation! Karl, what is this? Can you make out whose name is on this?"

Russell squinted at the fine print. "Can't tell," he said. "Looks like some lawyer."

"The name there is *Scruggs,*" a voice said from behind us. "Lloyd V., I believe. See, I told you we couldn't figure this business out without Cedar Creek."

We both jumped, and I dropped some papers.

"Eddie, god*dammit!*" Karl shouted, flicking the flashlight on him. "You scared the *shit* out of me!"

Eddie mugged in the pale beam as if it were a spotlight. "I always *loved* dramatic entrances," he said.

I fumbled for the dropped papers. "Eddie, what happened to you today?" I said. "On the phone?"

"Oh, that. A state trooper drove by, looked right at me. Spooked me, it did. But he kept on going. I guess it's like the sheriff said, they're not all terrified of strangers down here. Not yet. It's still a safe place."

"Oh yeah?" Karl retorted, "then how'd I get my goddam car stolen in broad daylight on I-81?"

Eddie grinned again. "Probably some fairy from inside the Beltway, out cruising the Valley boys," he deadpanned. "But say, thanks for letting me borrow it. I had to use your American Express card a bit too, and your computer. Listen, honey, that new faxmodem attachment is really something. Turned my motel room into a regular library research center."

"I know," Karl said. "The Commandos have two laptops in our motel room."

"Aren't they great?" Eddie said. "How many libraries have room service *and* cable TV?"

"Room service," Karl repeated flatly. I could tell he was apprehensively estimating the size of his Amex bill.

"Oh, don't worry," Eddie said, "I didn't order the steak. I'm a vegetarian, remember? Really, Karl, I do appreciate your leaving the stuff in the trunk--and your not reporting anything stolen."

"Strictly for the cause," Karl said. "Believe it. And we'll talk about the Amex bill later. But did you have to wear my best Duck Head slacks?"

"Do you really think they fit?" Eddie turned and struck a model's pose. "They *feel* great, but I'm not sure they're exactly my color. Everything else is back in the trunk."

"I want the pants *cleaned,*" Karl said briskly. "And watch the crease."

"Um, I hate to interrupt this fashion show," I said, "but what's this stuff in the folder?"

Without skipping a beat, Eddie was all business. "Tax and property records for the land we're on now," he said, "plus ten more acres, all zoned for business, and all owned by TLB Properties now."

"Jesus," I said, "how did you get all this stuff, from a motel room?"

Eddie snorted. "My man, all this and much, much more is on many a database, and yours for the asking. That's what they've been teaching me at the Center for Privacy. All you need is a phone, a modem, and a credit card. Lawyers get this stuff every day. I even turned up some of the financing information, and checked their credit records too. Did you know that Dr. Goode had six credit cards, with a total outstanding balance of $17,000? Thought I was on to something for a minute, but they're all current."

He riffled through the papers. "Let's see, the financing--it came from Rockingham Trust in Harrisonburg, and some West Virginia S & Ls."

"Rockingham Trust?" I pondered a moment. Then it came back: Reverend Phillips at Good Shepherd church across the street from Goode's old homestead. Bernie Carruthers of the big belly and bright red suspenders, who would tell us nothing. "The Temple's bank."

"Right," agreed Eddie. "And TLB is Tommie Lee Brewer, of course. I didn't think he'd make it that easy; a little arrogant of him if you ask me. But TLB is a subsidiary of Cedar Creek, whose real ownership is represented by a trustee."

"Lloyd Scruggs, Esquire," Karl deduced.

Eddie nodded. "Of Scruggs and Brewer, Beckley, West Virginia. The Brewer is Kenny Brewer, younger and probably smarter brother of Tommie Lee. And the small print pages are records for eight more pieces of property between here and Winchester. Altogether they're assessed at more than ten million dollars. The market value would be a lot more. There's more property south of Harrisonburg, but by when I got to that the print was getting too faded."

"That's a lot of real estate," I said. "Where do you suppose Tommie Lee is getting the kind of money you need to buy it all?"

167

"Good question," Karl said. "Did you find anything about that?"

"Nothing solid," Eddie admitted. "My hunch is that he's been playing around with Dr. Goode's bank balance somehow. They must have a pension fund, and it would have been easy to use that for leverage. He could 'borrow' some pension money, use it to buy a nice plot of land, sell it later at a profit, return the 'borrowed' money to the pension fund, and keep the difference. That was the eighties thing, after all. And he's the Temple's chief operating officer, right?"

"Yes, but--" I started.

Eddie pushed on. "So my theory now is that Goode found out about what he was up to, and Brewer killed him."

"It does have a certain Reaganite elegance," Karl said thoughtfully, as if appraising a crystal vase. "It even makes a kind of sense." His brows furrowed in the flashlight glare. "All it's really lacking," he concluded, "is any shred of evidence."

"Yeah," I chimed in, "it's just as likely that Brewer was acting on Goode's behalf in all of this, and the deals were strictly on the up and up, at least as far up as those deals get. Goode could have wanted his name and the Temple kept out of it for image reasons. Real estate speculation does seem a bit tacky as a hobby for a man of God."

"Tacky, maybe," Karl added, "but it's not illegal, and nothing new. Ask the Vatican. This is all very interesting, Eddie, but it doesn't explain why the guy got killed."

Karl opened the folder and shoved the papers into the slot. "Which, my little fugitive, is also to say that so far, there's nothing here that will keep your cute ass from getting strapped into Old Sparky."

Eddie began to look a bit deflated. I wasn't anxious to make him more paranoid, but there was no time for tact. "Besides," I said, "I found another possible lead today. Goode's first wife was--"

Headlights came over a rise to the north. We all noticed that they were going slower than the other cars that had come by. Without a word, Karl flicked off the flashlight and we were all pressed against the wall of the laundromat when the car passed, going quite slowly.

"Looks like this is my cue to say that's all folks," Eddie said, straining for a jocular tone.

Karl said, "Wait. We'll run interference for you. Come on, Bill, maybe it's time for a chase scene."

He sprinted past the stores, gravel spraying behind his pounding sneakers. When I slammed the door, he was gunning the engine, and creeping forward, lights off.

Just as the other car came slowly over the rise again, he flipped on the lights and hit the gas.

The tires screeched, gravel clattered against the old dumpster, and we careened onto the Pike headed south. I was still fumbling for a seat belt when Karl swerved left, onto a side road, skidding and accelerating.

I managed to click the belt, hung onto the armrest for dear life and looked over my shoulder. The other car was still there.

"I think he's gaining on us!" I called.

Karl seemed cool, even pleased. "Good," he said. "The closer he is to us, the farther he is from his real prey. Steady now."

With no more warning he swerved again, right this time, back onto gravel and straight for what looked like a solid wall of trees. I reeled back, throwing up my arms. But then the road sank and curved and the trees flashed harmlessly past my window.

I took a breath and looked back again. Dust was swirling in our wake. The knot on my head was pounding. The other car was still behind us, but falling back. "Why aren't there any red lights?" I shouted at Russell.

"Probably because they aren't cops," he yelled back. The Sentra splashed and bounced through a shallow stream that was wearing its way across the gravel and I clung to the armrest again.

Karl flashed me a quick smile, amused at my roller coaster rider's terror. "Not to worry, friend," he said. "They're not gonna catch us. And I'm not gonna kill us either. I know this road. I was out here last summer."

I looked back at him, still gripping the armrest as the car swayed and jounced. "You were?"

"Yeah. At night too." His grin widened. "With a deacon's son."

"You *slut!*" I cried. "I shoulda known. Told the sheriff you were a strict Catholic. Oh sure, but first chance you had you were out here doing sixty-nine with some nice Baptist boy."

"Hell, worse than that," he laughed. "Then I was reading to him from the *Baltimore Catechism.*"

But his confession did relieve my panic. We came to a fork and Karl veered to the right, then abruptly slowed and pulled into a broad farm driveway, stopping under the overhang of a large, dark barn. He switched off the motor.

We heard our pursuers slow at the fork. Then the sound of their engine faded.

Russell raised an admonitory finger. "You see, it pays to take the road less traveled. This one here loops around to within a half mile of the Pike. Our unknown friends are taking the scenic route, and if they don't watch it, they could be gone all night."

He backed out, and we sped off down the narrow lane.

I let go of the armrest and took a couple of deep breaths. My head was still pounding. Russell was still driving too fast for my taste. But the worst, I hoped, was over.

The road curved again, heading into another grove of trees. Just as we came to them, a sudden arc of tan and white flashed across the headlights. A buck, six-pointed and magnificent, bounded gracefully across the road not twenty feet ahead of us.

I didn't have time to gasp, Karl didn't have time to brake, and it was gone.

But then a smaller doe sailed out of the trees behind it, and right into the Sentra's hood.

The impact threw the deer up, so it hit the top of the windshield and vanished. It crashed heavily on the roof. The ceiling sagged and a crack appeared across the top of the glass. Then Karl was skidding and fish-tailing to a stop, and I had the door open and was running back through the churning dust to crouch where the doe lay, quivering, on the grassy roadside.

The tawny skin, pale grey in the moonlight, was unbroken. But the big yellow eyes were staring, blood was running from its half-open mouth, and if it wasn't dead, I hoped it soon would be.

I stroked a soft round ear helplessly. It twitched once under my fingers.

After a minute or two the quivering faded away. I rose and wiped my hands on my pants. I stood looking at it for a moment, breathing hard, then walked back to the car.

Karl was examining the hood. "God, we're lucky tonight," he said. "Some dents here and in the roof, the antenna gone. But everything still works, I think."

He drove more slowly after that, up to the asphalt road and then back to the Pike.

"What'll you tell the rental agency?" I asked.

He shrugged. "That we hit a deer. What the hell, it's even true. And the sheriff himself said they were way overpopulated around here. Fortunately I signed up for the extra collision coverage."

With the sight of that lovely, dying animal still vivid for me, his wisecracking tone rubbed me the wrong way. "A lot of good that does the deer."

He shrugged again, and pointed. We were passing the strip of stores. Where the Camry had been, the gravel lot was deserted.

I took a deep breath and let it out slowly. Now I could understand some of his carefree tone: Better that hapless deer, quick if not painless, than Eddie rotting on Death Row.

But my head still throbbed.

CHAPTER TWENTY-FIVE

Your own proud land's heroic soil
Must be your fitter grave;
She claims from war his richest spoil
The ashes of the brave.

> --Verse on a plaque in the Winchester National Cemetery

Another day, another committee meeting. The final session of the Planning Committee was set for 9:30 Friday morning.

Such is the exciting life of the dedicated Quaker. The story is told that Friends observe their own version of Groundhog Day the week school starts in the fall: Our plain grey rodent sticks his head up from his burrow and sees, not a shadow, but nine months of committee meetings stretching all through the academic year. No wonder our numbers are few.

For Friendly conference junkies, this liturgical peculiarity can easily be stretched through the summer to fill the entire calendar.

I'm not really that sort of addict. I get my share of committees at home in Washington Meeting, and only hit one or two summer gatherings per year. There I avoid the endless panels on "Friends' Response to" this or that crisis of the month, of which there are always plenty, and look instead for the sessions centering on what we media people call "soft news": A meeting for healing; or one on "Finding the Light In Your Work"

(I'm still somewhat in the dark on that one); or maybe Women in the Gospels.

Actually, anything on women is good, as long as it's open to men too. It's a chance to meet people. Which is what, for the unhitched Quaker, our conferences are really all about.

Which is why I sought out Rita in the Mott Hall cafeteria Friday morning at breakfast.

I wondered if my momentary martyr status, certified by the knot on my head, would still be worth some sympathy points. It only hurt now when I touched it; but I was right about its effect. She smiled warmly at me as I came to her table, reached up to flip the richness of her braid over her shoulder with one hand, and pulled out a chair with the other.

"Hey," she teased, "the hero of the day. Sit." When I clanked my tray down, spilling a bit of my orange juice, she added, "Ready for another round?"

"What?"

"You missed CNN this morning, I see. More action," she said. "Downtown. And cops in eight states are hunting for your friend Eddie."

"Eight states?"

She nodded. "Besides DC, Maryland, Virginia, West Virginia and Pennsylvania. Now they've added Delaware, New Jersey and North Carolina, in case he's gotten that far, and alerts are out across the country. Meanwhile, the Queer Commandos are bringing in more troops in the lavender baseball caps, and the Christians--"

"They're not the only kind of Christians," I said, repeating Karl's line from the Holiday Inn.

"Right. The *Temple* Christians are rolling into town by the carload. They're both saying they're gonna march again today. The Commandos still wanna get to the Stonewall Cemetery, and some folks claiming to represent the Rising Sons of the Confederacy swear they'll never let it happen."

I sipped the juice and mopped the spill with a paper napkin. "The Rising Sons of the Confederacy?"

"Yeah," she made a face. "They looked more like a chapter of Virginia Beer Bellies of Tomorrow to me. But that's not the worst of it. Last night somebody bombed the North Valley Women's Health Center. Only place in three counties that does abortions. Did abortions. Burned to the ground."

"Jesus."

"And the governor announced he won't tolerate any more violence. He's sending in the National Guard."

I groaned. "What have we started here?" Rita was as welcoming as I could have wanted. But any thoughts of potential romance were quickly being crowded from my mind again. Maybe some other lifetime. "Is the Conference still gonna start today?" I wondered.

"Funny you should ask," Rita said. "It seems Friends are not of one mind about that. With all the turmoil, some people are saying we should pack it in and go home. I know several who have already left. They were scared, and I don't blame them."

She shook her head and stirred a listless-looking bowl of oatmeal. "Frankly, I lean toward calling it off myself," she said, "but I feel like I've got to stay and see what happens. After all, Metropolitan Half Yearly Meeting helped pay for my ticket, and they'll want to make sure they got their money's worth."

She nibbled at a piece of tasteless white bread toast and pondered our plight. "Oh well," she concluded, "at least it'll make for a change of pace in our committee reports at business meeting next month."

"What about Lem?" I asked.

"Poor guy," Rita sympathized. "He looks like a trapped animal. A deer in the headlights."

I winced at the simile, but nodded.

"He feels he has no choice but to go on. The evangelicals are adamant, as could be expected. And it's hard to argue with them: You and that bump are the best we unprogrammed types can claim; they've got a real live corpse.

My scrambled eggs were cold. The hash browns were congealing in a rime of beige grease. I pushed the plate away.

"This is a perfect setup for the Fourth Battle of Winchester."

"The fourth?"

I glanced at her. "I guess you missed my history tour. The first three were in the Civil War. The other civil war, that is."

Murder Among Friends

"Well," she said, looking at her watch, "you know what they say: When the going gets tough--"

I finished for her: "--The tough Quakers go to a committee meeting."

She stood and picked up her tray. "See thee there?"

"In a few minutes," I said. I left my notebook in the room."

On the way back from the room, I cut across the parking lot outside Mott toward the grassy expanse of the oval, trying to trim a few seconds off the walk to Woolman Hall beyond it. It didn't work, though, because in the row nearest the sidewalk I saw something on a cream Ford sedan that caught my eye: Dark splotches behind both sets of wheels.

Something about this made me pause, then step around behind the car. The license plate had a yellow Hertz Rental frame, and the blue and white dealer sticker on the trunk said "Cedar Creek Ford."

I regarded it a moment. This was surely pure coincidence, but it was one too many Cedar Creeks for me. Opening the notebook, I jotted down the plate number. And then I started making a list of all the times the words had come up in the past week:

Goode's dying words, or so Eddie thought.

The Civil War battle his grandfather fought in.

His birthplace, more or less.

The name of his real estate holding company.

A gypsum factory that was closing.

And a car dealer with a Hertz franchise.

I ran my fingers through my beard, as I often do when concentrating intensely on something. It was getting toward the scraggly stage, I thought distractedly. It's about time to get it trimmed.

Then an idea was there, in my mind, like some creature that had been stuck for days in a locked basement and had just now managed to pick the lock on the trap door.

It might be nothing; it might be something. But it pulled at my mind, yanked at my attention, shouted in my inner ear:

Now. Don't wait. Time is short. *Come on.*

I gazed back at Mott Hall. The building was quiet, its worn

175

red bricks soaking up the morning sun.

There, the voice in my mind kept yelling. In there.

I flipped the notebook shut and walked back to the dorm.

The place was mostly deserted; a few people were in the lounge, leafing desultorily through the Winchester paper, or canted in a more interested angle toward the overly pink face of an anchorman on the big screen TV. None of them seemed to notice me going past them toward the stairs.

But I disturbed them when I came back twenty minutes later, clattering as I rushed down, and almost falling on the final landing.

"You all right?" someone called from the lounge as I stumbled past.

"Yeah, fine," I gasped. "Just in a hurry." A desperate hurry.

There were pay phones in an alcove next to the cafeteria. I snatched one up, stuffed it with a quarter, hit the keys. I asked the Holiday Inn operator for Karl's room.

"Hello," said a voice I didn't recognize.

"Karl? Karl Russell?"

"Gone," the voice said. "Downtown. The march starts in an hour."

"Shit!" I barked.

"What?"

"Look," I said urgently, "I'm a friend of Eddie Smith's. I think I've just found something that can clear him. But I need to get to a computer with a faxmodem, right away to check it out. I know you've got one there."

"Yeah?" The voice was cautious. "Do I know you?"

I wanted to moan. "No, probably not. I'm not one of the Commandos. But Karl will vouch for me. Isn't there any way to get hold of him?"

The voice was silent a moment. "I'm supposed to be security here," it said at last. "But I'm going downtown too in a few minutes, and I'll see him." A pause. "How about this? If he says you're okay, I'll call the motel and tell the desk to have a key card for you."

"That'll work," I agreed.

"All right. What's your name?"

I told him.

"And...something else, something that would identify you. Social security number?"

"He wouldn't recognize it." I was getting frantic; we didn't have time for this. Then it dawned. "Wait--here's something! Tell him I said to ask what former sheriff of Rockingham County lives in Fort Valley? The answer is Wilbur Byrd Hanson."

"Got it," the voice said.

"Write that *down!*" I shouted. "And just *do* it!" I hung up, whirled to leave, and realized that every face in the TV lounge was turned toward me.

I shrugged at them, grinned sheepishly, and raised one hand to my forehead, where the lump was pounding again. "In a hurry," I said lamely.

"You feel okay?" someone asked.

"Fine," I called back, rushing toward the main entrance.

Pushing heedlessly through the door, I almost bowled Rita over.

"Hold on," she said, "where you going?"

"Downtown," I answered breathlessly. "I gotta get to the Holiday Inn."

"How do you plan to do that?" she asked.

I remembered that my Toyota was back home, in Washington. "A cab?" I said weakly.

"That'll take hours," she said. "Half of downtown is blocked off, and with all the media in town you'll be lucky to get one by sundown."

I was feeling frantic again. "You know anybody with a bike?"

"I can do better than that," she said. "A group of the women got together after breakfast, skipped the Planning Committee and did a little planning of our own. We're gonna have a peace vigil at the Valley Women's Health Center. Sarah Scattergood has a van, and we're leaving as soon as we can get directions. We'll drop you off."

It was nearly noon when I waved goodby to Rita and dashed into the Holiday Inn lobby. At the desk the clerk, painfully cheerful in her navy polyester blazer, took forever looking through little slots.

"Nothing," she said, now cheerfully apologetic. "I'm sorry. Would you like me to page Mr.--"

"Russell," I hissed. "Karl."

She picked up a small microphone and took a breath. But then a heavy blonde stuck her head around a partition at the far end of the counter. The right headphone of her headset had been pushed back from her ear. "Did you say *Russell?* Something about a key?"

"Yes!"

She had a message form in her hand. "He just called. Said to ask you, let's see--" she peered at the form. "Okay, *'What was the Baptist deacon reading on the road to Cedar Creek?'*" She stared at it again to make sure she'd read it right. "Now what can *that* mean?" she wondered.

I just stared blankly back at her. It didn't compute. Seeing my confusion, skepticism began to cloud her expression.

"Wait--" I said. Then I laughed. That wise-ass. "The Baltimore Catechism, of course! What else?"

"Of *course,*" she shrugged. "What else?" She moved her headphone back and nodded to the clerk. "Give him the key."

CHAPTER TWENTY-SIX

The first that the General saw were the groups
Of stragglers, and then the retreating troops...
He dashed down the line mid a storm of huzzas,
And the wave of retreat checked its course there, because
The sight of the master compelled it to pause.
With foam and with dust the black charger was gray;
By the flash of his eye, and his nostril's play,
He seemed to the whole great army to say,
"I have brought you Sheridan all the way
From Winchester down, to save the day!"

--Thomas Buchanan Read, Sheridan's Ride

It would take, I figured, divine intervention to head off the
Fourth Battle of Winchester.

And divine intervention was what we got, in the form of a
thick front of severe thunderstorms, which formed over the
Alleghenies and bore down on the Lower Valley like some
relentless celestial cavalry.

When I was finished on Karl's computer, the rain and wind
were tapering off, and I switched on the TV. A reporter for Your
Valley Christian Station, reporting live from the scene, explained
from under her umbrella that the downpour and high winds had
kept the planned picketing to a small, thoroughly-soaked hard
core. But the various forces were still around, she said, and

179

when the storm passed, anything might happen, so stay tuned.

I didn't. I had what I needed, and it was time to get back to the campus. It was also something like divine intervention that brought a cab to the main entrance just as I came through the lobby. A reporter got out, wet, wrinkled, and disgusted. I slid in right behind him.

The driver, a grizzled black man wearing a vintage Baltimore Orioles cap and a weary expression, shook his head. "Sorry, suh, ahm on call back down to the courthouse."

I waved a twenty at him. "Take a detour."

"Where you wanna go?"

"Valley State. Quick."

His gaze shifted from me back to the twenty. "You got five mo'?"

I felt for my wallet. Three, four, five singles. "You're bleedin' me dry."

He gave me a slow, half-grin. "Times is tough for everybody," he murmured. "Got to get it when you can."

He took the bills. "Get in."

Outside Woolman Hall, a TV truck was parked. Your Valley Christian Station again. Several reporters and camera operators were browsing the lounge, as they had the morning after the murder. Evidently the rain delay downtown made our conference the hottest, or at least the driest, news spot in town.

Planning committee members were guarding the doors to the auditorium. I glanced at the clock--almost three-thirty. The opening was set for five. A bit late for the evening news feeds, but they could still get something. I nodded and pushed into the auditorium.

On the platform, which was illuminated by stage lights, Lem Penn was stage-managing a run-through of the opening ceremony, referring to a sheet held by Tommie Lee Brewer, who was offering whispered directorial advice on just about every item. I saw Rita off to one side; her braid looked damp. Her vigil had presumably been a washout too, I figured.

Fred Harrison was standing at a lectern, saying, "I'll welcome you to the campus and thank you for sticking around through

180

such a difficult week. It won't take more than five minutes."

"Good," Penn said. "Then I formally open the meeting, and I'll introduce Horace, for the spoken prayer. Horace?"

Horace Burks surprised me, by coming forward in a nearly white suit, set off by a scarlet hankie in the jacket pocket. I had the feeling this was his stadium crusade costume, rather than his telemarketing duds. I also suspected, since this was not California, that Brewer would have some sartorial counsel for him between now and the session.

Burks stepped up to the lectern in the center of the stage. "Dear heavenly father," he intoned into the microphone, "we come to thee this evening....How does that sound?"

"Great," Brewer put in. "Just fine. About two or three minutes will be about right, I think."

"Then I introduce the members of the Committee?" Burks asked.

"Yes," Penn replied. We're making a list of those who are still here for you. You'll introduce Lyndon last."

Lyndon Coffin took Burks's spot, now, as always, plaid to the hilt. "Are the hymnbooks in the seats?" he asked. Penn nodded.

"Which two have you chosen?" Brewer inquired.

Coffin was flipping through the book. "Number 83," he said, *"Onward Christian Soldiers.* And Number 272, *Once to Every Man and Nation.* These seemed familiar," he said, "and suitable to the occasion."

Penn looked stricken at this, but Brewer nodded contentedly. I saw Rita, off to one side of the stage with the rest of the committee, rolling her eyes.

Suitable to the occasion? Rita, honey, I thought, that's what happens when you skip the last Planning Committee meeting. You get an opening to a Quaker gathering that starts with a patriarchal prayer, then one hymn that's blatantly sexist and another that's overtly militaristic. But at this point, these seemed like some of the more minor outrages of the week.

"Then you introduce Rita," Penn said.

Rita stepped forward. "May we now," she said into the mike-

"A little louder, please," Brewer interjected.

Murder Among Friends

Rita glared at him and cleared her throat. "May we *now* gather in the *original* Quaker manner of worship," she boomed, "for a few moments of *traditional* silent waiting on God?"

I loved her subtle accent on "original" and "traditional." With luck and some chutzpah she would stretch out the quiet, and give time for the bad smell of the hymns to dissipate.

She looked up. "That sound better?"

"Perfect, Rita," Penn said gratefully. "After you comes Gus Murray, to make a few remarks and introduce Dr. Brewer."

Murray stepped out of the shadows and into the spotlight. He pulled a sheet of notes from the inside pocket of his jacket.

But just as he was about to speak, I clumped loudly up the stage steps and walked over to the mike.

"Excuse me, Gus," I said casually, careful to make sure the mike picked up the words, "I think there's some notes you forgot."

"What?" Brewer said, but I had stepped away from the lectern, toward the other side of Penn.

Murray glanced down at the paper I'd given him, then seemed to stumble for a moment. But he recovered quickly, mumbled "thank you," and started to put the sheet in his pocket.

"Oh, no," I insisted loudly, "you need to practice reading them. To us, here. They're rather important to our conference, don't you think? I'm sure Reverend Brewer would agree."

"What are you talking about?" Brewer snapped.

I stepped back toward the lectern. "Well," I said, "if Dr. Murray won't read the statement, I will. It's what Dr. Goode would have wanted, after all. What he *really* wanted, that is."

I pulled a sheet from my pocket and began to read into the mike. "'*Today,*'" it began, "'*after intense prayer and reflection, I want to announce that I have heard God calling me, as He called Abraham out of his own country, and as He called to Paul on the road to Damascus, to change my agenda, and to reshape my plans.*

"'*While many problems in our society cry out for remedy,*'" it went on, "'*and the forces of Satan are loose in*

182

our land, I hear God calling me to lay aside grand plans for national political campaigns, and to turn my eyes to the hills, as the Psalmist said, to the hills from whence comest my rest. These are the hills and the mountains of the Blue Ridge and the Alleghenies, the borders of the Shenandoah Valley, my beloved home.'''

"Give me that!" Murray snatched the sheet out of my hand.

But I grabbed the edge of the lectern and kept speaking into the mike. "It's okay," I said, "I don't need the text to tell you what it says. It says that Dr. Goode--" this time the title didn't gag me-- "planned to drop out of your Crusade for Family Values, Gus, and turn instead to a campaign to rehabilitate the economy of the Valley."

"Where did you get that?" Brewer demanded.

I ignored him. "It seems Dr. Goode had a revelation, namely that unemployment is probably the best friend the devil has nowadays. Yes, even better than liberals, gays and abortion clinics. That's because it smooths the way for all the other evils he preached against for so long. And he saw it spreading across the Valley month by month, like everywhere else. But he couldn't fix everywhere else."

I gave Brewer a sidelong glance. "What was it that turned him around, Tommie Lee? Was it the closing of the Cedar Creek Gypsum Plant last weekend? An awful thing to have happen to a company right after he joined its board of directors, don't you think?"

Brewer just glared, and I pulled another sheet from my pocket. "That's right, he'd just gone on the board last spring. It wasn't exactly headline news--he was on a lot of boards. But my computer found out."

I checked the sheet. "Says here he only joined it last spring. Bet he missed meetings, too, being so busy, and then the plant was gone. Just like that, three hundred and fifty more jobs--the mainstays of three hundred and fifty families--gone." I snapped my fingers for emphasis. "Just like that."

"They couldn't help it, the market was sluggish," Brewer said thickly. "Recession. It's everywhere."

"Sure," I said, "but this was close to home. Maybe too close. Was it then he felt called to do something for the Valley? I'll bet it was. And the best, cheapest way he could see to do that was to leverage its historical heritage, by creating a privately-sponsored Cedar Creek Historical and Cultural Program, headquartered *here*, at Valley State."

"You mean--?" Fred Harrison gasped. But I kept talking.

"He wanted satellite centers along the Valley Pike, including Kernstown, as far as the Cedar Creek battlefield itself. The properties are already in place, and the battlefield itself would be left undeveloped. He wanted to link up with existing Civil War museums and preserved sites as far south as Staunton, to create a Valley-wide network."

"It's a truly visionary idea," Fred Harrison said reverently.

"Ultimately," I continued, "the Cedar Creek Program would employ over a hundred people directly, and he thought it would draw a million new tourists to the area each year, supporting hundreds more jobs."

"This is fantasy," Brewer shouted. "You're making this up."

"Am I?" I retorted. "Am I making up the fact that Dr. Goode planned to stand at this pulpit last Tuesday and announce a grant from the Good Life Temple Ministries to Valley State of five million dollars, to endow the Israel P. Goode Cedar Creek Museum, named after his great grandfather."

I glanced around. Horace Burks and Lyndon Coffin looked like they were in shock. Burks wiped his face with the red handkerchief, and spoke. "What's this all about?" he asked Brewer.

"It's a fabrication," Brewer barked. "A *total* fabrication."

"No it isn't," I shot back. "It's the truth. It's what was on the other sheet that was torn from the Crusade announcement found in Goode's hand the night he was murdered."

I lifted the sheet and pointed to the corner. "It's still got the staple in it. And *you* knew about it, Brewer, because you handled all the property transactions through your TLB Corporation."

Lyndon Coffin looked toward Brewer, whose face was

crimson under his slicked down hair. The Indianan's eyes narrowed, and his adam's apple was working. "Tommie Lee," he said plaintively, is this true?"

But I wasn't finished with my questions. "Why didn't you want him to go through with it, Brewer?" I demanded. "You had a job either way. But you worked overtime to kill the idea. You cancelled Goode's appointment with Fred Harrison last Monday, and probably told Goode that Harrison had canceled."

"That's a lie," Brewer spat.

"And you and Murray argued with him that night," I hurried on, "told him he couldn't back out of the Crusade. But he said he was, right? I'll bet it was the closing of the Cedar Creek gypsum plant that did it for him, right? But finally you came to blows, or at least one of you did, smashing him with the baseball bat. That was a nice touch, setting up a fairy to take the fall. Which one was it that hit him?" ·

"You're full of it," Brewer yelled. "I'm not talking to you."

"My guess," I persisted, "is that you did it, Brewer. But why was the Crusade so important to you? Was it because you had a kickback deal going with the Center for Public Renewal?"

"That's slanderous," Murray snapped. "I'll sue you if you repeat that."

"*Is* it slander?" I retorted. "I'm not so sure. After all, Gus, the Center's tax records show a big drop in income over the past three years. Was it bad management, or just the passing of the Reagan era glory days? I mean, let's face it, the Cold War is over, Gorby is fading. Times are tough at home, and getting tougher every day. Even your yellow ribbons are starting to wilt. Isn't it getting to be a harder sell, blaming everything on Jimmy Carter, ten years later, and the Sixties, twenty-five years on? Though of course you'll never give up trying."

"Get out of here," Murray hissed, and tried to push me away from the lectern. But my grip on the edge was firm.

"The Crusade was gonna save your bacon, wasn't it?," I goaded. "A three million dollar windfall, just in the nick of time. And in the bargain it would put you and the Center back in the spotlight. How much were you gonna give Brewer back under the table, Gus? A quarter of a million? Half?"

Murder Among Friends

"I don't have to listen to any more of this," Murray said. He started to walk toward the steps.

"Before you go," I said to his back, "you'll need to explain to the police how this sheet, which was stapled to the one found in Goode's hand, got into your suitcase in Mott hall?"

Murray whirled and glared at me. I raised my hands in mock confession. "Yes, forgive me for prying, But your room was unlocked. You know how trusting people get at Quaker conferences. But tell me: Did you put it there *before* or *after* you planted Eddie's baseball bat back under his mattress?"

I rubbed my chin, pretending to think. "My guess is you did it right after I left you in the men's shower room that afternoon. It wasn't until today that I realized there was something strange about that--most people shave when they get up in the morning. But you needed an excuse for being up there late in the day, when your real mission was prowling around our rooms, planting evidence to incriminate Eddie and hiding anything that would incriminate you and Brewer. Did you hide the bat for Brewer, Gus? Or was it for yourself?"

Murray's chest was heaving, his fists were clenched. But he stood silent.

"It was a good idea," I taunted, "but it wasn't perfect, was it? Is that why you followed us last night, Gus? Oh, it had to be you. That was your rental car out there this morning with mud stains on the fenders where you went through the little creek. They're washed off now in the rain, but I checked the tags."

Murray raised an arm and pointed at me. "Stop this," he said in a tone of quiet rage. "You don't understand anything."

He took a step toward the lectern. "What typical liberal superficiality," he said contemptuously, "to think our budget shortfall had *anything* to do with this."

He pounded a fist on the lectern. "This wasn't about money, for God's sake! It was about saving American culture from itself. Saving it from the likes of *you,* and your degenerate friend Smith."

Now he tapped the lectern with a stern finger. "I told you Tuesday: one side has to win, and the other will lose. There's no middle round."

"Bottom line?" I asked sarcastically.

His eyebrows rose behind his glasses. *"Yes!"* he hissed, stabbing the finger now at me. "Bottom line. Zero sum. Sheridan or Early. The new civil war, just like we said. There's no escaping it." Now he pointed toward the back wall, in the direction of--what? Harrisonburg? Cedar Creek? Stonewall Cemetery? "Goode understood that," he said.

"Did he?" I questioned. "It sounds to me like he'd decided to be a conscientious objector in your war, Gus."

"No!" he shouted. "He wouldn't. I couldn't allow it."

"And you didn't, did you? But then there was the small matter of finding a designated fall guy. Excuse me--that's not proper liberal talk--a fall *person.* And Eddie's flap with Goode gave you the perfect opportunity. You needed him back in jail, taking the rap for you, on the way to he chair for you."

I opened a brochure from my pocket. "The Center for Public Renewal supports the death penalty, doesn't it, Gus," I jabbed. "It says here you held a symposium and published a book on it. Let's see, *Return to Justice,* that was the title, right?"

I folded the brochure up again. "That's for other people, though, right, Gus? But what will you say when the police find your fingerprints on this sheet, and in Eddie's room? What will you say when they strap *you* into Old Sparky? Will all our Quaker meetings get the letters asking for appeals to the governor for clemency? Or will you go to the end insisting that you did it to win the Second American Civil War? Or maybe that you did it to save some tacky scheme of Brewer's?"

Murray glared at me, then at Brewer, cold fury working in his face. Brewer looked back coolly and shook his head.

Then Murray shouted, "You scum!" and made a sudden lunge toward me. The lectern crashed to one side under his blow and he snatched the paper from my hands. He tore it in pieces, then whirled and rushed at Brewer. "I'll kill you, too, you bastard, you're setting me up!"

As they grappled, Lem Penn cried out and tried to pry them apart. Murray reacted with a fist that caught Penn's ear and sent him sprawling. Then I leaped on them, but Murray's knee caught me in the stomach and I crumpled to the floor.

I was still trying to catch my breath, staring at the scuffed tan floorboards, when I heard shouts and running feet in the aisle, and turned just enough to see a flash of lavender graze the spotlight. Then there were thuds and grappling sounds, loud cries and a couple of heavy thumps, then muffled gasps.

By the time I managed to stand up and turn around, Karl Russell and another well-muscled man in a skintight wet tee shirt and a lavender baseball cap were standing over Brewer and Murray, who were flat on their bellies, each with an arm pulled up and twisted around behind as if in a some careless, horizontal ballet gesture.

I instinctively hobbled over to where Penn was sitting on the floor, rubbing the side of his head with a checkered cloth handkerchief. He mouthed that he was all right, but couldn't speak.

Karl grinned at me, and touched his cap with a free hand. "We heard you on the PA system," he explained, "and figured you might need a little non-pacifist help."

He pointed to Lem and said, "Uh, Mr. Penn?"

When I nodded to confirm his guess, he added, apologetically, "These are Aikido holds, sir, and they're almost nonviolent. No blood, no broken bones, no permanent damage--"

Brewer started to struggle, cried out in pain, and subsided.

"Err," Karl corrected, "that is, none as long as they hold quite still." He peered down at his charges. "Would you try to remember that, please, gentlemen? Thank you."

He looked toward the rear of the auditorium. "Oh, and you with the videocamera," he called, "You can turn it off now. I think the excitement is over."

"A camera?" Penn was alarmed. Keeping the press out of the preliminaries had been firmly agreed upon by the committee.

But Karl just grinned at him. "Insurance, sir," he said. "We couldn't let this one get away, so we invited one of the cameras in. I promise it won't happen again."

He glanced back at me. "What about your piece of paper, Bill? He's kind of destroyed it."

"Not to worry," I answered. "That was a copy. I put the staple in for effect."

"Ah, very clever," Karl said. "Now would someone please call the police, before my hand gets too tired?"

CHAPTER TWENTY-SEVEN

I was not embraced in the terms of General Lee's surrender...and...as soon as I was in a condition to travel, I started on horseback for the Trans-Mississippi Department to join the army of General Kirby Smith, should it hold out; with the hope of at least meeting an honorable death while fighting under the flag of my country. Before I reached that Department, Smith's army had also been surrendered, and...after a long, weary and dangerous ride...I finally succeeded in leaving the country.

--Jubal Early, Autobiographical Sketch

"I should have guessed," I told Karl. His Camry was winding through thick stands of trees on Cool Run Valley Road, just west of Berkeley Springs, West Virginia. Winchester was thirty miles and a couple of planets away.

"Here," I pointed to a big resort Chalet that loomed suddenly out of the pines on our left. "Coolfont." He pulled in.

"Hey, where else would I go?" Eddie insisted a half hour later. We sat in the chalet's dining room, which jutted out over the side of a hill that sloped down to more woods.

High clear windows ran along three sides of the room. Well-stocked bird feeders hung at eye level every dozen feet or so in the big old maples and oaks that towered over the building. As we ate the excellent Sunday buffet, cardinals and chickadees and goldfinches seemed to add a feast of feathered color to the meal.

"The location is superb from a security standpoint," Karl grudgingly admitted. I could tell he was still thinking about his American Express bill. "You're within ten miles of four states, with lots of back roads to get lost on."

"I suppose so," Eddie agreed. "But I really came here because it's got the only decent vegetarian menu within fifty miles. Plus I knew they had cabins back in the woods with phone hookups and a jacuzzi. Besides, it was started by a Quaker."

"A jacuzzi," Karl repeated. "If the cops could have put together that many associations, they'd have tracked you here in an hour."

"But they didn't," Eddie grinned. "They're not that smart. I like this place. Oh, and did I mention the massage? Comes with the deal."

"Massage," Karl said.

I'd heard enough of a sales pitch. "About the warrant," I said pointedly. "It's been vacated. So you can come out of hiding now. If you call this hiding."

He nodded distractedly. "I heard. But I think I'll stay until the indictments come down on Brewer and Murray."

"Until *what?*" Karl's voice rose. "That could take days."

Eddie spread his hands apologetically. "Well, I'm still having nightmares about Old Sparky. And they offered me a great discount on the two-week package."

"You--" Karl's face was red.

"*Kidding!*" Eddie said quickly. "Just kidding. I'll go whenever you're ready. After lunch, that is." He turned to me. "Who was it that actually hit Goode?" he asked.

"Murray," I said. "He had the most to lose, and argued the loudest with Goode when he saw the new announcement, which wasn't until the night before they got to Winchester. Despite all his talk about a new civil war, without the Crusade money his Center was essentially broke. Not only that, it was his chance to join the big leagues of right-wing apparatchiks."

"Well," Eddie deadpanned, "he can always get born again in prison, write a book and start working his way back. But wait--nope, he's already a Christian."

"That won't stop him," Karl said. "Being born again is like having an orgasm: If it really feels good, once is never enough."

"God," Eddie marveled, "why do you have to be a Christian to wanna start a civil war over gay rights and abortion?"

"You don't," I objected. "That's a rank stereotype. Some of my best friends--our best friends--hell, even Ben Goode was getting over it."

"Okay," he conceded. "I take your point. But then why didn't he tell the college president, what's his name?"

"Harrison. He was going to. Goode figured out somehow that Brewer had torpedoed the meeting with Harrison Monday, hoping they could talk him out of the idea at the last minute, or at least get him to put it off. You know, first the Crusade, *then* the Cedar Creek Center. Something like that. They went after him again at dinner somewhere Monday night, but he wouldn't budge, and said he was gonna call Harrison Tuesday morning himself."

"What time did all this happen?" Eddie wondered. "I came back to the dorm around ten-thirty, and it was quiet. I found Goode in his room just a little later."

"I think you came within half an hour of walking in on a murder," I said. "Murray followed Goode into the dorm, tried our door open, looked in and saw your bat sticking out of your bag. He slipped in and grabbed it, went to Goode's room, threatened him quietly, then hit him. He's physically strong, I found that out Friday. So he only had to hit Goode once."

"And after that," Karl guessed, "he and Brewer got together and figured they could quietly sink the Center and go ahead with the Crusade as Goode's memorial. Clever."

"Right. Brewer figured he could handle the Temple board, and after the kickoff speech, the die would be cast. But they needed to keep a lid on things. Brewer called Rockingham Trust and got them to clam up just before Penn and I got there. And Murray was nervous about Eddie."

"Yeah," Eddie spoke bitterly, "he wouldn't be safe until I was on Death Row." He shivered, and changed the subject. "So how's the conference going?"

"Limping along, at best," I said. "Poor Lem Penn. After

Murder Among Friends

Friday they had to delay the opening again, since they'd lost their second keynote speaker. The evangelicals conferred for hours, and finally picked Horace Burks to do the honors, white suit and all. He preached on family values, of course. But Rita persuaded Lyndon Coffin to drop *'Onward Christian Soldiers'* from the hymn list. Did *'Amazing Grace'* instead."

"It's a good old song," Karl said wistfully. "That and *'Just As I Am'* are my favorites."

"Even Horace Burks restrained himself," I went on. He hardly mentioned homosexuality." A memory came to me. "Oh, and your Lavender Friends Fellowship display is back by the door, where it was supposed to be. Penn put his foot down: enough was enough, and fair is fair."

Eddie brightened. "Good man," he enthused. "How'd he manage it?"

"The evangelicals were too shell-shocked to fight it. The big Temple rally was canceled, of course, and the National Guard was sent home."

"But don't forget," Karl put in, "the cops let us Commandos march to Stonewall Cemetery yesterday, even if it was in single file, with no signs, and no rally. Then we sent everybody home." He smiled. "Just a quiet week in Lake Wobegon."

"So with all this sweetness and light," Eddie said, "is Penn making any progress? Are American Friends doing any of the healing and forgiveness that the whole thing was supposed to be about?"

I shrugged. "Who knows? Maybe. Let's see who talks to me at the ice cream social tonight."

"Right," Eddie said. "I'll call you tomorrow."

"Tomorrow," I sighed. "Why did you have to mention tomorrow?"

"You mean you won't be glad to be back at work?" Eddie taunted. "After this long and boring week of arguing over obscure church history and arcane theological disputes, who wouldn't be happy to return to the thrilling world of maritime policy?"

"Please," I begged, "don't rub it in." I turned to Karl. "What about you?"

"Oh," he said airily, "I think I'll stick around the Valley a few days, now that I have my credit cards back. There's a librarian I should visit down in Harrisonburg." A slow grin. "And some young Baptist deacons I'd like to get to know better."

"You *slut!*" Eddie hooted. But I could tell he was jealous.

CHAPTER TWENTY-EIGHT

It is well that war is so terrible, or we should grow too fond of it.

--Robert E. Lee, to Stephen Longstreet,
at Fredericksburg, December 13, 1862

I

Rita had to leave before the ice cream social, to catch her ride to DC and the Metroliner to Manhattan. I caught up with her as she was loading her bag into Sarah Scattergood's van.

"Well," I said, fumbling for something witty or memorable to say, "it's been quite a week, I guess."

Profound, Leddra, I berated myself. You're a real charmer.

She didn't seem to mind. "I wish I could stay," she said. "But the library needs me. Special collections demand a lot of work."

"Umm, we should keep in touch," I ventured. "I get up to New York now and again." Actually, I hadn't been there in over a year.

"Please," she said encouragingly. "I've got your address on the attender's list. But would you like my office number? I have a direct line."

"Sure." She told me and I wrote it down.

There was an awkward moment of silence. "Uh, Rita," I said,

"I never told you how great I thought you were at the demonstration. And thanks for coming to the infirmary with me. I never got knocked out before."

This was all the opening she needed. Her hands reached for mine, and then closed around my back. I buried my face in her hair, then leaned back far enough to find her lips.

We stayed in the clinch until Sarah Scattergood coughed and said tentatively, "Uh, Rita, I really need to go."

Rita moved her lips to my left ear. "Come see me," she whispered. "We just got the private collection of Edwinna Kinsey. I've been working on it at home. I'll read you some from it."

I was a little nonplussed. "Forgive me," I whispered back. But *who* was Edwinna Kinsey?"

She giggled. "Mrs. Alfred Kinsey, silly. The Kinsey Reports?"

"The sex doctor?"

Another quick kiss. "You're catching on."

"But was she in on that?"

"They were partners in *everything*. But her specialty was high-class erotica."

She kissed me again, lightly this time, and pulled away. "Call me at the office sometime, and we'll make a date. I'll be with my son tomorrow, and back at my desk Tuesday at nine."

Tuesday at nine, I thought, as the van drove off. Well, certainly I wouldn't call her then. I mean, there's a proper rhythm to relationships, which has to be respected. Especially in the nineties, and particularly with these independent, strong Quaker women. One mustn't rush into things.

Right. So nothing precipitate for me. No calls to New York on Tuesday at nine.

No way. I knew better than that.

I'd wait until at least a quarter to ten.

II

Since Lem had called ahead, Reverend Phillips had real lemonade waiting when he arrived at Good Shepherd Church late Sunday afternoon. They approached it slowly, through the garden along the side of the building, now even more rich with

196

color and provender. The big sunflowers still strained toward the sun, there were warm green snap beans to sample, and after a moment's consideration, Phillips plucked a pair of big, deep red tomatoes for slicing and sharing with his guest.

Penn noticed more about the interior of the trailer this time: A venerable dark blue overstuffed chair and sofa dominated the tiny living room, each with a finely detailed white antimacassar on its crest. End tables were crowded with pictures in leafy silver and goldtone frames: Phillips and a large grey-haired woman; younger images of both of them with two deferential-looking children, boy and girl, dark eyed and stiffly-dressed.

The room was cozy, but the film of dust on most objects in it showed it hadn't been used much recently. Probably since his wife died, Penn guessed. As before, Phillips led him through it to the kitchen, which was clearly his preferred living area.

Penn appreciated the homemade lemonade, with the tiny translucent sacs of lemon pulp floating in it, bursting tartly when squeezed between his tongue and the back of his front teeth. He told Phillips this, and enjoyed his appreciative laugh.

They ate thick tomato slices sprinkled with salt, and chatted of this and that for awhile. Phillips was interested in Penn's account of the extraordinary events of the past week. To each anecdote, his response was a shaking of the head and the same comment, "Ain't that somethin, *ain't* that somethin."

But he knew, as Penn knew he knew, that the white man had come back to this black church to do more than drink his lemonade, eat tomato slices, and tell stories, though each was content to wait until the moment seemed right before getting to the actual point of the visit.

Finally Penn felt the time had come. "Reverend," he asked, "I been wondering about something you said when that young fella and I were here before."

"Bill," Phillips remembered. "Name was Bill."

"Right," Penn agreed. "Yesterday I picked up a copy of a book of Dr. Goode's sermons up at the College library, and I've been reading it."

"You don't say."

"I do," Penn continued. "And it turns out that one of his

favorite Bible verses was John 13:35."

Phillips leaned back a little, and recited: *"'By this shall all men know you are my disciples, if you have love one for another.'* One o' my favorites too."

Penn sipped the lemonade, and thoughtfully chewed a bit of pulp. "And one of the first sermons in his book was preached on that text in early 1963."

"That so."

"I believe that was just about the time you all had the trouble with him over building your church here."

"Little afterward," Phillips said quietly. "It was just all over by then."

"Right. What that sermon did, Reverend, it made me wonder about that money that showed up in your mailbox when you were behind on the mortgage."

"Uh-huh," Phillips murmured.

"Was it really some liberals at Valley State who put it there, do you think? Or Mennonites from down toward Harrisonburg?"

Phillips looked at Penn for a moment, then leaned back, laced his fingers behind his head, and gazed up at the low ceiling. His lips pursed, then widened with the hint of a smile. Finally he raised his shoulders in an exaggerated shrug.

"Well," he said slowly, "that was only guessin'."

"Or was it somebody else?" Penn pressed.

Phillips surveyed the ceiling again. "Well, Mr. Penn," he said after a moment, "you a pretty good guesser yourself. What do you think?"

III

The man knew that WVCR-105FM, your Full-Power Valley Christian Station, was set to go on the air at 4:00 AM Monday morning, as usual. It had to; much of its core audience still followed the farmer's routine. Thus for the first hour, its sermons and hymnsings were interspersed with commodity price reports and other farm news.

He knew all that. He'd heard it many times. Too many.

Murder Among Friends

But before the first round of bulletins on the price oscillations of pork bellies, sorghum and spring wheat, each day's broadcast began with a tape of Dr. Ben Goode reciting from Psalm 118:24: "'This is the day that the Lord has made,'" he blared. "'We will rejoice and be glad in it.'"

Goode paused for effect, then shouted, "Say 'Amen!'"

And a thousand voices chorused back, "Amen!"

The enormous organ then roared on cue, and the Good Life Temple Choir broke into "The Star-Spangled Banner."

The man knew all that, too.

The recording featured a particularly piercing soprano, who threw her voice up an octave for a sustained vibrato emphasis on the climactic line, "O'er the land of the free...."

The man didn't know who she was, but that didn't matter. He imagined her as large and heavy-bosomed, pouring a lifetime of sexual undernourishment into that last, pseudo-orgasmic peal.

But what the hell, she might be young, skinny and great in bed.

It didn't matter.

That one, overreaching note was all that mattered. It would awaken a tiny microcircuit, tuned painstakingly to precisely that frequency, set it into sympathetic vibration, and evoke from it the merest flicker of an electrical charge.

Just a flicker. But it would be enough.

The security fence around the broadcast tower looked fearsome from a distance, topped with coils of razor wire that glinted when the daylight sun shone on it. It was a legacy of the first tower bombing.

But like most everything else about the Temple, it was mainly for show. The chain link fence under it was not wired, and at night the Temple security car came by less than once an hour. After midnight, it rarely stopped.

So it had been easy to cut an eighteen-inch opening at

199

the bottom of the fence with his quiet bullcutters, and slip inside. The opening was plenty big enough to get him and his payload through.

The payload wasn't much. Four foot-long metal mailing tubes, one with a new walkman taped to its skin. The walkman was tuned to 105FM, and on its palm-sized circuit board the special microcircuit and the detonator had been carefully, lovingly grafted.

Each mailing tube was filled with smokeless black powder, the common variety for reloaders, available anonymously from a thousand gun shops.

Thank you, Virginia, *the man breathed,* **for your wide open, anonymous gun market. Where would we be without the Old Dominion?**

Each tube also contained a dollop of old C-4, to make it look like the work of a 'Nam era grunt. Semtex would have been better technically, he knew, but he didn't want the job to look too expert. It should be mysterious and unsolved, like the last one.

Now, to quickly attach the tubes, one on each of the four columns supporting the big tower. Ordinary packing tape would hold them. The two on the north side would go at shoulder-level; the others about ten feet higher. That should make the collapsing tower fall away from the station offices, as the first one had, into the grass beyond the fence, minimizing the chance of injuries.

Unless, of course, somebody came out here, say for a smoke, at just the wrong time. Or, less likely but possible, if a strong north wind suddenly came up and pushed the tower the other way.

Well, there were always risks in a war, even to the innocent.

If you could call anyone involved in Goode's operation **innocent,** *the man thought bitterly.*

Murder Among Friends

He checked his watch: 1:47 AM. His van was parked by the Seven-Eleven at the mini-mall half a mile north on Highway 11. Ten minutes' walk. Then up to the wagon which was sitting outside the Wal-Mart in Winchester, by the all-night supermarket. Switch there, and by the time two hours and thirteen minutes had elapsed, he would be--where?

He hadn't decided yet. West Virginia? Maryland? Pennsylvania? Or maybe DC. DC was a good place to get arrested, if it came to that.

Which it wouldn't. There was nothing here to trace, except ordinary materials in ordinary containers.

The only extraordinary part, the skill that put them all together, was the one ingredient that left no traces at all. It would leave them all suspicious of each other, doubting, pointing fingers, ratcheting up the tension.

Just what you needed for a war.

He taped the last tube in place, then swung around to face south, hanging on to the tower framework with his left hand and foot.

He raised his right hand in a smart, silent salute, rotating from south to east in the directions of the graves of Robert E. Lee, Stonewall Jackson, Jubal Early, and, who could forget, John Singleton Mosby. Oh, and don't overlook Phil Sheridan and Golden George Custer, though their graves were far away.

Fellas, he whispered, this one's for you. Remember Cedar Creek! Then he dropped lightly to the ground.

Headlights turned into view beyond the station. He ducked behind the transformer unit.

The security car rolled slowly past the station office, made a U-turn in the parking lot next to it, then hummed quietly away.

The man was through the fence before it was out of sight, trotting easily back toward the highway, and the van.